THE STRANGEWORLDS
· TRAVEL AGENCY ·

The Edge of the Ocean

By L.D. Lapinski

The Edge of the Ocean

THE STRANGEWORLDS

· TRAVEL AGENCY ·

The Edge of the Ocean

L. D. LAPINSKI

Orion

ORION CHILDREN'S BOOKS

First published in Great Britain in 2021
by Hodder and Stoughton

1 3 5 7 9 10 8 6 4 2

A CIP catalogue record for this book
is available from the British Library.

ISBN 978 151 0 10595 9

Printed and bound in Great Britain by Clays Ltd, Elcograf S.p.A.

The paper and board used in this book are made
from wood from responsible sources.

MIX
Paper from
responsible sources
FSC® C104740
FSC
www.fsc.org

Orion Children's Books
An imprint of
Hachette Children's Group
Part of Hodder and Stoughton
Carmelite House
50 Victoria Embankment
London EC4Y 0DZ

An Hachette UK Company

www.hachette.co.uk
www.hachettechildrens.co.uk

For Molly
and
for every girl who fell in love with
The Pirate King, Elizabeth Swann

'Dead men tell no tales.'
Hiram Beakes,
Eighteenth-century pirate of Saba

PROLOGUE

People called them 'pirates'. And the sailors who lived in the world of The Break wore that title with pride, because when you live on a ship, and your life includes a lot of skulduggery and skally-waggery, what else would you call yourself but 'pirate'?

Every one of them certainly looked the part, and the crew who called Nyfe Shaban their captain were not without style. The sailors' appearance was as artful as it was necessary. Prosthetic legs were carved with delicate rising waves, and eyepatches were made of softened leather with the crest of the ship sewn onto them. Captain Nyfe's own eyepatch, nestled in the hollow of where her left eye used to be, had a spray of blue embroidered on it, a homage to her flagship the *Aconite*, named after the poisonous blue flower.

That night, Nyfe was engrossed in a map in front of her. She had not looked at the clock in her cabin for some time. Clocks were very important in The Break because the sunrises and sunsets were so unreliable. Nyfe had been poring over a collection of maps and charts for most of the day. A half-eaten meal had been buried under an unfurled scroll several hours ago.

Nyfe ran her hand over the map. It was circular, coloured in vivid inks and sealed with varnish. The surface shone and crackled. It was a map of her entire world. The world of The Break.

A knock sounded on her cabin door.

'Yes?' she said, keeping her eyes down.

'Captain.' Jereme, the second mate, stuck his head around the door. 'It's getting dark and there's still no sign of the *Nastur*.' He paused, shifting the weight of the truth he carried before dropping it. 'The ship's gone, Captain.'

Nyfe looked up from her chart. For a moment, worry flickered behind her eye. Then it vanished, replaced by her usual unreadable chill.

'Tell the crew to batten down, and get themselves

some food. If they can't find the ship in the light, I doubt they'll find it in the dark.'

Jereme nodded, and excused himself.

Nyfe leant back and adjusted one of the markers on her map. In the centre of the mostly blue world was a brown island that looked like a round of bread torn open: The Break. The largest island in the waters, and the one Nyfe's world was named after.

A splatter of other islands spiralled out into the blue, but none of them rivalled the land mass of The Break. A sailor would need more than a day to walk from one side to the other.

There was a time, when Nyfe was younger, that the map she was looking at had been twice the size. Over the years, the map had been trimmed down, cut away as the sea became smaller. It had been happening for so long now, that Nyfe couldn't remember a month going by when the map had stayed as it was.

Nyfe Shaban took out a thin blade from the collection at her belt. She stabbed quickly into the edge of the map, and skimmed the blade around the edge of the circle, shaving off a slice no wider than her thumbnail. She picked up the hoop of chart, and crumpled it in her hand, before dropping it into the wastepaper basket.

'The world is shrinking,' she said to no one. Then, she took out a piece of thick recycled paper, and a writing set.

She had a letter to send.

No – not a letter.

A summons.

CHAPTER ONE

Flick twirled the magnifying glass between her fingers. The brass handle was speckled with little marks and imperfections. There was a deep scrape close to the round lens, there were little scratches running down the slender, pen-like handle, and a dark smudge of something that refused to budge, no matter how often Flick cleaned it.

She looked over the little instrument, not through the glass itself for the moment, enjoying the anticipation. Looking through the magnifier was a treat to be savoured.

She spun the handle quickly, tripping it through her fingers in a practised movement that she'd spent far too many nights perfecting. She was lying on her bed, the pink glow from the agate slice on top of her old lamp lighting up the room in a way that reminded her of the gentle glow of a forest made of crystal and magic, a whole other world away. A world she had walked in.

Flick closed her eyes, and took a steadying breath. Then she raised the magnifying glass to her right eye, keeping her left closed. The first time she had tried this, lying on her bed, she had dropped the instrument on her head.

Because this was no ordinary magnifying glass. And Felicity Hudson was no ordinary person. The magnifying glass in Flick's hand contained glass that came from another world, and the little instrument had been made by someone who knew the nature of the enchantment.

To look through it – if you had the right gift – was to see a hidden magic. Quite literally. And as Flick looked through it, she smiled.

The air around her swarmed with magic. Glittering, golden, white-crested glimmers on the air that drifted silently, unseen by everyone but her. Flick's smile grew into a wide grin as she watched the golden sparkles swirl and ballet-dance around her bedroom. They rolled and dived through the air like glitter in water, tumbling in a swarm of magical particles.

Flick raised a hand, and the swarm of magic floated soundlessly over to her, draping across her hand, fitting around her fingers like a glove. Flick could feel nothing at all, even when she squeezed her fist around some of the particles.

Flick lowered the magnifying glass and pressed the round bit of it to her mouth. It was cold, and tasted a bit like a two-pence coin she'd once licked, just to see what it was like.

The magnifying glass had been made over one hundred years ago, and had once belonged to a member of her friend Jonathan Mercator's family (the initials N.M. were scratched into the rim of brass). The magnifying glass wasn't exactly magical by itself – it was merely a way to see the magic that was already there. Magic, Flick now knew, was everywhere in the whole world.

But that wasn't all that Flick could see.

She got up off her bed and clicked the bedside lamp off before peeping through her curtains. With the light off, she could see past her own reflection, right into the garden and the housing estate beyond.

The rows of houses looked dark and gloomy in the overcast night. It had been a hot and muggy day, the air full of moisture that refused to condense into rain. There was no moon to be seen, and the sky was the sort of deep purple that promised a thunderstorm later.

Flick pressed a palm to the glass, and wondered if that static feel in the air you got just before a storm really *was* just static, or something more magical. A prickle crept over her back at the thought. It was entirely possible that storms stirred up magic in the air. Anything was possible, really.

She stared out at the dark for a few minutes, watching the occasional light come on in a house she didn't recognise. She waited until she couldn't stand it any longer, before raising the tiny brass magnifying glass to her eye once again.

This time, the effect was electric.

A bright scratch of light lit up the play area in the centre of the housing estate. It was jagged, like a lightning bolt drawn by someone whose hands were shaking. The line in the air glowed with yellow-white light, tiny particles of magic moving in and out of it. It was carved into the air about two meters above the top of the slide, just waiting.

A schism.

A tear in the fabric of reality.

A gateway to another world.

A massive shiver ran over Flick's body. She had spotted the schism the day before yesterday. Although it wasn't hurting a soul, the schism reminded Flick of what *could* happen. And what she had done, only a few weeks ago, in another world.

Flick stared at it until her eye started to water, then lowered the magnifying glass and rested her head on the window. The cold glass felt nice against her warm skin, and as she listened to the creaking night-time sounds of her home, gradually the frightened feeling gave way to a soft calm. She was safe here, and loved, and with the family she had come so close to losing. The memory of that near loss was now for ever associated with schisms. Even looking at one through the magnifying glass made her feel sick with nerves.

Flick had only found out about schisms recently, when she had joined the secret society that was part of The Strangeworlds Travel Agency.

A place of travel, and magical objects, and the home of the only friend Flick had made since her family moved to Little Wyverns.

The Strangeworlds Travel Agency was also the reason she was grounded right now. Her parents were acting as though Flick had gone out and robbed a bank, when all she'd really done was disappear for a day and a night.

Flick pulled a face. She wished she didn't understand why they were so mad. But she did. She hadn't expected to be grounded for the whole of the summer holidays, though. There was only a week and half left, and then she'd be off to her new school and would only have the weekends and holidays to visit the travel agency.

In the distance, a siren sounded and blue lights flashed. She jumped slightly at the sound, knocking a mostly-empty piggy bank off the windowsill and onto the floor with a crash.

She stayed still, listening.

From her parents' room, she heard a cough and the creak of their bedframe. She ought to be back in bed.

Flick left the piggy where it was, pulled the curtains closed again, and slipped back into bed. The magnifying glass was still clutched tightly in her hand.

CHAPTER TWO

The kitchen was so full of carrier bags and boxes the next morning that Flick wondered if they were moving again. Fortunately, it was just one of her dad's semi-regular attempts at a clear-out. This time, he was planning on taking things to the flea market at the town hall.

'Last chance saloon,' he said, as Flick shoved some fruit loaf down into the toaster and took a swig of orange juice directly from the carton on the table. 'Any old clothes, shoes, toys, books, get them bagged up. And don't do that,' he added, nodding at the orange juice. He stacked another box onto a cardboard tower. The box at the bottom sagged. 'Your mum doesn't like it.'

'We've all got the same germs.' Flick rolled her eyes

and went to get a glass. 'Besides, you kiss Freddy and he should be condemned under the public health act.'

Isaac Hudson looked at his son, who was currently sporting two green, candle-like protrusions from his nose. 'Maybe you do need a wipe, young man, eh?'

'Put him in the steriliser,' Flick suggested.

Freddy laughed, and Flick felt mollified. At least someone was prepared to humour her for her jokes. She felt a lot more affectionate towards Freddy these days, despite the snot.

Moira Hudson came in then. She was wearing jeans instead of her Post Office uniform. 'Aren't you ready yet, Felicity?' she snapped.

Flick paused with her fruit toast halfway to her open mouth as she tried to remember what it was she was supposed to be ready for.

'It's Saturday,' Moira sighed. She clicked her tongue in the way that usually meant trouble was coming. 'You said you were going to come with me into town.'

'But—'

'The shopping needs doing.'

'But—'

'And Freddy needs some more trousers; he's wearing through the knees with crawling.'

'But—'

'So get ready, and don't spend half the day in the bathroom, you're beautiful enough as it is. Chop-chop.'

Flick resignedly shoved the rest of her breakfast in her gob.

*

Ever since Flick had failed to return from The Strangeworlds Travel Agency a few weeks ago, she'd had about as much freedom as a spider trapped under a glass. She had turned up at home in the small hours of the morning, with no reasonable explanation. And understandably, her parents had questions.

In an attempt to stop them giving her the third degree every five minutes, Flick had eventually come up with a half-hearted lie about getting 'lost' in Little Wyverns. Her parents hadn't bought it for a second of course, but they seemed to prefer even an obvious lie to no explanation at all. Her dad had stopped being angry after the first week or so, but Flick's mum was like a pot of water simmering on the hob – anything could turn up the heat and send her boiling over, so Flick had been trying to just do as she was told. Her parents, and her mother in particular, were determined to keep her busy. But Flick's parents didn't know about Strangeworlds, and Flick had no intention of telling them about it, either.

She had made it back to the travel agency twice. The first time, shortly after her disappearance, she had managed to skive off a piano lesson to tell Jonathan she was grounded semi-permanently. The second time, Freddy had chosen the pavement outside Strangeworlds as the perfect spot to throw one of his Mega Tantrums™, giving Flick the chance to wave frantically through the glass as her mother wrestled with him.

Though Flick was grounded, apparently there was no harm in her leaving the house to entertain her baby brother around the shops.

Since it was the holidays, the supermarket was packed full of parents and their offspring, who were either being kept quiet with crisps, or screaming because they *weren't* being kept quiet with crisps. Freddy was among the latter, alternating between bleating like a goat and trying to swallow the trolley's connector key. Flick wandered over to the soft fruit whilst her mother complained loudly to no one that now the cucumbers were not wrapped in plastic, they didn't last as long. There had been an argument at home about single-use plastics the day before, when

Flick crossed cling film off the shopping list in a moment of feeble rebellion. Flick was wondering why her mother thought a firmer-for-longer cucumber was more important than the great whales when she saw a familiar tousle of dark hair, and a terrible tweed waistcoat that could only belong to one person. She peered around the banana display, hardly daring to hope.

But it was.

It was Jonathan Mercator.

Flick's heart soared.

He was really there! Out of his precious travel agency, standing looking at fruit as though he was as boring as everyone else in the multiverse.

Well, not quite as boring. Though it was August, and everyone else was in shorts, Jonathan's only concession to the weather was to have left his suit jacket off. Even his shirt was still buttoned to the neck. Flick felt weirdly tickled. Seeing Jonathan in the supermarket was like seeing a turtle out of its shell.

She walked over.

'Hey,' she grinned. She suddenly felt as though her legs were filled with springs. 'It's so good to see you!'

'Oh!' Jonathan blinked rapidly behind the lenses of his glasses and a smile spread across his face. He put the avocado he'd been examining into his basket. 'Hello.'

Flick glanced over to where her mother was trying to wrestle her shopping list out of Freddy's mouth. 'It's been like trying to escape Alcatraz at home. How are you?'

'Better, thank you.' He patted the back of his head, where there was a ridge of scar where a rock had hit him only a few weeks ago. It was a reminder of the dangers of his line of work.

Jonathan's travel agency was the only one like it in the world. And Flick was one of only a few people who knew the secret – that when The Strangeworlds Travel Agency sent you on a trip, they didn't send you on a plane. The old travel agency was filled with an assortment of old suitcases, each one different from the last. And each one of those suitcases could transport you to another world; all you had to do was step inside.

Flick glanced at the contents of Jonathan's basket. There was a tin of vegetable soup keeping the single avocado company. It was weird to think of Jonathan doing anything as mundane as eating meals.

'Does my shopping meet with your approval?' he asked.

She laughed. 'I guess. So, how's business?'

'Slow and steady, as the saying goes,' he shrugged. 'I revisited the City of Five Lights, recently. The place seems to be getting better. Thanks to you.'

'Thanks to Nicc DeVyce,' Flick said, suddenly missing the pink and gold city and her red-cloaked Thief friend with a heart-aching intensity. 'She was the one who agreed to release the stolen magic back into the world. She could have kept it.'

'Not everyone is that kind of Thief,' Jonathan said. 'I spoke to Miss DeVyce, as it happens. She's heard nothing of Overseer Glean, or her cronies. It seems as though you trapped them in that other world for good.'

Flick stared at some kiwis, the heavy feeling in her chest dissolving into liquid guilt.

Jonathan seemed to sense how she was feeling. 'You saved yourself, saved Strangeworlds Society members, and ultimately the world of Five Lights itself. Without you, Overseer Glean and her Thieves would have journeyed to another world and drained the magic – the life – out of it.' He adjusted his grip on the shopping basket. 'That doesn't mean you have to feel good on a personal level about trapping people in another world.'

Flick hummed. 'Still not even sure how I did it.'

'Have you tried to do anything since you've been away?'

Flick shook her head, feeling as though spying through the magnifying glass didn't really count.

'No experiments, with your gifts?' Jonathan's eyebrows rose. 'Why ever not?'

Flick shifted awkwardly. During her time with Jonathan, it had become clear than she was magically gifted, more so than he was, and more so than he had ever seen before. On her last adventure with Jonathan, she had done the impossible: torn open a schism between two worlds – and survived. But back in Little Wyverns, quite possibly the most mundane village in the multiverse, it barely seemed real.

Jonathan smiled. 'I do miss you being there, you know. You should have come in, the other week. I saw you waving.'

'Oh.' Flick blinked and smiled. She didn't think she'd ever had a friend say they missed her before. It made her feel shy, but in a good way. 'I would have come in, but I was with my mum. She'd only ask questions. That's pretty much all she's done since I didn't come home that night.'

'Ah. Understandable. Still, that's—'

'Hey – Jonathan, isn't it?'

The two of them turned around to see a very tall, broad-shouldered young man in a rugby shirt. He was holding a four-pint bottle of whole milk in one hand, and he was grinning good-naturedly.

At the sight of him, Jonathan seemed to shrink. He grasped his shopping basket tightly in two hands. 'H-hello,' he said, his voice slipping upwards several octaves.

'Hey,' the young man said again. 'It *is* Jonathan, isn't it?'

Jonathan nodded like he was one of those dolls you keep in the back window of a car. 'Yes. And – and you're Anthony.'

'That's me.' Anthony looked at Flick, and then back to Jonathan. 'Are you going to introduce me to your . . . sister? Friend?'

'This is Felicity,' Jonathan said, his eyes staying on Anthony like they'd been glued. 'She's just a friend.'

'Nice to meet you, Felicity-just-a-friend.' Anthony shook her hand and she smiled. It was like shaking hands with a friendly giant.

'Nice to meet you too. So, how do you know Jonathan?' It seemed incredibly unlikely that this cheerful, freckled mountain of a young man was a member of The Strangeworlds Society, but she wasn't about to rule it out either.

'Oh, I'm a student rep, I work at the college up the

road.' He gestured with a thumb. 'I was helping out at the open day, and Jonathan here was one of the few people who didn't laugh at my efforts to tell people about courses.'

'You were very good. Knowledgeable. I mean,' Jonathan said. His cheeks had gone rather pink.

Anthony rolled his eyes, but seemed pleased. 'Thanks. Did you sign up for a course?'

Jonathan seemed to shake himself. 'Er, yes. I signed up for the modern geography module in the end. That was an excellent suggestion.'

Anthony nodded. 'No problem. Well, I'll leave you guys to your shopping. It was nice to meet you, Felicity, and I'll see you soon, yeah?' He smiled at Jonathan.

'Yes, I – I'll see you at – at college.'

Anthony nodded and Jonathan gave a little wiggly-fingered wave as he turned away.

As soon as Anthony had rounded the corner, Jonathan covered his face with a hand. 'Oh, *God*. Is there any chance you could be persuaded to never mention that encounter ever again?'

Flick grinned. 'Really? You want me to pretend I never saw you do *this*?' She mocked his little wave.

'Felicity, I'm begging you.' He dropped his hand. 'Please.'

'All right, fine,' she said. Then smiled. 'For what it's worth, he seemed nice.'

Flick's mother came over then, her trolley rattling as one of the wheels tried to go the opposite direction to the other three. 'Come on, Felicity, let's get going,' she said. She looked at Jonathan. 'Have we met?'

Jonathan gave what could only be described as a winning smile and stuck his hand out. 'I'm Felicity's friend, Jonathan. I must say,' he added, 'I'm rather sorry Felicity never came back to help in the shop.'

Flick's heart stopped.

Her mother's eyes narrowed. 'What do you mean?'

'I run a local travel agency. Felicity said she was keen to start a summer job, did a brilliant first day, and then she never turned up again,' Jonathan lied, as smooth as cream. 'I thought she'd changed her mind.'

Flick's heart started up again. She shook her head. 'No, I just haven't been able to get down there. I'm sorry.'

'You never said you were looking for a summer job,' her mum said suspiciously.

'I've not been allowed to explain anything, much.' Flick knew that wasn't true, but it was important to steer her mother away from any possible connection between Jonathan and the night she had failed to come home.

'It's a shame,' Jonathan went on, 'because she was such an asset. You don't find young people as willing to work that hard, even in Little Wyverns.'

Moira Hudson fluffed up at the praise of her daughter. 'Yes, well, Felicity has always been very mature for her age. Very responsible.'

Jonathan's crowd-pleaser smile stayed plastered on his face. 'It's testament to how well brought up she is, I think. A real reflection on you.'

Flick wouldn't have thought her mother would be so easily suckered by such obvious flattery, but she was actually preening a little. After weeks of anger and upset, she was being smoothed over like icing on a cake. Maybe flattery was Jonathan's super-power, or maybe there was only so long you could carry on being annoyed with someone. Either way, it was amazing to watch her mum's shoulders relax for the first time in weeks.

Jonathan carried on. 'It would be a shame for the training I started to give Felicity to go to waste. Computers and systems and such. The sort of thing that would really shine in a CV.'

Flick saw something flicker behind her mother's

eyes. Moira Hudson knew enough about college and university admissions to recognise how useful this would be. She gave her daughter a shrewd look.

'I'll improve my timekeeping,' Flick said. 'Promise.'

Her mum took a deep breath in through her nose. 'All right,' she said. 'But if you *ever*—'

'I won't,' Flick said quickly. 'Cross my heart and all that.'

'We'll talk about this later,' her mum said, but Flick knew she had been won over. Freddy blew a raspberry. 'Come on, Felicity. We've only got another hour on the car park. Nice to meet you, Jonathan.' She nodded at him and started back down the aisle.

Jonathan let the grin drop off his face. He fixed his tie and raised his eyebrows at Flick in a question.

Flick winked at Jonathan. *See you tomorrow*, she mouthed.

Jonathan tapped his watch. *Ten sharp*.

CHAPTER THREE

The walls of The Strangeworlds Travel Agency were filled top to bottom with large, rectangular holes, or slots. And each of these slots contained a suitcase. There were small ones and large ones and wicker ones and leather ones, and ones where the locks had been welded shut with some sort of gloopy metal that felt cold to the touch.

One of the suitcases – specifically, a sunshine-yellow one made of thick, varnished cardboard – began to fidget. It shuffled and inched, as if trying to escape from its hole. This was no easy task, as the space had been built to fit exactly, and the wriggle-room was mere millimetres.

But gradually, oh so gradually, the case pushed itself

out of its space in the wall and tumbled to the floor with a thud. Immediately, the top was flung open and a girl stepped out, arms held as wide as her smile.

'Ta-dah,' she trilled, to the empty shop.

Then she let her arms drop. 'Oh.'

Outside, a streetlamp shone. The clocks on the mantlepiece ticked, and the shop was in gloom, for, as the largest clock-face stubbornly told her, it was two o'clock in the morning.

Avery Eldritch pulled a face. 'Hm.' She folded her arms and went behind the desk. She gave the untidy desk a once-over, snorted derisively, then turned to the faded novels in the bookcase behind her, and chose Terry Pratchett's *Night Watch*.

She pulled it off the shelf, and three other books came with it, tumbling to the floor with loud thumps that made her wince. She swore under her breath, watching the doorway to the kitchen.

Before too long, a varnished cricket bat came into view, held by a hand protruding from the sleeve of a rather fetching maroon dressing gown. 'I have to warn you,' a voice squeaked, 'I am armed, and quite prepared to—'

'It's me,' she said. 'It's Avery.'

The cricket bat lowered a little, and Jonathan, hair

on end from sleep, peered around the door frame. His mouth dropped open. 'A – Averina?'

Avery smirked as she took in his dressing gown and moulting slippers. 'Surprised?'

'Extremely.' Jonathan pushed his glasses up his nose. 'What are you doing here? Is Portia here?' He looked around.

'No, Mum isn't here, just me. What's wrong? You're not excited to see your cousin?' She grinned nervously.

Jonathan gave a small laugh. 'Sort-of cousin.'

'True. I think I'm actually your aunt-several-times-removed or something.' She folded her arms tightly, like she was hugging herself. Her expression became somewhat apprehensive. 'It's been a long time.'

'Three years. Since Mum died, in fact.' Jonathan put the cricket bat on the end of the desk. 'I wasn't sure I'd see you again. Does your mother know you're here?'

'Pretty sure she'll soon figure it out if she doesn't know already.'

'Will she come after you?'

'She can't stand to be in the same room as our suitcase, so, I doubt it. What happened to your mum really got to her.' Avery scuffed the floor with her boot. 'They forbade me from coming here, after that. But, a few weeks ago, we heard about your dad.'

Jonathan looked up. 'Oh?'

'Mum got a letter from one of the old Strangeworlds Society members. Quickspark?'

'Oh yes, Greysen and Darilyn in Five Lights.'

'They explained what had happened to your dad, and how you were looking for him. Wondered if we had any information. Which we didn't, I'm afraid. It was the first we'd heard of it. I said I wanted to come through and see you, but Mum and Dad said no, it was too dangerous. So, I waited until they weren't looking.' She sniffed. 'I figured I'd been kept from seeing you for too long, anyway. And they're too cowardly to come after me, so . . . I've run away, basically.'

'Which isn't stupid at all,' Jonathan smirked, though without malice. 'I'd be lying if I said I wasn't glad to see you, Averina.'

They smiled stupidly at each other for a minute, before Avery went in for a hug, which Jonathan tolerated for three whole seconds before pushing her gently away. 'Care to explain the hour?'

'Miscalculation. Sorry.'

'Not to worry,' Jonathan yawned.

'Anyway,' Avery said. 'I didn't just come here to say sorry about your dad. Which I am, by the way – but there's something else. Something important.'

Jonathan's yawn disappeared and his mouth snapped shut. 'What?'

'The House on the Horizon,' she said, with an air of mystery.

Jonathan stared, unimpressed. 'The Strangeworlds Society Outpost? In the Desert of Dreams? What about it?'

'Heard from it lately?'

Jonathan tightened his dressing gown belt, before pulling the enormous Society Register from the bookshelf and crashing it down onto the desk. 'I haven't heard from *anyone* lately. Besides, I don't even know for sure if it's manned.' He caught Avery's eye and said, 'Peopled, I mean. Staffed.'

Avery gave a small smile. 'I overheard my parents talking about it. About a man named Thess who apparently lives there. Mum said he's been part of The Strangeworlds Society since the beginning.'

'That would make him a seriously old man,' Jonathan said, flipping through the pages of the register, 'so I'm assuming he's not from my world, at least.'

'But if he's been part of the Society from the start . . . I thought maybe he could help find your dad.'

Jonathan looked up from the book, sharply. 'What makes you think that?'

'He's been around for a long time. Maybe he knows something we don't. Or you don't.'

'I don't know a Mr Thess.' Jonathan shrugged. He looked back at the list of names. 'But, if he's a Society member, his name should be written down.'

'The thing is . . .' Avery paused. 'My mum says he's dangerous. He's been seen around Five Lights and other worlds too, asking questions – and not being polite about it. Someone said he had a gun.'

Jonathan paused, a memory coming back to him. 'The children in Tam's forest said they'd seen a man who had a gun. He came out of a suitcase.'

'Could it be him?'

'I hope so,' Jonathan said. 'Last thing I need is *two* armed gunmen running around in and out of suitcases. A-ha.' He turned the book around. 'Thess. Danser Thess. It says here he was the Strangeworlds Custodian at Phaeton's Trading Post before Mr Maskelyne. I was there, recently.' He touched the back of his head, remembering the pain of falling onto rocks, the abandoned mountainside, and the landscape that was bare – no outpost to be seen. 'The entire outpost was gone,' he said to Avery. 'Nothing left except snow and rocks. And the ledger doesn't say where Thess went after that.'

Avery leaned forward to see. 'Apparently the Quicksparks heard him telling people he's guarding the House on the Horizon.'

'Well, if he is, he hasn't bothered telling me,' Jonathan said. 'It says here that that contact for the House on the Horizon is lost . . .' He trailed off.

'Another lost person,' Avery said thoughtfully. 'Or maybe not lost, but unable to be contacted? How *do* you get to a place that's always on the horizon?'

Jonathan frowned. 'Wait – always? The House is *always* on the horizon? So, if you move forward, it moves further away?'

'Exactly. You can see it, but you can't get to it.'

'But The Strangeworlds Society must have had a way of getting to it,' Jonathan said. 'It's an outpost – there would be suitcases stored there. There must be a suitcase here that can take us there. Unless someone has moved it.' He glanced up at the empty slot in the wall of suitcases, which had been relieved of its case by his father, Daniel Mercator, just before his disappearance.

'So . . . should we try and go there?' Avery prompted.

Jonathan rubbed at his forehead. 'Maybe. I suppose it's worth a shot. I have no idea where the right suitcase might be, but we can start searching in the morning. It shouldn't take too long, with the three of us.'

'Three of us?' Avery asked in surprise.

'Oh, yes,' Jonathan grinned. 'Didn't I tell you? I've recruited a new Society member.'

CHAPTER FOUR

Flick got to Strangeworlds bang on ten.

It was a joy to be out of the house, alone, with no Freddy to be pushed in a pram and entertained, and no Mum or Dad nagging at her to stop scuffing the heels of her shoes.

Flick felt positively bouncy on her good mood. She grinned as she watched people hurrying past the travel agency as though it wasn't there. Their eyes slid from the second-hand bookshop on one side, to the church on the other, without blinking. The place did have the occasional visitor, of course; not everyone was so dull in the mind that they didn't notice it. But rare were the people like Flick and Jonathan – the people born with the ability to see magic.

Strangeworlds' bright red sign blared over the bay

window, confidently broadcasting the name of the travel agency to the public. The gold letters looked polished and gleaming, and Flick wondered if Jonathan had given the sign a scrub since the last time she was there (though it was difficult to imagine him up a ladder, or doing manual labour). Flick glanced at the tattered red patch she'd safety-pinned onto her sleeve. A magnifying glass embroidered in gold, with a slash of lightning in the middle of the lens shining against the red fabric. She felt a flush of pride. She felt as if she was coming home.

She pushed open the door, and went straight in.

'See, right on time, just like I promi—' She stopped and stared.

Instead of Jonathan sitting behind the desk, there was a girl about Flick's age. She had short black hair that stuck up at the front as though she'd been electrocuted. Her face was round, her dark eyes were sharp, and she looked suspiciously at Flick. The girl was wearing all black, including thick boots that laced up the front.

'Can I help you?' she asked, in a tone of voice Flick found very familiar.

'Um,' Flick said, aware she had been staring at the girl as though she was an escaped cobra. 'I was looking for Jonathan?'

The girl brightened. 'Oh! OK.' She came over. 'I'm Avery.' She offered a hand. 'Avery Eldritch,' she said. 'Not heard of you, yet.'

'I'm Flick,' Flick said, shaking the pale brown hand briefly. 'I help out?'

'At Strangeworlds?'

'Well, yeah.'

'Really.' Avery made a face that said *sure you do* in no uncertain terms.

The two girls stared at one another. Something about Avery reminded Flick of the girls at Lawrence Academy, Flick's old school, who would go silent and just wait for you to say something, anything. And then when you did they would laugh at you. So Flick kept quiet, teeth clamped together in case a word tried to sneak out.

'Jonathan didn't tell me he had an assistant,' Avery said eventually.

'I'm not his assistant. I'm . . .' Flick wondered if she was allowed to mention The Strangeworlds Society to this girl. Surely she was, if she'd been left minding the shop. A sudden burst of annoyance flared inside her. Jonathan had replaced her! After only a few weeks! And he'd acted so eager to have her back. Was that all a ruse? Was he lying to her, yet again?

Flick realised she hadn't finished speaking, and went red. 'I'm a . . .'

Avery raised her eyebrows. 'You're a what, exactly?'

Fortunately, Jonathan chose that moment to come into the room, fastening one of his cuffs as he walked. 'Ah, Felicity,' he said, as if everything was normal. 'Nice of you to turn up. I see you've met my cousin, Averina.'

Flick raised her eyebrows. 'Cousin? I thought you said you didn't have any family.'

'All right, you pedant. She's a sort-of cousin A Mercator married someone from Avery's world, as I understand it.' He looked at Avery. 'I think my great-great uncle is your great-great-great grandfather?'

'Something like that.' Avery shrugged. 'Back in the day,' she looked at Flick, 'when The Strangeworlds Society was all over the place, in every world you can think of, they were doing more than simply exploring. Let's just say there are more than a few of us with real blood-ties to this travel agency.'

Flick felt herself going red again. 'Oh?'

'Blood's pretty distant now, though,' Avery added. 'And my parents aren't Strangeworlds Society members. They don't even know I'm here.'

'My parents don't even know the Society exists,' Flick said, getting one up on Avery. 'It's a secret.'

'Wow, that must be tough,' Avery said. 'I'm so glad I could talk to my parents about it if I needed to. It's essential to have that closeness and support in your life, I think.'

Flick bit back something unpleasant, and flashed a fake smile instead, before going to sit in one of the armchairs.

Jonathan, apparently oblivious to the mood in the travel agency, straightened a few papers. 'Felicity, Averina has brought us news of something we – I – might need to investigate.'

'The House on the Horizon,' Avery nodded. 'It's part of The Strangeworlds Society.'

Flick folded her arms. 'Like the travel emporium in Five Lights?'

'Quicksparks? No, the House isn't like that, exactly. It's not just storage. The House on the Horizon is a safe house,' Avery said. 'As safe as you can get. You can't physically get there, you see?'

Flick blinked. 'What do you mean?'

Jonathan began to explain how he thought the House worked, but it made Flick's head ache.

'. . . so the location might be relative to the position of the person attempting to—'

'OK,' she said, wincing. 'I get it. You can't get there. Probably.'

'Unless we can find a suitcase that takes us to the house itself,' Jonathan mused.

Flick looked at Avery. 'And you think this Danser Thess person who lives there might know something about Jonathan's dad.'

It wasn't a question.

Avery shrugged. 'It's worth a shot, isn't it? Someone who's been part of the Society from the beginning might know more about Daniel than any of us.'

'Then, you'll need me,' Flick said.

Avery raised her eyebrows. 'You?'

'I would need your assistance, yes,' Jonathan said, ignoring his cousin. 'We need to look at all the suitcases with the magnifying glass.'

Flick nodded. 'So, what's the strategy once we find the right suitcase? We go to this Horizon place, and then what? I'd quite like a plan this time.'

Avery looked begrudgingly at Flick. 'She's right, Johnnie, we need a plan of attack.'

Flick looked up in delight. *Johnnie?*

Jonathan ignored the nickname. 'Yes, I shall do my research before we take off. The House isn't going anywhere, and until we know what might await us there, neither shall we. This Danser Thess character sounds like someone to be wary of.'

Avery stretched, her shoulder and spine clicking like castanets. 'Right, then. Pop through to see me if you find anything out. I'd best be getting back. My mother'll be wondering where—'

Her words dried up.

Flick looked up, following Avery's eyeline. There, at the bottom of the wall of suitcases, was a glittering light, just visible through the keyhole of a large trunk. For a moment Flick thought she'd suddenly developed the ability to see magic without a magnifying glass, but if she had, then Avery and Jonathan had too, because they were all staring at it.

Something tiny and golden and glowing like a firefly drifted lazily out from the keyhole of the trunk. The trunk was, like everything in the travel agency, not simply luggage. The trunk led to the Back Room – the immense storage space where the masses of suitcases that wouldn't fit in the main area of the shop were kept.

The golden spark drifted upwards, until it was head-height with Avery, and hovered in the middle of the room. It looked like a glowing pom-pom.

Jonathan steepled his fingers. 'What are you?' he asked, softly.

At the sound of his voice, the glowing spark seemed to turn, and floated over to him, bobbing on the slight breeze coming through the single open pane of the bay window. It stopped in front of Jonathan's desk, as though it was a customer.

'Is it alive?' Flick whispered.

'I don't think so.' Jonathan reached out and brushed his fingertips over the glowing speck.

At once, the speck swelled, lengthened like a glow-stick, then unfurled like a scroll, dulling to a pale brown sheet of paper that floated down onto the desk.

There was smart calligraphy on it, and a smudged blue stamp in one corner.

Jonathan picked it up. 'It's a letter. Sent through the keyholes. A little water-stained, but how marvellous.'

'Who's it from?' Flick stood.

Jonathan cleared his throat and read:

My good friend Mercator,

I hope this letter finds you in fine winds and fair weather. We fare not so well. You will be aware, I imagine, that the circle is falling away year by year, but I must stress that the speed at which it crumbles is now of the utmost concern.

We lose swathes of sea by the week, and only yesterday the Nastur failed to make port.

I find myself in the position of being forced to bend a knee and ask your help. We are four ships lost, and have heard nothing from the freemariner sailors who are our allies.

I have arranged a parley-meeting with the Mer-folk at the new moon, and would request your presence as a noted expert in these matters. You have my word that you shall not be harmed by myself, or any of my crew.

I await your arrival at The Break. I trust you will do us the honour of attending, but if you do not, I hereby curse you to sleep uneasily for the rest of your days, knowing you have sent us to walk with the corpses that dwell in the dark beneath.

Yours,
Nyfe Shaban
Pirate Queen, and Captain of the Aconite

'The pirates of The Break,' Avery said, taking the letter. 'They're being awfully polite.'

'Polite?' Flick spluttered. 'That letter included a curse!'

'Only one for disturbed sleep. This is their best manners,' Avery said. 'They must be desperate.'

Flick wanted to ask how she knew, but the fact remained that Avery *did* know these things, and Flick didn't. She found herself wishing rather hard that Avery had gone back home before the letter had arrived.

Jonathan had his hand at his mouth, one finger tapping his chin. He was thinking. He didn't move when Flick leaned over and lifted the letter from his hand.

'They want your help?' she asked, skimming the letter again.

'They want help in general,' Jonathan said. 'But it's not that which concerns me. I'm Head Custodian, my job is to help other worlds to the best of my ability. But *the circle is falling away . . .*'

'What does it mean?' Flick asked. 'What circle?'

Jonathan licked his lower lip. 'The Break is a tiny world,' he said. 'It's very old. And very small. And,' he smiled, 'circular.'

'Well, our world is circular,' Flick said.

'No, our world is a sphere – a globe,' Jonathan said, condescendingly. 'At least, our planet is a globe. I wouldn't like to hazard a guess as to the shape of our universe as a whole. It could be shaped like a butternut squash for all it matters. The point is, the world of The Break is a *flat* circle. A thin plate, or a disc, covered in water from edge to edge. No outer space, no other planets, not even a sun. The place is lit by rips and tears in the darkness of the sky that let in light from other worlds. There's no way to predict day or night, it just depends which worlds are passing by at the time. I gather they live very much by the clock, rising and going to bed when it tells them to, rather than doing what the sky says.'

'And the only land worth talking about is a little island at the centre of all the ocean. There are a few tiny islands, but the people don't really live on them. They stay on their boats all the time,' Avery added.

Flick blinked. 'But, if the circle is falling away, that means . . .'

'World-collapse,' Jonathan said. He took the letter back. 'A meeting with the mer-folk is proof this is serious. The pirates and the mer-folk have been merrily killing one another for centuries. A parley – a meeting – means they are prepared to put their differences aside for a threat bigger than their ancient squabbles. This letter implies they're suffering from world-collapse. That means everyone in that world is at risk.'

'Why is it collapsing, though?' Flick asked. 'Is it like Five Lights? Has everyone been bottling magic?'

Jonathan looked uneasy. 'Not that I know of. Bottling magic isn't something I remember being part of life on the seas. We'd have to check the relevant guidebook. But no matter the reason, I need to go.' He folded the letter and put it into his inside jacket pocket. 'This is Mercator business, and I have been summoned.'

'You're not going on your own,' Flick said.

Jonathan opened his mouth to argue.

'No, you're not,' Avery said. 'Not for one second, Johnnie.'

'My name,' he snapped, 'is Jon. A. Than. It's three syllables long, I am perfectly sure you can stretch to it.'

'Only if you call me Avery,' she smirked back.

They stared at one another for a moment, then Jonathan looked away with a sigh.

'Fine,' he said. 'The name you choose is up to you, of course.'

'You should know that,' she sniffed. Then she brightened. 'So, pirates. What do we need?'

CHAPTER FIVE

'They call themselves *pirates*,' Jonathan said to Flick, once Avery had gone back to her world to get a change of clothes, 'but they aren't really. Not if you want to get technical. They're not committing piracy, as such. There's no king or queen with a navy for them to be pirating against.'

'That letter was signed *Pirate Queen*,' Flick pointed out. They were hunting for appropriate wet-weather clothes in Jonathan's wardrobes, which seemed to contain only second-hand suits and hideous knitwear. But she was pleased to have Jonathan to herself for a little while, at least. She couldn't put her finger on exactly why Avery had got under her skin. In terms of personality she was quite similar to Jonathan, and she seemed clever and was even a bit funny. But Flick felt like keeping her at arm's length (and possibly further) for now.

Jonathan gave a small laugh. 'Oh, *Pirate Queen* is a chosen name. Every leader picks one. There've been all kinds of names . . . Painted Soul, Wandering Eye, Davy Jones' Bride . . . Pirate Queen is just another title. But Nyfe won the right to use it in what was probably not the fairest of fights.'

'So she's not to be trusted?'

'I think we should be wary, at least. She might not be a true queen, but she has a fearsome reputation as a ruler. She's always respected Strangeworlds, and the world-hopping we do, but she's never been exactly friendly.'

'And what about the mer-folk?' asked Flick. 'Is there a king of the sea?'

'A queen,' Jonathan said.

'A pirate queen, *and* a mer-queen?' Flick felt a swell of pride at the women holding positions of authority in that world.

'Just so.' Jonathan picked up his small backpack. He was wearing his usual deep blue tartan trousers and matching waistcoat, though without a tie, and he had put on heavy leather boots instead of his usual brogues.

Flick was trying to ignore the prickling anxiety in her stomach. It had been a few weeks since she had travelled via suitcase, and although she had missed it terribly, she suddenly felt nervous and slightly seasick. 'Is time the same, there?' she asked, to avoid thinking about stepping into a world that was almost entirely water.

'No,' Jonathan said. 'It moves faster. And it's difficult to track if you don't have a clock with you, due to the unpredictable light and dark. They measure a twenty-hour day, and a ten-day week.'

'What's the conversion rate for time?' Flick asked, frowning. 'I can't stay out past six in the evening, our time. Mum will brick up my bedroom door.'

'Relax,' Jonathan drawled. 'For every one of our hours, The Break experiences *eighteen*. I'll keep my watch running to our time. If we're going to overstay, I'll know about it.' He shrugged the bag onto his back and clipped the strap across his chest.

'Your dad went there,' Flick said, suddenly remembering the list of worlds that had been jotted down in Daniel Mercator's notebook. The notebook was something Flick had found in a silent world with an island and a lighthouse – the only clue to his disappearance. Flick did not like thinking about that place, it gave her the shivers. 'The Break was on his list, at least.'

'He went there fairly often,' Jonathan sighed. 'It's a popular place for people to visit, you see? High seas adventure. I'm sure if he was still there they wouldn't have bothered writing to the travel agency.'

Avery knocked, and looked around into Jonathan's room. Jonathan had advised that layers were best, since The Break could be any temperature, depending on whether or not a sun was shining onto it, so Avery had come back to Strangeworlds wearing several T-shirts, and some waterproof trousers over her black jeans. She still had her black leather boots on, with thick woollen socks folded down over the tops. They looked *serious*.

Flick was suddenly very conscious of her teal and pink leather Converse. She had one of Jonathan's old yukky hand-knitted jumpers on under her splash-proof jacket, and it came down to her thighs.

'I think we look the part.' Avery nodded at them. 'Except Jonathan, who looks like he's taking the rest of the local parish council on an afternoon hike.'

'I have standards,' Jonathan sniffed, hitching the backpack up.

Avery smirked. 'Can you both swim?'

Flick nodded, but Jonathan looked as though she'd asked him to lick the sole of someone's foot.

'I have no desire to enter water that has played home to someone else's bunions, thank you,' he sniffed.

Flick's mouth did a good impression of a goldfish's. 'But the whole world is water, Jonathan.'

'I don't care. I don't swim, and I don't particularly enjoy even being wet.'

They all clattered down the stairs. Flick noticed that Jonathan touched the frame of his dad's photograph as they passed it. Avery checked the front door was locked, and Jonathan cleared a space to lay down the suitcase to The Break.

The case was water-damaged, black, and peeling in places. The latches were orange and brown with rust, and the handle's leather was softened and worn with the ghosts of old grips. It looked well-used, and, Flick thought, loved.

'Ready?' Jonathan asked.

'Ready.' Avery checked her coat-cuffs in a way that was so Jonathan it unnerved Flick for a moment.

'You may wish to stand back a little,' Jonathan warned. 'Last time this suitcase was opened a rather aggressive octopus tentacle came out.'

Avery backed up against the wall. Flick forced herself to stay where she was. She was a real Strangeworlds Society member, and she definitely wasn't afraid of tentacles, no matter how slimy they might be.

Jonathan undid the latches.

Immediately, a wave of water splashed out of the case. It was mercifully tentacle-free.

Jonathan pulled a face. 'I'll bring the suitcase through, if you don't mind.'

Flick nodded, and steeled herself, before gritting her teeth and stepping down into the watery suitcase.

The world rocked for an instant, and Flick flung her arms out for fear she was about to tumble into the sea. She staggered out onto a skinny jetty, no wider than a small car. The boards beneath her feet were rotting and sodden, green slime and seaweed hanging down from them into the sea like drapes.

Avery erupted from the suitcase next, catching hold of Flick and apologising as they both wobbled awkwardly on the jetty. Flick grabbed a thick wooden pole to steady them, then immediately wished she hadn't. The pole was covered in slime and scratchy barnacles, and the stuff clung to her hands.

Avery pulled a face. 'Thanks for the catch, but at what cost?'

'Uh, I know, right?' Flick tried to wipe her hand off on a clean-ish bit of wood.

Jonathan came out as gracefully as ever, quickly pulling the suitcase through after himself. 'Let's get somewhere less damp, shall we?' he asked, looking at Flick's slimy hands. 'According to the guidebook, this is the main island of The Break, so there should be someone around here who can point us in Captain Nyfe's direction.'

Avery handed Flick a tissue for her hands but walked off before Flick could say thank you.

The wind blew straight off the sea as they trotted down the jetty onto what could generously be called a beach, but would more accurately be described as a pile of boulders with some sand in between. There was a promenade of sorts on the flattened rocks above, where small wooden booths stood gloomily overlooking the sea. Old rope and nets were tangled here and there, along with broken lobster pots and heaps of sack-cloth weighted down by rocks planted on the tops of them. Running down from the walkway to the beach was a pathway, which had been smoothed deliberately to allow boats to be slid down into the water. A thick stripe of seaweed marked the beach in a permanent line, the older stuff rotting beneath newer plants. The seawater bobbed constantly back and forth, leaving a dent where it kissed the sand.

'I'm not entirely sure of protocol,' Jonathan said. 'But I believe we should make ourselves known.'

'There's no one about,' Avery said, looking at the deserted booths and the empty lobster pots and nets strewn about. She fastened the top button of her jacket and folded her arms across her chest as the wind blew.

'Perhaps it's night.' Flick looked up at the sky. Instead of stars, there were thin strips of light shining through the blackness, like rips in dark velvet showing white silk beneath. There was enough light to see by, though oil lamps were lit here and there along the seafront. 'By their clocks, anyway, I mean.'

'Very possible.' Jonathan nodded. 'Still, someone will be awake. A night watchman, or someone. We need to let Nyfe know we have arrived.'

They walked up further, past the empty booths that advertised shellfish soup, tentacle chips and stuffed crab-heads.

Flick stuck her tongue out slightly at the menus. 'Stuffed heads? Sounds vile.'

'Stick to the soup,' Jonathan said.

They didn't have to go much further before they found a man snoring loudly in a wooden hut. A hand-painted sign beside him told the three of them that when he wasn't asleep, he had a job:

Adam Quillmaster

Scribe

Letters of note, declarations, advertisements

also Express Pigeon Service

Jonathan tapped him on the forehead.

The man snorted but didn't wake up.

Jonathan did it again. 'Hello?'

Suddenly, the man's right arm swung out like a pendulum. He smacked Jonathan in the side, sending him cartwheeling to the floor. The man stood quickly, pulling a short knife from out of nowhere. Flick and Avery stepped quickly back.

'You young hoodlums,' he snarled, showing long, yellow teeth. 'Curse on your heads. Don't you know you'll bring the ill measure of the sea on your heads by waking a sleeping scribe?'

'Don't you know it's terrible luck to hit a fellow wearing glasses?' Jonathan countered from the ground.

Adam Quillmaster considered. 'In that case, I reckon they'd cancel out, sir?'

Jonathan picked himself up. 'How fortunate.'

The man flicked his fingers, and the knife seemed to disappear. 'Right. So, how can I be of service?'

'We need to send a message to the Pirate Queen,' Jonathan said. 'Urgently.'

'I see. I charge extra for the captain, you know.' Quillmaster reached behind his booth and lifted out a sleeping pigeon. 'Wake up, you cur,' he said to it.

The pigeon opened one eye, and gave him a cool stare, before pecking hard at the hand that held it.

The scribe ignored it. 'And what do you want saying?'

'Tell her . . . tell her Jonathan Mercator has arrived to parley,' he said.

Quillmaster was rummaging in his booth for paper, but he paused.

The bird pecked him again.

'Then no need for the bird, young man. As it happens, I'm planning on attending the parley myself. Give me a minute to lock up the bird and I'll row you out.'

CHAPTER SIX

The scribe locked up his pigeon and his booth, and led them along the promenade to a marina, where a whole host of boats floated like shiny, upturned beetles.

Quillmaster waved them over. 'I'll take you in the *Rooster*. Enough room for four in that. Can you all swim?'

'If the occasion calls for it, and I certainly hope it will not.' Jonathan raised his eyebrows.

'Can't guarantee nothing in these waters,' the scribe said darkly. He got into the bright green and orange boat, and helped Flick and Avery in. Flick took hold of the suitcase so Jonathan could use both of his arms to balance as he boarded.

Quillmaster took his seat at the pointy end of the

boat. 'Now, you've arrived a bit early for the parley with the Mer-Queen,' he said, as they pushed off. 'But lucky that you did, I reckon. Because tonight is a gathering of the ships. Anyone who calls themselves a captain or a first mate will gather to hear Captain Nyfe's plan. Then, we'll sail where she points us, to the parley with the Mistress of the Deep.'

'Mistress of the Deep? You mean the Mer-Queen?' Flick asked. Jonathan gripped the side tight as the boat rocked drunkenly.

'Aye, that's one name for her. The Queen of Weeds, that's another. Leviathan's Bride, the more fanciful call her.'

They rowed out from the island into the sea proper, and then along the line of the coast. The water was calm. As they skirted around the island of The Break, the beach dwindled until it vanished altogether. There were only sharp juts of rock and cliff that dropped suddenly into the dark water. Flick sensed that the ocean would always be dark, even if the tears in the sky overhead shone through with the most brilliant white light.

'Why did you call your boat the *Rooster*?' Avery asked, patting the painted side.

'Chickens is important,' Quillmaster said, as though

it was obvious. 'Very industrious bird, the chicken. Keeps on giving through its whole life, never a complaint.'

'That's hens,' Avery said. 'A rooster doesn't lay eggs.'

'Ah, but without the rooster in the coop, there's no more chickens and therefore no more eggs.'

'So, the cockerel does one job and gets a boat named after him, and the long-suffering hen gets what, exactly?'

Quillmaster rubbed his chin. 'Eaten, eventually.'

Avery opened her mouth, probably to object, when there was a thud, and the boat gave a sudden violent rock.

Everyone froze. Jonathan dug his nails into the bench and the blood drained out of his face. Flick could feel her arms buzzing with tension as she tried to keep as still as possible. She gripped the suitcase handle tightly. A chill breeze lifted spray from the ocean and fogged it over their faces in a fine mist.

Quillmaster lifted the oars from the water, and the boat drifted slightly on the swell. 'Hush,' he said, unnecessarily, as everyone was still frozen in silence. 'Mer-folk. They might just nudge the boat and be on their way.'

Flick's eyes searched the dark water. She couldn't see anything. No faces, no fish tails.

Quillmaster relaxed slightly. 'We're best to—'

The boat tipped.

As though lifted by a giant, the vessel arched onto its side. Avery screamed. Flick somehow remembered to take a huge gulp of air before all four of them went crashing into the water, the boat up-turning itself on top of them.

The force of the boat sent Flick spinning. She kept her eyes open, the saltwater stinging them as bubbles tickled her skin, racing ahead of her to the surface. The suitcase swung from her hand, no help whatsoever. For a second Flick was outraged that it wasn't acting as a floatation device, but of course this wasn't a normal suitcase.

She kicked hard, trying to right herself as the water buffeted her to and fro.

She didn't know which way was up.

She felt her lungs burn. Panic lanced though her. The suitcase was twisting in her fingers, dragging her deeper into the water as it sank down—

No. As it was *pulled* down.

Flick gave a shout of horror, losing precious air as she saw just what was trying to yank the suitcase out of her hand.

When Flick had imagined mer-folk, she'd thought

of cartoons, where the characters had impossibly skinny waists and curtains of red hair which matched their underwater lipstick.

The creature that blinked back at her was nothing like that.

The mer-person's skin was a mottled, scaly mixture of blue and grey. There was no hair on its head, though there were thick fronds, like fins, growing down its scalp and neck. There were four, deep, blood-red gashes on the creature's throat, which had to be gills, two jet black eyes and when it blinked – as it did now – Flick could see the creature had two sets of eyelids for each eye, one set a clear covering that looked like plastic, the other pair the same shade as its skin.

It gave a sort of stretch of its mouth, which Flick thought might be a nasty smile.

She pulled hard at the suitcase.

But the mer-person had more than two arms to use. With a twist of its body, it lifted four of its eight tentacles and yanked at the suitcase.

Flick was no match for it. The mer-person had more than twice as many limbs as she did. And she was drowning. The suitcase handle was wrenched out of her hand.

She watched the mer-person shoot out of sight, the suitcase held tight to its chest.

Flick flailed, her heart hammering in a panicked fight for oxygen.

She could kick in the wrong direction, swim down or across and never breach the surface. She'd promised her parents she'd be back this time . . .

A hand grabbed her wrist. It pulled her, hard.

Up.

Flick's head broke the surface, and she gasped, eyes open, water pouring down her head. Her chest raged in an effort to get air back into it, and black spots burst like dark fireworks in her vision as she kicked in the water.

She turned, trying to find the *Rooster*.

Just in time to see a boat the size of a mountain bearing down on her, cutting through the water like a scythe. The curved wooden prow was moving faster than Flick would have thought possible. A carved figurehead of a skeletal mer-person grinned down at her, glaring with empty eye sockets.

Flick yelped, kicking hard to get out of the path of the ship. But the water was dragging her into it like she was a leaf, ready to be smashed against the hull—

Strong arms grabbed her around the middle, and she was pulled swiftly out of the path of the ship, which never slowed down. Flick, safely out of the way of the ship, watched in silent shock as the ship's windows, cannons, and the swollen curve of its enormous body washed past her. She'd seen big boats before, but this was something else.

'Oh my god.' Flick tried to breathe. She turned, treading water as the rescuing arms let go of her. 'Thank y . . .' Her words shrivelled and died before they made it out of her mouth.

Another mer-person, this one with brownish-red mottling running down their chest, stared back at her.

Flick foolishly looked down for the suitcase. But of course, they did not have it.

'I am sorry. About the suitcase,' they said, blinking with those strange, double-lidded eyes. 'We had to.'

'You *had* to?' Flick coughed.

The creature gave a nod, then pointed behind her. 'Your boat.'

Flick looked and sighed in relief at the sight of the *Rooster* heading towards her, three very wet figures sitting inside it.

'Felicity!' Jonathan – a picture in his sopping wet suit – called.

When she looked back, the mer-person had gone.

Moments later, Flick was being pulled into the boat. Quillmaster, Avery and Jonathan were as wet as she was. Avery's spiky hair was glued to her scalp, and Quillmaster's clothes had taken the opportunity of a good dunking to release a smell comparable to a million wet (and possibly dead) dogs.

Jonathan was leaning against the side of the boat, a hand to his ribs. He was breathing hard and was even paler than usual.

Flick turned to look, but the creature in the water was nowhere to be seen.

'Any injuries, girl?' Quillmaster asked Flick.

'No.' She started to shiver as her skin woke up and realised it was freezing. The word *hypothermia* came to mind, and her shivering got worse. What were you supposed to do if you fell into water? Quillmaster handed her a soaked blanket. 'It'll keep the wind off you at any rate. We'd best get on. The ship that just passed us was the *Aconite*. The flagship.'

'That was Captain Nyfe's ship?' Jonathan asked, wrapping himself in a blanket.

Quillmaster snorted. 'Yes. Headed to The Break in a hurry.'

'Good,' Jonathan shuddered. He winced as he sat

up, his wet shirt translucent, showing his binder underneath. He still had a hand clamped to his ribs, and Flick wondered if his water-logged layers were making it difficult for him to breathe. 'I don't understand why the mer-people attacked us. We weren't doing anything. What did they want with us?'

Flick swallowed. Guilt rose in her like nausea. 'They wanted the suitcase,' she said in a small voice.

Avery looked up, and Jonathan's eyes widened like saucers behind his glasses.

'They wanted the *suitcase*?' Avery looked at the empty floor of the boat. 'It's gone?'

'You let them take it?' Jonathan rasped. His hands twitched as if he was trying not to jump up and shake her.

'I didn't *let* them do anything,' Flick said, but it sounded pathetic. 'I tried to hold on to it, but they pulled me down. I had to let go.'

Avery sat back, shaking her head. 'Why did they want it?'

Flick looked out at the water. 'I don't know. One of them pushed me to the surface, and said "I'm sorry, we had to" and then swam away.'

'*Had to?*' Jonathan repeated. He took his glasses off and pressed the heels of his hands into his eyes.

'Wonderful. Just wonderful. And now, we're *stuck here*!' He thumped the side of the boat and hurt his hand. 'Ow!'

Flick buried her nose into the blanket. If they never found the suitcase again, she'd cursed them to stay here for ever. There was no way to know where the merpeople had gone with the suitcase, or even why they wanted it so badly. There was no way of following them, either.

Flick's throat contracted hard with the sharp dry feeling of wanting to cry.

It was all her fault.

CHAPTER SEVEN

They sailed in the wake of the *Aconite*. The motion from the larger ship meant their own boat bobbed and dropped in a way that made all four of them swallow hard. Avery and Jonathan had wedged themselves together for warmth, and Flick was quite jealous, wrapping her arms around herself and tucking her legs up to try and make herself as small as possible beneath the blanket, which seemed to be doing less and less by the second.

'I'd be a gentleman and offer you my j-jacket,' Jonathan said. 'But I'm using it.'

'Hilarious,' Flick said, her teeth chattering.

Quillmaster gave them a look and shook his head. 'We're here.'

They looked up and saw the great looming darknesses of the anchored galleons. Flickering lights from stinking oil lamps shone here and there. The galleons might have been anchored, but they were not still. They moved and bobbed on the water like restless beasts, so Quillmaster kept a distance from them – their great curved wooden sides could have knocked the *Rooster* into splinters.

The bay led into a network of caves, where rock arched out over the water like a ceiling. The low tide had exposed flattish sections of rock that acted as walkways. A channel of water ran into the largest cave, bordered on either side by these walkways.

Quillmaster tied off the *Rooster* beside a number of small vessels, and everyone disembarked. Flick tried to get her legs moving again, but it was as though her blood had congealed into cold cement. She was still shivering and felt rough with guilt at losing the suitcase.

Avery stamped her feet hard and scrunched up her nose in distaste at the squelching noise. Even her heavy boots had been no match for the ocean.

'This way,' Quillmaster beckoned. 'I can't hear any shouting, so I don't reckon the meeting's started yet. Do you good to introduce yourselves afore it starts. And get dry and warm, of course.'

They walked on slippery rock, passing several groups of sailors who looked at them with interest.

'Quillmaster.' A man with meaty forearms hailed him. The man's tanned skin was marked with dozens of short lines, tattooed into his skin like tally-marks. Flick wondered what they were keeping count of. 'You going to see Nyfe?'

'Delivering these young 'uns, aye. Why'd you want to know, Jask?' Quillmaster sniffed.

Jask dug a nail between his teeth. 'My crew's been talking. If The Break's going the way we think it is, it's proper leadership we need.'

Quillmaster's face stayed expressionless. 'And you think you're the man to lead the armada, do you?'

Jask shrugged and spat whatever he'd picked from his teeth into a corner. 'Better me and my crew than someone who spends time talking with fish. "Talk to the mer!" Like they're human! S'a waste of time.'

Quillmaster clicked his tongue. 'Careful, Jask. You challenge Nyfe, you're liable to end up with no chance of passing your name on.' He glanced back and jerked his head. 'Come on.'

Flick, Jonathan and Avery filed past Jask, whose expression was somewhere between amused and annoyed. Flick didn't like the look of him, or the sound of what he had been talking about. Challenge the Pirate Queen? Tensions were clearly already stretched to breaking point amongst the pirates.

They walked further into the passageway. The temperature started to increase from the amount of bodies walking about and the fiery lamps that lit up the gloom. The lamps, Quillmaster told them, were made of whatever bits of whales they couldn't eat, wear, or turn into weapons. The stuff in the lamps was the real dregs, wrung out and already used, rotting even as it burned. The stink was the sort of sharp smell that went straight for your eyes and the back of your throat.

Flick did not want to be stuck in this world, smelling whale-stench for ever. She fell back to walk with Jonathan, who was hunched over and glaring daggers as he walked. 'I'm really sorry about the suitcase. I didn't mean to—'

'I know you didn't mean to, but it still happened. I'm always, *always*, telling other people not to lose their luggage. "Don't lose your luggage!" I might as well have it tattooed. And then what do you go and do?' He gave a sort of breathy hysterical laugh.

Flick felt utterly miserable. 'We'll get the suitcase back,' she said, though she had trouble believing herself.

'I suppose,' Jonathan said, not sounding very convinced either. He brightened slightly. 'At least it's not just the two of us this time. Avery will have some good ideas. She got us out of all kinds of scrapes when we were younger. Though, to be fair, she usually got us into them to begin with.'

Flick found that she was scowling slightly.

'I'm glad she's come back now, even though her parents didn't want her to. Bit like you, really,' Jonathan went on. 'She's always done the right thing, even if it's unpopular.'

Flick looked back at Avery, who was stepping carefully on the wet rocks. She felt the hostility she'd been nursing over her begin to slip, just a little.

'Who goes there?' A sharp voice came from ahead.

'Adam Quillmaster, at your service,' Quillmaster said.

A woman came forward. She was dressed in what looked like a huge leather cone, which expanded outwards from her neck. This might have looked amusing, but for the cutlass in her hand, and the blue-black tattoos all over her face, which flowed in some delicate script Flick couldn't read down her forehead, dripping down her face and over her cheeks to her chin. Glossy purple-red lip-paint completed the decoration.

'Who's this?' she asked, pointing at the three travellers with her sword.

'They want to speak to the Pirate Queen,' Quillmaster circumnavigated the question. 'They've the right.'

'She sent us a summons,' Jonathan added.

'Very well. Bring them through.' She nodded at them. 'My name is Edony.'

'Jonathan, Felicity, Avery,' Jonathan pointed at everyone quickly. 'I don't suppose you've any way of drying our clothes?' he asked. 'We're suffering, I don't mind telling you.'

'Drape them on the hot-stones.' Edony nodded at an area lit by oil lamps, where several items of clothes steamed on tables of stone. 'There's a fire-mountain below the ocean, here, and the heat comes up through the stones, see? You can choose something to wear from the slop chest for now and then I'll take you to see her. There's a wee bit of time before the meeting begins, yet. Most of the captains are here, we're just waiting for a few stragglers.'

'We can choose clothes from the *what*?' Avery asked. But Quillmaster nudged her shoulder, and led them all through into the lit part of the cave.

Flick wrinkled her nose. The smell of rapidly drying clothes mixing with the stink of the oil lamps made the air so thick you could chew it.

'Best get stripped off,' Quillmaster said, starting to undo his coat without preamble.

Flick felt her face ignite, and Avery's eyes widened into saucers.

'What on earth happened to privacy, man?' Jonathan spluttered.

Quillmaster paused, his shirt open to his collarbones. Enough wiry, grey chest-hair to stuff a pillow was escaping. 'Fine, if you're all airs and graces.' He pointed. 'The slop is out there by that outcrop, and there's a bit you can hide behind, if you're bothered.' He went back to undoing his buttons, and Flick, Jonathan and Avery all fled.

'What in the name of Pan's pipes is the *slop chest*?' Avery whispered.

'It's where they keep clothes. Spares, and stolen,' Jonathan said. 'It's usually a store on a ship, but I suppose there's been a crate or two brought ashore for this meeting. Nothing too disgusting, I hope.'

The slop chest wasn't an actual chest, it turned out. It was crates and boxes of clothes, shoes, drinks and bottles stacked up against a damp wall of the cave. There were a great number of silk and jewelled dresses, and Flick was initially tempted by them before she saw Avery grab a pile of sensible, waxed trousers, shirts, woollen jumpers and thick jackets. Avery shoved some of them into Jonathan's arms.

'You go first, you'll probably be ages.'

Jonathan carried the clothing behind the tall stone screen, and Flick heard a sigh of relief as though he'd sunk into a hot bath. There was a comical throwing out of clothes, and then a pause as, presumably, buttons were done up. He eventually sauntered around from behind the outcrop, and the sight of him made Flick grin stupidly.

'Oh, don't start.' He brushed at the waxed trousers that were bunched around his ankles. 'They're not exactly to size.'

'I wasn't going to laugh,' Flick said quickly. 'You look amazing!' She beamed.

Jonathan adjusted the deep blue jacket he had on and tried not to look too smug. He had on two shirts and a thick, grey, knitted jumper under the jacket and was finally standing straight again. With his curls unbrushed and drying in a way that seemed to defy gravity, he looked rather like a naval officer who had decided it was a pirate's life for him, but wasn't quite willing to give up the finery. The only thing that let him down was the sour smell of the unwashed sailors who had worn the clothes before.

Flick went behind the screen next and stripped down to her pants. This wasn't what she had expected to be doing just before going to meet a pirate queen. She decided that she was going to keep her pants with her, even if they were wet. The last thing she wanted was for a pirate to see them drying on one of the hot-stones. She stuffed them in her backpack and checked over the contents. The only things entirely dry were the biscuits she'd brought, safe in their plastic packaging. She zipped the bag back up, and pulled on the thick trousers, which creaked and smelled of old blood, then put on three of the huge sail-like shirts before pulling on a jumper that came down to her knees. She hung her shoes off one of her backpack straps by tying the laces together, and walked out barefoot.

Avery followed, copying Flick's method with the shoes. Jonathan had merely loosened his laces and changed his socks.

'I'm not putting my feet anywhere where other people's feet have been,' he said, and that was the end of it.

When they got back to the hot-stones, Quillmaster had changed into similar clothes, and he was clearly fed up with waiting for them.

'Look lively,' he snapped, standing up. 'She's heard you're here. She's a-waiting for you.'

CHAPTER EIGHT

Quillmaster led them through the cave down a natural corridor of rock, worn smooth by centuries of rising tides and howling winds. The floor was pitted with dents worn from the constant ceiling drips, and Avery cursed as her foot slipped into a deep puddle.

Eventually, the pathway widened again, and the channel of water that was beside them widened too, into a pool. Around the edge of it was a wide walkway illuminated by fat-lamps drilled into the walls, the stinking, yellow light making watery-white reflections dance on the ceiling.

Edony, the woman in the conical coat with the tattoos was waiting for them. She gave a nod, taking in their new, dry clothes. 'Better.'

'Thank you for your generosity,' Jonathan said. He glanced over the woman's shoulder. 'Is our host available?'

'The Pirate Queen is ready to see you,' she said. 'But she's not the host. This is no one's land to claim. We only come down here to discuss. Never to reign. This way. And watch your tongues.'

Quillmaster waved goodbye as Edony led the rest of them around the walkway. Her conical coat was, Flick could see, rather more practical that it had first appeared. Edony had billowing trousers on beneath it, and the coat was soft, not stiff – if she had to climb in a hurry, the coat wouldn't impede her movements. It was genius, really.

'Captain,' Edony said as they approached a group of four pirates who were talking in low voices. 'Captain, the Mercator child is here.'

The Pirate Queen, Nyfe Shaban, turned around.

She was the largest woman Flick had ever seen. Easily over six feet tall, with a neck broad and thick enough to break a hangman's rope. Her shoulders could have supported a bridge, and though her clothes were the finest of anyone around, the trousers and shirt were almost straining at the seams with the woman's obvious muscle. Her black hair was cropped short, and her brown face was entirely free from make-up, though she had a swirling tattoo on her throat. There was a black eyepatch over her right eye, embroidered with a blue petal.

She smiled, and it was as though she'd drawn a blade. 'Mercator.'

'Pirate Queen.' Jonathan gave a bow, though not a deep one, and he maintained eye contact.

Flick, too shy to look up properly, kept her eyes on Nyfe's belt buckle, which was a stylised fish with a hook through its lip as the fastening.

Nyfe glanced at the pirates she had been talking to, then jerked her head towards the exit. The pirates walked away without argument, though with curious looks at Flick, Avery and Jonathan. All except Edony, who stayed, leaning against the wall of the cave.

'So, you received my summons,' Nyfe said once they were alone. She folded her arms over her chest.

'Most ingenious, I have to admit,' Jonathan said. 'I've never seen a message like that before. How does it work?'

'By using blood-magic.'

Jonathan blinked. 'Excuse me?'

Edony held up what looked like a marble, except that it was softly glowing in the gloom. Flick recognised it as being the same sort of glass container as the Thieves had used in Five Lights, though this one was much smaller. 'We don't use a lot of magic,' Edony said, 'but this technique is useful for sending messages long-distance. The marble is broken onto the letter, you see? And the released energy is activated to find the named person.'

'Ah,' Jonathan nodded. 'It's a homing pigeon.'

'Correct. Homes in on the named individual, or their closest blood relative.'

'Well, it worked. I received your letter. The circle is collapsing, you said. Quite the claim to make.'

'It's not a claim,' Nyfe said. 'It's the truth. You've seen the boats floating on the water. I ask you: Where are the forests that grew the trees each plank is made from? Where are the mines that donated the iron for arrowheads, for bullets, for nails and buckles?'

'Where?' Flick asked.

Nyfe's dark eye slid over to her, and she stared at her for several seconds. The temperature seemed to drop. Flick wondered how the pirate they'd passed in the cove, Jask, thought he could take on this woman. She was *fearsome*. She made you feel *fear*. 'Those parts of the world have fallen away, girl,' she said. 'Gone into the ether before my time, or my grandmother's.'

'Do you know why?' Avery said.

'No.' Nyfe shook her head. 'World's always been shrinking, but those who lived in the past looked at it as a problem for the future. Not their job to keep us safe, they thought. Others would sort it out, one day. Well. Now we *are* the ones in charge. And it's happening too fast to stop it now. We've run out of time.' She looked away, and Flick had to remind herself to breathe.

Jonathan frowned. 'What is it you plan to do?'

'We talk, first of all.' Nyfe indicated the water. 'It's taken me a long time to convince the mer-folk to parley with us. I plan to tell them there is still hope, and a way out. Which is where you come in.'

'Me?' Jonathan went pale.

'You own the means of transportation.' She waved an impatient hand. 'The suitcases. The way out. For all of us.'

'You own a suitcase, do you not?' Jonathan asked. 'How else would have you sent me that letter?'

'The ruler of The Break has access to one case only.' Nyfe raised a finger. 'The case is passed from leader to leader as a sort of talisman. It was a gift, so they say, from the Strangeworlders back when my grandmother captained my ship. And using that suitcase is how I sent your summons – the message travelled from our world through that one, and then another and another until it found what it was looking for. But the land inside the suitcase is useless to us for any other purpose. It leads to a sand-covered world – a sweltering desert of nothing that is suitable for no one. We would not even survive travelling through it. We need another suitcase. One we can all travel through. One that leads to a water world. You can provide it, so we can move to another world to begin our lives again.'

Jonathan shook his head. 'I'm afraid I can't do that.'

'You must.'

'I can't,' he repeated. 'Living in a world that you were not born in is impossible.'

'Not impossible,' Nyfe sniffed. 'We know of people who have.'

'Yes, but their lifespan is so greatly reduced that—'

'And you think our lives are not about to be greatly reduced here?' Nyfe raised her voice.

Flick and Avery shrank back in alarm, but Jonathan kept his skinny shoulders as square as he could.

'Look,' he said. 'The truth is, I'm not in a position to help anyone at this exact moment.'

'What do you mean, Mercator?'

Jonathan spread his hands. 'Do you see a suitcase in my hands, Pirate Queen?'

Nyfe's expression went from annoyed to shocked in an instant. 'How came you here, then?'

'Oh, we *came* here through a suitcase.' Jonathan snorted. 'But we were capsized by mer-folk on our way here. One of them stole the suitcase.'

'Stole it?'

Flick hunched slightly, wanting to disappear from view.

Nyfe frowned. 'There is bad blood between them and us. I'd thought we might be able to work together on this, but if they're attacking my visitors before we even begin . . .'

'But they saved me,' Flick added quickly. 'I couldn't find the surface, and I was panicking. They could have let me drown, but one of them pulled me to the surface, and then out of the way of your ship. They saved me.'

'That just makes it a robbery without murder.' Edony shrugged. 'Just because you're keen on one doesn't mean you'll happily do the other.'

'Unless there's more to it,' Nyfe said. She looked thoughtful; her formidable expression had softened slightly. Flick wondered if the Pirate Queen's ferocity was real, or whether it was an act to cover her true feelings.

Nyfe unfolded her arms and planted her hands on

her hips. 'Don't mention that your suitcase has been stolen to anyone else, do you hear? Unless you want to feel the flat of my blade across your face.'

The mood was lightened somewhat by Avery, whose stomach let out a growl that rumbled around the cave like thunder. She blushed.

Nyfe gave a snort that might have been a laugh. 'I need some time to think and you evidently need something to eat. Let's talk again after the meeting. And remember, you are here only to observe,' she repeated, pointing a finger at Jonathan like it was a cutlass. 'This is my armada, my crew, my people, and my world. Understand?'

'Yes, thank you,' he said, as if he'd been offered some luxurious Belgian chocolates.

'Ed,' Nyfe said, addressing Edony. 'Take them to Jereme.'

CHAPTER NINE

Jereme hardly seemed like a pirate. He was incredibly well-spoken and moved like a dancer, dodging around other pirates and skipping over puddles without a single pause. He accepted Flick and her friends from Edony, who looked glad to be rid of them, and led the three of them to a curve of rock at the back of the cave, where there was a table, several benches, and various pots bubbling over banked-up fires. The warmth was delicious, and Flick sighed as her bare feet touched warm rock and the heat began to spread into her muscles.

Jereme lifted the lid of one pot and inhaled the steam.

'What are the choices?' Avery sank onto the ground

in relief, spragging her legs out in front of herself. Flick flopped down beside her, suddenly exhausted. The adrenaline from earlier had clearly worn off.

'Well,' Jereme said, checking the pots, 'there's confit, or tafelspitz, or—'

'Tafelspitz?' Jonathan frowned.

'Meat and apple stew,' Jereme said. 'It's good if you add some buckthorn berries to it.' Jereme scooped up a spoonful and tasted it. 'Been cooking long enough. Carrots are a bit soft, mind. Here . . .' He picked up what Flick had assumed was a disc of dried tar, pulled a knife from his belt and deftly slit the thing in half, then opened it up like a pita bread. 'Once this is filled with hot tafel, you tell me that it isn't worth crossing an ocean for.'

He did the honours and handed Flick one half of the black bread, now steaming with tafelspitz.

She licked at it. It tasted only vaguely of apples, mostly of carrot and some other unidentifiable green. She took a nibble and decided that it was probably safe. The black bread had an aftertaste like liquorice.

Avery bit into her bread-half without preamble, and then hastily fanned her open mouth, giving everyone a good look at some half-chewed black bread. 'Hot,' she said, unnecessarily.

Jereme smiled. 'We're supposed to make it with beef,' he said, handing Jonathan a half, and taking the last one for himself. 'But it's been many a year since I ate cow. None left, any more.'

Flick swallowed, looking at the strips of red-grey meat in her pocket of bread. 'Then what meat do you use?'

'Depends what we can get,' Jereme shrugged. 'I think this is—'

'I'd really rather not know, if it's all the same to you,' Jonathan said, false cheeriness making him sound slightly hysterical. 'I'm supposed to be vegetarian; this is testing me enough as it is. Let's just pretend it's chicken and be done with it.'

'It might be.' Jereme shrugged. 'Your guess is as good as mine.'

Everyone fell silent, and Flick swallowed her food quickly, trying not to let her brain fill in the blanks about the nature of the mystery meat. Avery clearly didn't care what it was. She had found a spoon from somewhere and was scooping out the last of the stew from her bread. When she asked for more, Jereme gave her a helping of what he called 'casso', which he promised was made of seagull meat and nothing else.

'Seagulls are basically rats,' Avery said, blowing the steam from a hot spoonful.

'If it's rat you're interested in,' Jereme said, 'I know that Cook likes to finely chop the tails and add them into the—'

'NO,' Jonathan boomed, killing the explanation. 'No, thank you. Let's not sit discussing which vermin are in which pot.' He examined what was left of his black bread, before popping it into his mouth. 'No chance of a dessert, I suppose?'

'A desert?' Jereme frowned.

'Desserrrrrrrrrt,' Jonathan drawled it out. 'A sweet. Afters. Pudding.'

'Cook does a stomach-and-blood pudding,' Jereme said, innocently.

Even Avery said no to that. Instead, they washed their meal down with cold tea, having refused the alcoholic-smelling cloudy juice Jereme offered around (though Avery had a swig of it when Jonathan's back was turned. She later told Flick it tasted like paint-stripper, though Flick had to wonder how she knew that). Then, they gathered their things, and headed back towards the largest cave.

The meeting of the captains and Pirate Queen was about to begin.

CHAPTER TEN

The walls of the tunnel leading back to the main room were a blur of stalagmites and stalactites, which blended together into ridges of rock. It was like stepping into the island's ribcage. It was cold. It was the sort of cold that dripped down your throat into your lungs and made you want to cough it out, as if the cold was an object lodged in your chest, stealing your breath.

Flick was grateful her trainers and socks had dried out enough to be pulled back on – she hadn't felt her toes for a while. The cold was only slightly offset by the flames of candles that had been balanced into every little nook and cranny imaginable. Lamps swung from hooks drilled into the rock, and there was scattered gravel on the floor, clearly added to make walking on the damp, slick surface a bit easier.

Soon, the cave's narrow shaft opened up like an upside-down bottle, and the interior space rose up into a large cavern, high enough to fit a house inside.

'Keep with me,' Jereme said to them. 'There's more folks than we anticipated. Still not everyone, but here we are.'

'How many people live in The Break?' Flick asked. She brushed against a pirate's arm and muttered an apology, getting a hard stare in return.

'Don't know if anyone keeps count, to be honest. Less than there used to be. More lost ships, fewer babies. People don't want to bring life into a world that might not be here for the child's old age.' Jereme sighed as they passed one nursing mother – her baby strapped to her by means of a long strip of fabric, wound around and around so it left her hands free to do other things. Right now, she was polishing a cutlass. 'There's always exceptions, of course.'

People made way for them, grudgingly, until the press of bodies got so close that they were stuck.

'If you can get up on those rocks, you'll be able to see.' Jereme indicated a spot to their left where the cave walls sloped enough for three young people to clamber up. 'Wedge your feet hard against the stone and you'll not slip. I need to be at the Pirate Queen's side.'

Flick forced her way through the crowd. The tension in the room was contagious – Flick felt her scalp prickle in anticipation. She led the way, pushing past pirates who were wider at the shoulder than she was tall, until she reached the slippery rock wall.

It reminded her of climbing over the car-park wall as a shortcut to get into the park back at the flats she used to live in. And this was easier because the stone was lumpy and had places to put your feet in. Several other pirates clearly had the same idea of climbing up high to see better, but they were weighed down with their heavy equipment, and Flick, Jonathan and Avery were able to squeeze past them and up onto a crop of rock that wasn't so much a seat as a shelf. They ended up sort of leaning against the cave wall, their knees at the height of the heads of the pirates below.

Flick looked down at the scene.

In the centre of the crowd was a raised stone dais or platform, like a stage. It was empty. There was a sudden shout from the direction of the walkway, and all heads turned in that direction at once.

Captain Nyfe walked out from the crowd with a

swagger only someone her size and build could ever hope to pull off. Her boots shone, the metal at her belt gleamed in the candle-light, and even her skin looked polished. She stomped up to the dais and stood on it, raising herself a foot higher off the stone floor, though she would have looked over almost every head in her stockinged feet.

Flick felt in awe of her. The Pirate Queen had complete command of the place, and she knew it. Nyfe radiated confidence, and Flick couldn't help wishing she herself had even a scrap of it.

Nyfe raised her chin as she looked around, as if waiting for quiet.

But the place had been silent and still since she walked into sight. These pirates knew their leader.

A drum banged.

Flick jumped, heart hammering, looking in the direction of the noise. Edony, who had removed her conical coat, was sitting cross-legged on a cushion, a skin-drum in front of her.

Nyfe raised a hand. 'Welcome to this sacred place. For those too young or too old to remember, this is the Whispering Cavern. The place our ancestors first found when they landed here, back when the world was new. They left their old selves here, and they entombed their bodies here – long before we learned the secret of sailing with the dead.'

'Sailing with the dead?' Flick whispered, a shiver running up her back.

Jonathan shrugged.

Nyfe went on. 'Our ancestors – those who came first – their spirits are still here. And if we need their input, they might choose to whisper to us. Everyone may have the chance to speak here, if they wish. But be aware – your words may not be your own.'

The shiver on Flick's skin turned into a cold grip. 'Spirits? Does she mean ghosts?' she whispered.

'Shh.' Avery nodded down at the speaker.

Nyfe looked around her at the assembled crew. 'I thank you, for assembling here. I trust you to relay what is discussed here back to your crews, and to let them all know they are welcome to join in our parley with the mer-folk. We sail tonight, around The Break, to meet them at the Cove of Voices.' She paused, and looked around, catching more than one eye as she did so. 'We have to decide. All of us. What is to happen with our world. What we can do to save it. And, if we cannot stop the coming end, how we can escape our fate.'

There was general mumbling amongst the gathered people.

'Has a cause been found, Pirate Queen?' a woman at the front asked. 'Do we know *why* our world is breaking apart?'

Nyfe adjusted her stance on the dais and sighed. 'Our world has always been impossible – the scours in our sky tell us as much. And yet, it has always existed. It has always survived. Now, something has changed. My advisors have assured me that the cause of the collapse is no fault of ours – it is an outside influence. Someone, or something, is taking whatever magic it is that holds our world in place.'

'Years ago, a man from another world came. He told us youngins stories about magic,' an old man piped up. 'He came from a world of crystal, he said. He gave us gifts.' He held up a necklace with a shaft of quartz dangling from it.

'Can you recall what he said, Old Mebby?' Nyfe asked.

Interested, Flick leaned forwards to see better. A world of crystal? Had the visitor paid a visit to the Crystal Forest and brought gifts from there? But you weren't supposed to take anything from one world to another, after all.

'I was only a boy,' Old Mebby said, apologetically. 'But I remember he said that magic is like water in a bowl, left out in the sun. Eventually, the water will dry up, you see?'

'Unless you pour more in?' said Nyfe.

'Unless it rains,' Mebby corrected, smiling with his gums. 'Sun dries up the water, but then it forms clouds and the sky lets it back down again. A natural process, you see, Pirate Queen? Always the same amount of water, just some in the bowl and some in the clouds.'

This made sense to Flick. Magic was a type of energy, so it could change just as light changed into heat when you left a lamp on for a long time.

She blinked, as another thought occurred.

If magic was like water stored in a bowl, what would happen if there was a leak?

Could it run out?

Worry lurched in her insides, and she gripped at the rock to steady herself. For a moment, she felt as if she could almost see the golden-white magic spiralling down into some sort of dark multiverse drain, never to be seen again.

Nyfe was thanking the old man, and putting a finger to her chin as she thought. Flick wondered if the voices in the cave were whispering to her. She didn't like the thought very much. Nyfe was enough of a force by herself.

'How can we leave our entire world?' someone called out, clearly unable to wait until his leader had finished considering.

'People have come here from other worlds before,' Nyfe said, shrugging.

'Yes, but we are no wizards. We are sailors. Fishers. Soldiers. We don't have a way of finding other worlds.'

Jonathan shifted on the rock, and Flick wished more than ever that she had the suitcase in her hand.

'And why do we need to parley with the Queen of Weeds, anyway?' someone else shouted. 'What's she giving us?'

'Nothing,' Nyfe said.

There was a sudden dull roar of activity, as everyone began to voice an opinion.

'The mer are our enemies!'

'An alliance would never work!'

'They're thieves and godless fish!'

'Hardly godless,' Jonathan murmured to Flick. 'My guidebook says the mer-people have over a dozen different gods for the tides alone.'

Nyfe folded her arms, and the hubbub died down. She glared out into the audience. 'I know nothing of the ways of gods,' she said, 'but I know the sea. And I know this world. It is decreasing every moment. Would you have me leave others to die?'

There was a current of uncertainty.

'It is time to make allies of our old enemies, to have them on our side. To figure out a plan – together.'

'You'd join forces with our enemies?' A man stepped forward. It was Jask, the man they'd passed on their way into the caves. Flick tensed all over. She'd been right to be worried about him. Jask sneered, his teeth sharp. 'You'd offer those killers – those thieves and murderers – safe passage? This could be our chance to get rid of them once and for all.'

'You'd rather have dead bodies than greater forces?' Nyfe asked, as if bored.

'Aye,' he said. 'I would. They've never given us reason to trust them, and if anyone has to offer the hand of friendship, it shouldn't be us. We might get bitten.'

There were scattered cries of 'AYE!' from the back of the cavern.

Flick pinched Jonathan's sleeve. He glanced at her, eyes wide, face pale. 'This could end badly,' he breathed.

Jask folded his arms. 'You've been a solid leader, Nyfe, but you've got the softness of a woman when it comes to the difficult decisions. I think you should reconsider your position.'

'I will not.'

'Then,' Jask put a hand to his cutlass, 'I'll ask you to step aside, Pirate Queen. If our world is in such a state as you say it is, we need firm leadership. Leadership that can withstand the future.' He inched the sword out, enough to show the blade.

The audience gasped, and there were shouts of displeasure at the scene. But there were also some scattered roars of encouragement, and that made Flick extremely nervous. Jask looked confident. If it came to a fight between him and Captain Nyfe, Flick had to admit that at first glance they looked equally matched.

Nyfe raised a hand.

Flick expected a sword to be put into it.

But instead, Nyfe swept her arm out in a clear invitation. She put her head to one side, and stepped down from the platform, so neither of them had the high ground. 'I see you challenging, Jask Irontasker,' she said. 'But you don't move. Do you yield before you've tried to strike a blow?'

'Your sword,' Jask said, uncertainly. 'You don't have it.'

'What does that matter?'

He glanced at the people watching. 'Nyfe, this isn't honourable. You're doing this to shame me.'

'Yes,' she said. 'I am.'

'Nyfe.' Jask unsheathed his cutlass completely and held it out. 'I don't wish to fight an unarmed sailor, but if I have to . . .'

'If you want me to step aside,' Nyfe said, stepping close enough for the sword to reach her, if Jask swung it, 'you *will* have to.' Jask was still. Nyfe reached up and adjusted her eyepatch. 'Not ready to fight an unarmed woman lacking an eye, Irontasker? You criticised my softness, but here you are the one pausing. How *soft* of you.'

There was some laughter from around the cavern. Flick realised the joke was on the man holding the sword. This seemed to flip a switch in his mind. He drew his arm back, and Flick saw his thick muscles tense, then he thrust the blade forward, hard.

Flick gasped.

But Nyfe moved like a snake.

She grabbed his sword-arm with one hand, bringing her other down like a lump hammer on Jask's tattooed forearm.

The CRACK echoed around the cavern like an explosion.

Jask screamed, his legs giving way. Nyfe lifted his broken limb higher, forcing Jask to try to stand. Avery was hiding behind her hands, and Jonathan had gone as green as Flick felt.

'Do you still want to fight?' Nyfe asked Jask.

'No!' he yelled, tears and sweat pouring off his face.

She looked at him impassively, still holding his arm. 'No?'

'No, my – no, Captain!'

That seemed to be good enough. Nyfe dropped him, and Jask screwed himself up into a ball, cradling his arm.

'You see?' Nyfe shouted to the onlookers. 'You try to harm an unarmed foe, and it comes back to hurt *you*. The mer-folk are our enemies, yes. We have a chance to drive a blow at them that they will never recover from, yes. But we will not. Fighting a dishonourable fight brings only pain. Back away when you can, when the world offers you the chance to change your actions. Not afterward.' She looked at Jask. 'Someone see to his arm. And who is first mate of the *Sola*?'

'I am, Pirate Queen.' A woman raised a hand.

Nyfe nodded. 'Take control of the *Sola*, Jennirum, until your brother is fit to turn the helm again.'

'Aye, Captain.'

'Does anyone else object to joining forces with the Queen of Weeds?' Nyfe called.

The answer came back instantly. 'NO, CAPTAIN.' Water droplets rained from the ceiling as the cavern shook with shouted calls and stamping feet.

Jonathan puffed out a breath. 'Well. That certainly shows us what we're dealing with.'

'Yeah,' Avery said, staring. 'A woman who can break a man's arm with one punch. I feel really reassured.'

Flick nodded, weakly. She felt slightly light-headed, as if she'd learned something she wished she could unlearn rather quickly. 'Yeah,' she said. 'Super safe.'

They looked back at the scene.

Nyfe had lit what looked like a sparkler. She was using it to draw in the air. But, unlike the sparklers Flick used on Bonfire Night, the shapes Nyfe drew didn't fade. They lingered in the air, a sort of burnt-orange glow of light against the cavern gloom.

'We sail tonight,' Nyfe said, still drawing what was now clearly a map. 'Around The Break. Larger ships to follow the smaller. We don't need to lose anyone in the wake. Smaller ships leave immediately, larger within the next two hours. Go around The Break and moor at the Cove of Voices. You will encounter mer-folk as you sail. Do not provoke them. We are allies. We aim for the same end. Understand me?'

'AYE, CAPTAIN.'

'Very well. Dismissed. Back to your ships, the lot of you.' Nyfe blew out the glowing sparkler, and a thin trail of smoke kissed over her face.

Jereme tapped Flick on the arm. 'The captain wants the three of you aboard her ship.'

'Really?' Flick felt her insides tense.

'Not an honour I'd refuse,' Jereme said plainly.

'Not more than once, anyway.' Edony appeared and nudged him aside. She had put her coat back on, and in the gloom she looked like a looming shadow. 'I'll escort you. Your clothes have already been taken aboard.'

The three of them scrambled down the rocks to the walkway and followed Edony out of the cove. She didn't seem to believe in politeness – she barged into the people ahead of her, expecting them to give way, and snorted and huffed if they didn't.

'Why does Nyfe want us on her ship?' Flick asked when they paused for a moment, caught behind a slow-moving family. After what they'd just seen, she felt safer with Edony than she would have if they'd been walking with Captain Nyfe.

'You're important people, you suitcase-bearers,' said Edony. 'Nyfe isn't going to leave any ship to shelter you. She wants you on the best there is.'

'Where she can keep an eye on us?' Flick suggested.

Edony grinned. 'That's part of it, yes.'

Flick did not feel reassured at that.

At that moment, Captain Nyfe stomped past them, Jereme at her heels. She gave them a curt nod as she swept past. Once out in the fresher air, she was stopped by a group of sailors, who crowded around her eagerly.

'Where is the ship?' Flick asked.

But her question wasn't answered. Instead, there came a frightened yell from the other end of the jetty.

'Captain! Look!'

Heads swivelled to look at a sailor, who was pointing out to sea, one hand to their hat.

'Look!' they shouted. 'It's happening . . .'

Everyone, Flick and the others included, crowded to the edge of the jetty. Nyfe took a collapsible telescope from her belt and pulled it to length before putting it to her eye.

But the telescope was unnecessary.

There was a sudden shaft of light on the horizon, shooting up from the dark ocean, splintering into the air. And along with it came a noise – a sound like the crunch of rock on rock, except one hundred times louder.

Flick gasped as a section of the seafloor rose above the edge of the horizon, the sea gushing from it like water pouring off a plate. Part of the edge of the world had broken away completely, and was rising up like it weighed nothing. It hovered in the air, a chunk of sparse, bare rock caught in the beam of light, and then the rock glowed bright white and vanished completely.

There was no twinkle or sparkle of magic (Flick cursed not getting the magnifying glass out of her pocket, but in the shock of the moment she simply hadn't remembered), no floating dust, not even a sound to accompany the disappearance. One moment the rock was there, the next it had vanished. The world of The Break was now smaller – Flick had seen it happen with her own eyes.

The horror of it was all-consuming; it felt as if she had been hollowed out and filled with cold cement. This was nothing like the breaking up of the City of Five Lights, where streets had vanished but the world had knitted together to hide the fact they had ever existed. This was a brutal breakage of the world for all to see.

It was awe-inspiring and terrible. The world of The Break was too far gone to save – Flick knew that deep in her soul. The pirates here didn't hoard magic, they barely used it at all. Like the old man had said, the magic in the world should be held safe in a bowl, but it was leaking away so fast it was taking huge chunks of the world with it at a time. There was no supply of magic to release back into the world – it was simply being stolen, taken away, removed. And it could never be replaced.

Flick tried to move, to back away from the frozen crowd of people, but she felt as if her cold-cement insides had now broken into stones, clacking together in her hollow shell.

The knowledge that she could not save this world, could not even try to, was bearing down on Flick like a crushing weight. She had felt helpless before, of course she had. Being trapped in the tiny false-world of the Waiting Room had been terrible. But this was worse. This was standing, suitcase-less, watching a world crumble before her very eyes.

And if the magic of The Break really was being stolen . . . then who was taking it?

Flick wanted to run away, but there was nowhere to go.

'How long does this place have left?' she whispered.

Jonathan's eyes were wide, staring behind his lenses. 'A month,' he murmured. 'Maybe less. We got here too late.'

Captain Nyfe turned, her face emotionless. The only sign that she was upset was a muscle throbbing in her cheek. 'Get to your ships,' she barked at the onlookers. 'Gawping isn't going to solve anything. Now!'

The sailors scattered, too disorientated and frightened to do anything other than follow her orders.

Nyfe jerked her chin at Flick. 'This way. The *Aconite* welcomes you.'

They finally made it down the jetty to where a large wooden dinghy was tied off, and Edony got them all seated. Once Nyfe and Jereme, neither of them particularly small, were seated, the boat seemed almost overloaded. Jereme and Edony took the oars.

Flick met Jonathan's eyes, and tried to say with her face how awful she felt – tried to get across some of the panic she had felt at the sight of The Break crumbling before her.

Nyfe barely glanced in their direction. She was running a finger over the raised embroidery on her eyepatch and her lips were pursed as if she was thinking deep thoughts. It hardly seemed possible that she had broken a man's arm only a few minutes before. But then, watching a piece of your world disappear could take someone's edge off, Flick imagined.

A few silent minutes later, they had reached the swollen belly of the great ship that had almost mown Flick down in the ocean earlier that day. The side of the ship stretched upwards higher than a house. Jereme stood and grabbed a bit of rope hanging down the side, holding it to steady himself and the little boat. He thumped the side of the ship.

A moment later, a skinny rope ladder unfurled from high above them. Next there was the squeaking of pulleys as two bigger ropes with hooks were lowered down to them, which Jereme attached to the sides of their boat.

'Everyone out and up the ladder,' Nyfe said.

Avery gawped at the ladder, her eyes goggling.

'Can't they just pull us up in the boat?' Jonathan asked.

Edony snorted, rolling her eyes so dramatically it was a wonder they didn't fall out of her head.

'Easier for the lads pulling the jolly boat up if it's not full of sailors,' Jereme said. 'So, up you go, like Captain said.'

Flick looked at the rope ladder. 'Up that?' she asked, her voice doing a wonderful impression of a squeaky toy meeting a heavy boot.

'You can sleep with the sharks, if you'd prefer.' Nyfe hauled herself up, taking the ladder steps two at a time. Her boots, Flick could see, had been scored with grooves on the soles to bend better and get a better grip on the wet, slippery wood.

'Should I go next?' she asked.

Avery hadn't moved her gaze away from the ladder yet, and Jonathan was rather green. 'Fine,' he said.

'Not that I'm desperate to get up there,' Flick said, 'but if you fall, you'll probably take me with you.'

'Oh, as long as it's only that you're concerned with,' he managed to smirk.

Flick took a hold of the ladder and began to climb.

The first few steps were easy. But as she went up, it became more difficult – you had to haul your whole weight up, plus fight against gravity, and you only had rope to hang on to. The steps were so slender your legs had to stay tensed the entire time, or else you might slip, and to top it all off the wind was getting up, and it clearly had a mind to blow Flick clean off the ladder and headfirst into the sea for the second time that day.

'Keep going, girl,' Nyfe looked over the edge of the ship's gunwale down at her. 'Bit higher.'

'I . . .' Flick tried to get her legs to move, but they were solid on the step, and refused to lift. 'I can't! I don't know how to do this!'

'You've done it this far!'

'Yes, but I wasn't thinking about it then!' The wind blew harder, making the ladder rise up and slam back down against the curve of the ship. Any harder and it would have banged Flick's white-knuckled fingers.

She was going to let go, she knew it.

'Felicity!' Jonathan yelled below. 'Don't you even think about letting go, do you hear me?'

She shook her head, frozen.

Something warm suddenly touched her shoulder, and she opened her eyes to see Nyfe leaning down over the side of the ship, one hand on a cannon to anchor herself, the other arm wrapping around Flick's underarms. 'How you lot get anything done I'll never know,' Nyfe said.

'I—'

Before she could protest, Flick was pulled smartly

off the ladder, and hauled onto the deck. Nyfe swung herself around on the cannon and got to her feet with the grace of a dancer.

Flick landed on her backside. 'Ow.'

Nyfe helped her up. 'You really would have clung there for ever, wouldn't you?'

'No,' Flick said. 'I would have fallen off, eventually.'

The Pirate Queen smiled.

Avery came up next, looking extremely relieved to have the climb over and done with, and Jonathan followed after her, helped (pushed) onto the deck by Jereme, who had donned a slick-looking mac.

'Thank you.' Jonathan put a hand on Jereme's shoulder, then took it away, looking at his palm in horror. 'Is this *tar*?'

'Keeps the capes slick,' Jereme grinned, and Flick could see now that the front four of his top teeth were capped in silver metal. 'Rains are coming in, you see?'

'Lovely.' Jonathan looked for somewhere to wipe his hand, settling for the front of his borrowed jacket.

'We've a few bunks spare for you and your girls, Mercator,' Nyfe said, leading the way across the deck.

'Avery and Felicity aren't my girls,' Jonathan said. 'They're my friends.'

'I belong to one person,' Avery said, her bravado

coming back now she was safely away from the ladder. 'And that's me.'

'A sensible girl.' Nyfe pushed open a door at the rear of the ship. 'First, we'll talk in my cabin. Then sleep. You've eaten, yes?'

'Yeah, but don't ask what it was,' Flick sighed.

Nyfe laughed. 'Nothing that'll kill you. Edony, cast off and get the crew working. Jereme, with me.' She held the door open, and the five of them went inside.

The cabin wasn't large – it was about the size of Freddy's room in their new house. There was a bed of sorts to one side – a blanket-covered mattress atop a chest of drawers – but the rest of the room looked like an office. There was a desk to the far end strewn with papers, and a small window behind that. There was a covered stove in one corner, and Flick realised why the window was so small – it was to keep the heat in. Flick wondered what it would be like to never be properly dry, to never get your land legs back, to always have the dark depths of the ocean beneath your boots.

Nyfe went behind her desk and sat in the chair, legs out in front of her, ankles crossed. 'So,' she said, looking at Jonathan, 'is he dead, then?'

'I'm sorry?' Jonathan frowned.

'Your father. Daniel Mercator. Is he dead?'

'My dad? I . . .' Jonathan paused. 'I don't think so. He . . .' He trailed off, looking confused. Flick met his eyes, and for a moment time seemed to slow down. Surely not. He couldn't be, could he?

Nyfe took her legs off her desk, sitting up seriously. 'My summons was for Daniel Mercator,' she explained. 'Him, or his closest relative. And . . . here you are.'

CHAPTER TWELVE

'**M**y dad isn't dead,' Jonathan said, words rushing out in one breath. 'He's missing. I – I've been trying to find out where he went.'

'This is most unfortunate,' Nyfe said. 'We could have used his expertise. Instead, we're stuck with inexperience.'

'We thought he might have come here, actually. The Break was listed in one of his books.'

'I haven't seen him for many of our years,' Nyfe said.

'But I don't understand.' Jonathan's brow was furrowed. 'Why did you think my dad was dead?'

'The spell we used to send the summons searches the multiverse, and heads for the addressee. Or the closest blood relative,' Nyfe repeated, 'if Daniel couldn't be found.'

Closest blood relative? The words sounded very loud in Flick's head. Closest relative meant next of kin, didn't it? *Which meant . . .*

Avery was frowning. 'Closest blood relative?' She looked at Flick. 'What does that mean?'

It means Daniel is dead, Flick realised. To her shock, grief suddenly washed through her bones, and she felt her chest seize in a tight agony. It was not, she realised, grief for Daniel Mercator – a man she had never met.

It was for the look that had crossed Jonathan's face as he too realised what Nyfe's words meant. His expression went completely blank and what little colour there was drained from his face, leaving his features looking as if they had been drawn on a crumpled paper bag.

'No,' he croaked.

Nyfe softened her tone, just a little. 'I'm sorry. That spell can search every world in the multiverse. If it couldn't find him, he must be d—'

'Stop saying that!' Jonathan shook his head. 'There must be some mistake. He's just *missing*!'

Avery walked over to him and reached to put a hand on his arm. 'Johnnie, it's OK—'

'Get off me.' He snatched it away. His eyes were shining behind his glasses. He stopped, putting a hand to his mouth.

Flick couldn't stand still either, she felt too awful. 'Jonathan, I'm so—'

'Don't,' he snapped. 'Just don't.' He marched to the cabin door and wrenched it open, slamming it shut behind him.

Flick looked at Avery.

Avery looked back, her expression of grief mirroring Flick's. Flick wondered if she ought to run after Jonathan, but the menace in his voice when she tried to speak to him told her enough – he needed to be alone, at least for now.

Nyfe sighed. 'I didn't mean to break it to him like that.'

Avery clicked her tongue. 'Done now, isn't it?' she snapped.

'Everyone dies, girl.'

'Yeah, but that was the only real family he had left,' Avery said, and Flick was proud and jealous of her being brave enough to back chat.

Nyfe said nothing and there was a long silence.

Flick rubbed the heels of her hands over her eyebrows. The people of The Break still needed

Strangeworlds' help and Jonathan wasn't in a fit state to help them. It was up to her now, she thought.

'We need the suitcase back,' she said to Nyfe. 'From the mer-people. If we can get that back, Jonathan, Avery and I can go back to The Strangeworlds Travel Agency, and try to find you a new world to live in. It would take some sorting out, but if you really don't mind the risk of a shorter life, you could all walk through a suitcase to start again in another world.'

Nyfe held a hand up to interrupt. 'And the mer-folk?'

Flick frowned in confusion. 'What about them?'

'The mer-folk cannot breathe outside the water. Some of them, the cephalopod-people, can survive for a very short time on land, but the fish-folk can only manage a jump from the water before they need to submerge again. They cannot *walk* through.'

Flick blinked, temporarily boggled. 'The mer-people . . . maybe we could have them swim from water to water, somehow. That wouldn't be too difficult.'

'And what about my ships? Do you have suitcases big enough for them?' asked Nyfe, demandingly.

Flick was taken aback. 'Your ships . . . they're too big. They'd never get through a suitcase. You'd have to leave—'

'No.'

'What do you mean "No"?' asked Avery.

'You could make new ships, couldn't you?' Flick chimed in.

'You can't just *make* a new ship,' Nyfe scoffed. 'You're thinking of these vessels like they're simply transport.'

'Well, aren't they?' Flick asked, who was starting to feel irritated.

Nyfe shook her head. 'These ships have been passed down by our ancestors. Yes, some parts have been replaced or mended. In fact, I doubt you'd find a single bit of the ship that hasn't been altered somehow over the years. But it's the same ship. It's not just a box to float over the water in. It's our *home*, for ever. Even after our bodies are gone from it.'

Nyfe saw Flick's confused face and went on. 'We are born, we live, and we die at sea. Our bodies? They get old and we pass them over the side to the beings that need them – the sharks, and other creatures of the deep. But our souls – they stay on board. And they remain as much a part of the crew as anyone.'

'They're ghosts?' Flick asked, feeling the hairs on her arms suddenly stand on end. 'There are ghosts on the ship?'

114

'You'd be a fool to think otherwise,' Nyfe said. 'Many a time there's been a man slip on the rigging and had his arm caught by a hand he can't see. Sometimes there's a glass of something left out in the morning, though the cabin-boys will swear they locked everything away the night before. The ship is crewed by those who came before.' She leaned forward. 'And I will not be leaving them behind.'

'But we don't have suitcases big enough to fit your ships!' Flick cried. 'I'm sorry. I think . . .' She glanced at the door Jonathan had slammed behind him. 'I think we need to do what's right for the people who are still alive, not listen to the wishes of the dead.'

There was a gust of wind. The lanterns swinging overhead were abruptly extinguished.

And then the wind dropped as suddenly as it had arrived.

Flick looked round but the window and door were both still shut.

Smoke from the lanterns drifted slowly outwards, reaching like fingers into the dark. And Flick could just see Nyfe's outline, shaking her head.

'Be careful how you speak aboard the *Aconite*,' she said. 'There's captains past in this cabin.'

CHAPTER THIRTEEN

Flick found Jonathan up the steps at the back of the ship. He was leaning against the edge of the surrounding railing, looking down at the iron-grey water with an unreadable expression.

'Jonathan?' Flick tried.

He turned his head a fraction to indicate he had heard her.

'There's food,' Flick said. 'It's vegetable soup, and it actually looks nice. Avery's waiting in the dining room. The mess, I mean.' She almost saw her words bounce off him. 'Are you coming?'

Jonathan took a deep breath, like he was trying to inhale the entire atmosphere. 'Later.'

'All right.' Flick wondered if she should try to persuade him more, but decided against it. Jonathan was in a world of his own right now, and wherever he was, he was out of her reach.

*

'Is he OK?' Avery pushed a bowl towards Flick.

'No,' Flick picked up the large mussel shell that served as her spoon. 'It's like he's not there.'

'Poor Jonathan.' Avery tapped the tabletop in a nervous habit. 'What do we do with him now?'

'I don't know.' Flick swallowed a mouthful of soup, which was rich and flavoursome. For some reason, that annoyed her. At a time like this, food should be bland and tasteless. She tried to enjoy it as little as possible. 'We need the suitcase so we can take Jonathan back to Strangeworlds, but Nyfe didn't say anything about helping us get the suitcase back.' Flick hesitated. 'And that whole thing with the spirits of dead captains . . .'

'Seriously creepy,' Avery said. 'Ghosts can't be more important than living people, surely?' She pushed her empty bowl away. 'You ask me,' she said softly, 'Nyfe's scared. She can't see what she *should* be doing. I don't think everyone here agrees with her, either,' Avery added darkly, looking at the sailors around them.

'What do you mean?'

'If there's one thing I'm good at,' Avery said, 'it's listening. I've had to be; my parents like to keep secrets. The trick is to look so busy that no one notices you're even there. And no one notices kids in a place like this, anyway.'

'So?'

Avery glanced about. 'I heard some of the younger sailors talking. There's another bunch of pirates, around the edge of the world. They call themselves the Buccaneers.'

'Are the Buccaneers bad guys?'

'Depends on who you ask. But the men over there,' Avery jerked her chin in their direction, 'they sounded worried. They seemed to think there's going to be a fight, though none of them were saying why. They reckon that's why Nyfe is gathering all her allies together. The Buccaneers are led by someone called Burnish.'

'Why would Nyfe start a fight now?'

'I'm not sure,' Avery said. 'But that's the last thing this world needs.'

'Nyfe said she wanted peace,' Flick pointed out. 'That she wanted the whole world's population to get out of here, not just her sailors.'

Avery shrugged. 'Looks like she's not being entirely honest. She is a pirate, after all.'

Flick pushed her bowl away. 'Do you think we can trust her?'

'Probably not,' Avery admitted. 'But do we have a choice? You saw what happened to Jask. We wouldn't get very far in this world going against her. We need to keep on her good side.'

'What we really need is our suitcase back,' Flick said.

Avery stretched. 'I don't suppose there's anything we can do tonight, except try to get some sleep. Shall we have another crack at Jonathan before bed?'

They went up onto the deck. Jonathan was now sitting on the steps between the lower and upper decks, his knees tucked close to his body. His face was wet with a mixture of tears and sea spray, but he wasn't crying at that exact moment. He was staring into space.

Flick and Avery glanced at one another. Flick wanted to go to her friend by herself, but Avery had known Jonathan for longer. She was family. He might need her, right now.

Avery patted him on the knee. 'Jonathan? We're going to get some sleep.'

'Right,' he said.

'Jereme said there's hammocks for us all below decks.'

Jonathan blinked, and raised his head as though it weighed twenty stone. 'Hammocks?'

'I know, I don't fancy it either.' Avery gave a falsely cheery smile. 'What's wrong with a decent floor, eh?' She held a hand out and Jonathan took her arm at the wrist, getting to his feet so stiffly it was like he'd taken root. 'Come on. You need some rest.'

Flick followed them, feeling more than slightly useless. 'What *is* wrong with hammocks, anyway?' she asked Avery.

'If hammocks were so great, the captain would be sleeping in one,' Avery said, shrewdly. 'I'll be on the floor.'

'Then I hope you don't mind mice.' Jereme had come over, holding a lantern. 'Some of them can get very friendly. Just ask Charlie-Two-Toes over there.'

'Hammocks are great, I've always thought so,' Avery said quickly.

Flick kept an eye on Jonathan as they were herded down to the sleeping quarters. He was walking rather robotically, as if his brain were elsewhere and his body was just doing as it was told by other people. She had never known anyone who had lost someone close to them. She had no idea how to try to make it better.

The sleeping quarters below deck were warm and

stuffy – the sort of atmosphere that makes it difficult to drop off to sleep, and even more difficult to wake up again. The hammocks were surprisingly easy to get into though, and Flick, still wearing her borrowed clothes, was soon settled into one, her own dry clothes on the floor beneath her, ready for the morning.

In the dark around her, there was only the gentle snore of the pirates, and the occasional sound of something pattering with tiny clawed feet over the dry floorboards.

Over where Jonathan slept, there was no sound at all.

Not a single breath, nor a snuffle.

It was a very loud sort of silence, Flick thought.

As if someone was trying their very hardest to be quiet as they cried.

CHAPTER FOURTEEN

lick gave it a minute, then climbed down and crept over to Jonathan's hammock. 'Hey. You awake?'

There was a moist snorting noise from amidst a heap of blankets. 'Go away.'

'Oh, all right then, I will. I'll just leave you here by yourself.' Flick rolled her eyes. 'Don't be stupid. You're upset.'

Jonathan's head appeared from the depths of the covers. 'Just leave it, will you?'

'No.'

There was a silent stare-off in the darkness.

Then Jonathan sighed. 'Go up on deck. I'll be a moment.'

Flick pulled her trainers back on and climbed the

wooden steps to the deck. The *Aconite* rose and fell on the ebb of the tide, and Flick kept her eyes on the wood beneath her feet to avoid seeing how the horizon bobbed about. Either side of the ship, specks of light glowed in the dark like fireflies. The other ships, Flick realised. They were on the move now, headed around The Break to the Cove of Voices.

Overhead, the sky was hidden by the billowing sails that stretched into enormous bellies as the wind strained at them. Flick sat up on a crate, and a moment later Jonathan climbed up from below deck, his borrowed jacket buttoned and his boots on, though unlaced. In the glazed light of the moon of another world, his nose and eyes looked pink. He didn't say anything as he sat up beside her, and for a moment it was nice for it to just be the two of them, the ship rocking the rest of the crew to sleep.

'I thought he would still be alive.'

Flick looked up at him.

'Isn't that stupid?' Jonathan gave a daft sort of laugh. 'But I really thought . . .' He stopped, and looked away, shaking his head. His mouth screwed up as he fought hard not to cry.

Flick's chest ached. She reached out, and patted Jonathan's elbow – the only bit of him that didn't seem off-limits. 'It's not stupid,' she said. 'It's never stupid to hope for something like that.'

'It wasn't even hope. It was a fact. In my head. He was still alive, in my head. It's like finding out our world is as flat as this one. It doesn't make sense.' He sniffed and took off his glasses before planting his face in his hands. 'And to find out like that . . .'

'I'm sorry,' Flick said. She didn't know what else to say. 'I really am so sorry.'

Jonathan just nodded, still hiding his face. 'That's it, then. No more Mercators. No more of *us*. No more Dad. Just me.' He lifted his head and put his glasses back on. He laced his fingers together, and then unlaced them, putting his hands flat on his legs. He didn't seem to know what to do with himself. 'What am I supposed to do now? Sort this mess out?' He gestured vaguely at the ship. 'And then what?'

'Then decide what you want to do with Strangeworlds,' Flick said. 'I guess.'

He sighed and leaned back, knocking his head deliberately on the crate behind. 'I know I kept on saying *I'm in charge*, but it never felt like it. Not really.' He gave her a contemplative look. 'When you were kidnapped in Five Lights, do you know why I ended up at Tristyan's?'

Flick shook her head.

'I was looking for a grown-up to ask for help.' Jonathan gave a sad smile. 'I needed an adult. A – a parent, really. And I didn't have one. And it felt awful.' He sniffed. 'That's what it's going to feel like for the rest of my life, isn't it?'

Flick wished she could say *no, it won't,* and be certain it wasn't a lie. But she wasn't sure. Jonathan was at sea. And she didn't know how to save him.

She patted his elbow again. 'It's cheesy, but you're not on your own, you know. Not really. You've got Avery and her parents—'

'Family so distant I barely remember what they look like.'

'—and you've got me,' Flick finished loudly. Then blushed, feeling embarrassed.

Jonathan blinked at her behind his sea spray-splattered glasses.

'So there,' she said, folding her arms. 'And you're allowed to be sad. That's OK. You can be as sad as you like for as long as you like. But you're not on your own.'

Jonathan nodded.

Flick smiled at him. 'Do you want to talk about your dad?' It seemed like the right thing to ask.

He huffed out a breath that might have been a laugh. 'I don't really know what there is to say.'

'Tell me about him. I don't know anything about him, really, apart from his name.'

Jonathan was quiet, for a moment. Then he cleared his throat. 'He's – he was . . .' His voice failed at the change of tense, and he stood up and took a few steps, as if he could walk away from whatever he was feeling. 'He used to tell me off for leaving books fanned open, instead of using a bookmark,' he said, half smiling. 'He was allergic to copper coins, of all things. And he would always manage to flip a pancake perfectly the first try on Pancake Day.' Then he paused. 'And . . . he really loved being a custodian. He wanted to make Strangeworlds somewhere to be proud of, he said . . .' He stopped, wincing as the words stuck in his throat.

'It's OK,' Flick said. 'You don't have to talk right now.'

He gave her a sad smile. 'Have you ever lost anyone, Felicity?'

She shook her head. 'No.'

'I hope you never do,' he said. 'When my mother died, I thought I could make it stop hurting by becoming cold-hearted. But it doesn't work. All that happens is anything else that hurts you chips away at the ice block in your chest until there's nothing left at all.'

The wind picked up and there was a spray of saltwater over the side. Flick wished she could think of something clever to say to make things better, but what good were words at a time like this?

'I can't believe I'm never going to find him,' Jonathan said. 'I *really* thought he'd be out there, you know? Lost, or waiting. I used to get so bloody *angry* with him for leaving me, and then I thought . . . Well, maybe he's been captured, or he's injured or sick, and he needs me. Maybe I should be looking for him, maybe he's lying somewhere, wondering why I don't come. Maybe I'm the one who's letting *him* down.' His eyes shone, and he wiped them quickly on his sleeve.

'You don't know what happened,' Flick said. 'But you didn't let anyone down, Jonathan. This isn't your fault.'

'I could have—'

'No, you couldn't,' she said quickly. 'You had no way of knowing any of this would happen. This isn't your fault.'

Jonathan shrugged and scuffed his boots on the deck. 'I can't even think about it, right now. We're supposed to be getting my suitcase back, and then, oh, doing the impossible and getting a few thousand people and their ships off this world. I should probably be concentrating on that.'

'*I'll* concentrate on that,' Flick said. 'You need to get some sleep. I'll think of something.'

Jonathan raised an eyebrow.

'Hey, I did last time.'

'That's true.' He nodded slowly. 'But The Break isn't a small world like the Waiting Room. And we want to *stop* it collapsing, not make it happen faster.'

Flick hopped down from the crate and stretched some blood back into her legs. She held out a hand. 'Come on,' she said. 'You need to sleep. Who knows what tomorrow might bring?'

CHAPTER FIFTEEN

I t was still dark when the bell on deck started to clang, though Flick supposed it must be morning by the clock, because she'd at least had a bit of sleep. Far from being nauseating, the rock of the ship was like sleeping in a big bassinet, and the motions of the waves had sent her to sleep. She'd heard no more crying from Jonathan, though she didn't expect that to be the end of it. Actually, she suspected that the grief she'd seen had barely been the tip of the iceberg. They needed to get him home. Flick flexed her hand in a sort of ghost-grip, reliving the moment the suitcase had been torn from her fingers. They had to talk to Captain Nyfe about searching for it, or else none of them were leaving this world in a hurry.

Just then, Avery fell out of her hammock and swore loudly, to the amusement of some of the crew.

'Up you get, girl.' A woman no taller than Flick lifted Avery with one hand. 'Those things are the devil to get out of when the Sandman's glued your eyes shut, they are.'

Flick climbed out of her own hammock more carefully, and noticed Jonathan had already changed into his own clothes and was lacing his boots. 'Did you sleep?'

'In a fashion,' he said. 'My neck seems to have corkscrewed itself into an interesting position.' He rubbed the back of it.

Flick pulled a sympathetic face. Then frowned. 'We're all right for time, aren't we?'

'We're fine.' He stifled a yawn. 'According to my watch, we've been here just over two hours in our world's time.'

'Oh, that makes my brain hurt,' Avery said, putting her fingers to her temples. 'I've been to sleep, I'm still tired, and yet I shouldn't even have gone to bed yet. This is what sends everyone round the twist. Going into a suitcase one day and coming out three days earlier.'

'Can that happen?' Flick asked.

'No, ignore her,' Jonathan said, standing up and

straightening his incredibly-creased shirt. 'Time is only moving in one direction.'

'That's what you think.' Avery checked her reflection in the underside of a brass pan. 'Uh. I look like I've melted.'

Flick snorted.

Avery looked at her. 'What?'

'You know you don't,' Flick said, feeling weirdly irritated. Her face had gone prickly. 'Not even slightly.'

Avery raised her eyebrows. 'Right.' She put the pan down. 'Well . . . same.'

She went quickly up the steps onto the deck, leaving Flick to pick up the pan and give her own reflection an assessment. She decided that Avery was absolutely lying because she had a massive crease down her face from the hammock, for starters. Her mouth tasted like something had died in it.

Flick followed the rest of the crew up on deck. The sky overhead was as dark as before, but she could see a weird grey-blue filtering through the torn holes in the sky. Somewhere, in some world, it was morning.

'Sleep well, did you?' Jereme appeared, a steaming kettle in one hand, and a stack of small clay cups in the other. He poured out some pale yellow liquid and indicated to Flick that she should take the top cup.

'What is it?'

'Tea.'

'Tea is supposed to be brown,' Jonathan said, taking the next drink. He sipped it, and his face fell like a piano dropped from the top of a building. 'Oh.'

'That nice, is it?' Flick asked apprehensively.

'Tell yourself it's medicine.'

Flick screwed up her nose and tasted it. It wasn't exactly awful. It was somewhere between the green tea her mother had tried for a few weeks, and mouthwash. It certainly stripped the bad taste from her mouth, though it felt as if it was stripping the top layer of her tongue off as well.

'Captain wants to see you first thing,' Jereme said. 'Get yourselves a breakfast and go as soon as you're ready.'

'Good,' Flick said to Jonathan when the first mate had gone. 'We need to remind her that we *all* need that suitcase back.'

'Maybe she has it?' Avery suggested. 'It could have been brought to her during the night, by one of the mer-people.'

'Seems a bit of a long shot,' Flick said. 'But fingers and toes all crossed that you're right.'

*

Breakfast turned out to be dried fish and black bread, along with some strange vegetables that looked like purple carrots, but tasted of mushy peas. Jonathan didn't eat much and it wasn't long before he made an excuse and vanished below deck.

'There's no such thing as *privacy*, here,' he thundered when he returned, as red as a postbox.

'Was someone watching you through the keyhole?' Avery asked.

'There wasn't a keyhole. There wasn't a *door*. Just a – a bucket behind a screen.' He shuddered. 'The sooner we're out of here, the better.'

'Maybe Nyfe *has* found out where the suitcase is,' Flick said hopefully. 'Maybe that's why she wants to see us.'

They finished breakfast and went over the deck to Nyfe's cabin. They were let in immediately, and Flick couldn't help feeling immensely jealous of the three empty eggshells on the captain's table. Clearly, the captain wasn't about to settle for black bread and mysterious root vegetables.

'Close the door behind you,' Nyfe instructed. Her clothes were clean, and different from the previous day's, although the seams were still stretched to bursting along her shoulders. Flick wondered if it was deliberate, to make her look intimidating – her clothes could have been made bigger, surely?

'Do you have my suitcase?' Jonathan asked.

'No,' Nyfe said, looking mildly surprised that he'd asked. 'I don't. But I *do* have information. And for that, you must come this way.'

She went over to the bed and grabbed the handles of the topmost drawers the mattress lay upon. To Flick's surprise, the drawers didn't pull out – they lifted, taking the mattress with them, revealing several steps vanishing downwards. 'Watch your step,' Nyfe said, swinging a leg over. 'The boards are old and thin.'

The three of them climbed over and down, Nyfe staying at the top to pull the mattress-board back into place before following them. The passage was narrow and the ceiling low – Jonathan had to keep his hand above his head and Nyfe was bent double, but they quickly came to their destination: a water-level balcony that had been carved at the rear of the ship, beneath the level of Nyfe's cabin.

'This is a picaroon pit,' Nyfe said, straightening up. The water washed over her boots, and Flick's heart sank as her trainers were soaked for the second time in as many days. 'Captains past have used it for secret trades, deals, and dropping off those they would rather not make a public spectacle of.'

'Dropping off?' Flick asked in alarm.

Nyfe ignored her. 'But today, we have a meeting.'

A grey-green head popped up from the surf, making Flick jump. The head gave a nod. 'Captain.'

Nyfe nodded at the mer-person. They swam over and took hold of the railing on the pit to steady themselves. 'What news, Merrow?'

'We began the search for that object you said had been stolen, Pirate Queen,' Merrow said. 'The handled box, with locks. Our spies report that it was indeed taken from a group of humans sailing close to the island of The Break.'

'That was us,' Flick said.

'And the object was then taken to the Depths,' Merrow finished. 'Unfortunately, we do not know what happened to it since. I understand it is of great value to you?'

'To us all,' Flick said quickly. 'We need it if we're going to get any of you out of here – we're not any help at all unless we can get back to the travel agency.'

'I see. Then you should also know that the mer-folk

who stole your suitcase are allied with the humans known as the Buccaneers.'

Avery nudged her foot against Flick's ankle.

'The Buccaneers?' Jonathan asked. 'Who are they?'

'Water rats,' Nyfe spat. 'An ill wind on the ocean.'

Jonathan blinked. 'I'm sorry?'

'They are humans,' Merrow explained. 'Humans with ships, much like Captain Nyfe's. Only they do not make berth in The Break. Their port is to the rim, where the Scattered Isles lie.'

'They are weed-scum on the skin of the sea,' Nyfe said firmly.

'But I don't understand,' Flick said. 'Why would they want the suitcase? Why wouldn't they just leave this world with your crew once we worked out how to get everyone out?'

Nyfe and Merrow glanced at one another, and Flick felt an unpleasant jolt of realisation.

'You weren't going to tell them about it,' she said. 'Were you?'

Nyfe did not even have the good grace to look ashamed. 'It is not that simple, child. There is too much bad blood between us and them.'

Flick gawped, disbelief rolling off her in waves. 'But – but they're as much a part of this world as you are!'

'You're talking about things you don't understand.' Nyfe raised a finger as threateningly as if it were a sword. 'And I do not intend to sit around idle and wait for them to leave us here in this crumbling world. If the Buccaneers have stolen your suitcase, it is war they are asking for.'

'Captain Nyfe.' Jonathan stepped forward. 'There is no need to start a fight over this. We can all help one another, here.'

'You can't even help me and my crew,' Nyfe scoffed. 'You said you can't sail a ship through a suitcase. Have you come up with a solution for that yet? And what of those mer-folk as large as ships themselves? You realise not everyone in this world is the same size.'

Flick didn't know what to say to that. To leave a ship behind was one thing, but to leave people . . .

'Until you come up with a solution, you will do as you're told.' Nyfe looked at Merrow. 'No one can leave this world without the help of the children on my vessel. That's the rumour your mer-spies will spread, anyway. Sow seeds of doubt into the minds of our enemies. Make it known that any ship or mer-folk who come to me and pledge to become part of my crew shall be accepted. If they don't fly my colours . . . they should prepare for war.'

'No!' Flick clenched her fists. 'We're not your bargaining chips any more than the suitcase is. Besides,' she added, grasping at straws, 'you said your ships were valuable, surely you don't want them damaged in a pointless fight?'

'We outnumber the Buccaneers,' Nyfe said. 'It would be a short fight, and one in our favour. Once their sailors learn that only I can help them, they will mutiny against Captain Burnish and any of his crew foolish enough to stay loyal to him.'

'Yesterday you said you wouldn't leave without your ships,' Flick spluttered, 'but now you'll leave *people* behind?'

'Ships carry the dead,' Nyfe snarled. 'They are priceless.'

'More priceless than people?' Flick stared at her.

Nyfe stared back. 'Some.'

Merrow adjusted their grip and gave a small cough to get everyone's attention. 'I shall do as you have instructed, Pirate Queen. I hope you know what it is you are asking.' They let go, dropping beneath the water with barely a ripple.

Nyfe turned to Jonathan. 'If you have a brain in your head, boy, you'll tell anyone who asks you that the mer-folk have returned your suitcase to us. We cannot afford for anyone on the ship to think poorly of them at this time. This parley we are sailing to has been hard won, and it could fall apart as easy as a dandelion clock.'

'This is despicable,' Jonathan replied. 'You're not a hero – you're only trying to save the people who agree to do as you say.'

Nyfe bared her teeth. 'I command these seas, boy.'

Jonathan pushed his face up closer to hers. 'Your command hangs by a thread. I could break it as soon as I step foot on deck. I could tell your crew we've got no way out of here and you're grasping at straws.'

'Do that, and you would risk a mutiny,' she countered. 'And leave us too busy fighting to leave this world. And that,' she pointed at him, 'would be your fault. You left it too late to save your father, I gather. Do you want to make the same mistake again?'

Jonathan backed away as though Nyfe was a shark. He leaned against the railing, his face ashen.

'That was uncalled for,' Flick snapped.

'That is life in The Break,' Nyfe said. 'For the sake of peace aboard this ship, keep your mouths shut. We will sail to the Cove of Voices for the parley, and from there to the Buccaneers, to get your suitcase back. Agreed?'

'I agree.' Jonathan nodded weakly. 'I shall say nothing, unless asked. And if I am asked, I shall lie.' He gave her a look of absolute loathing.

Nyfe gave a nod of acceptance, choosing not to acknowledge the venom in Jonathan's eyes. 'And you, girl,' she glared at Flick. 'I would mind your tongue about things you do not understand. This is not your world, and things do not work in the same way as you are used to.'

Flick wanted to argue again, but Avery was digging a thumb into her back. Just the day before she'd thought they were sailing with the good guys, and that the Buccaneers were the real pirates around here. Now, it felt as though things might be the other way around.

Their suitcase was out of reach. They had no way of escaping from the *Aconite*. And the captain they were sailing with was ready for war. Flick hadn't felt so at sea since she'd fallen into it out of Quillmaster's boat. But what could she do? Nothing, at least, not whilst Nyfe was leaning over her like she was. She nodded. 'Yes.'

Nyfe waited a beat, as if waiting for Flick to call her 'Captain', then let it go. 'Let's go back to the cabin, then. Before we are missed.'

CHAPTER
SIXTEEN

Flick managed to hold in her anger until she had Avery and Jonathan alone at the rear of the ship half an hour later. 'We can't let her start a war over a suitcase!' she hissed, keeping her voice down.

'I know. I know.' Jonathan looked exhausted. Ever since Nyfe had snapped at him, he seemed to have shrunk both physically and emotionally.

'She seemed to be spoiling for a fight with the Buccaneers anyway,' Avery muttered, cracking her knuckles. 'Just needed an excuse.'

'What does she even hope to get out of this?' Flick whispered. 'She has a whole load of ships calling her Captain, already. She'd honestly leave people here just because they've fought each other in the past?'

'She needs to grow up.' Avery rubbed her head, making her hair stand on end. 'But right now she's the one with the ships, the command, and everyone listening to her. We've got nothing. Literally, since the suitcase was stolen. We have to stay with her. Try and figure something out.'

'And save *everyone*,' added Flick.

'Everyone,' agreed Avery.

'Yes, that sounds the best course of action,' Jonathan said, staring into space. Flick had the impression he didn't really know what he was agreeing to.

Avery gave him a worried look, then turned to Flick. 'OK, so we save everyone. But how? We're in the middle of the ocean!'

Flick paused, an idea flickering into being. It felt rather impossible, but anything else would only keep them right under Nyfe's boot. 'What if we *don't* stay here with Nyfe? We could get off the ship.'

'You know how I feel about swimming,' Jonathan sighed.

'I don't mean swim,' Flick said. 'There are smaller boats on the side of the ship.'

Avery brightened a little. 'I'm listening.'

'We take one,' Flick said. 'We leave this ship and sail to the Buccaneers before Nyfe does.'

'And how would we do that?' Avery said. 'She's got a bigger boat. She could easily chase us down even if we managed to get away without her noticing at first.'

'We leave the parley at the Cove of Voices before it's finished,' Flick said, her brain beginning to tick faster and excitement building in her chest. 'Nyfe won't be able to leave the meeting immediately even once it's over – you saw how everyone crowded around her before. And smaller boats go first so they don't get knocked about in the wake of the bigger ones, remember? She'd have no choice but to give us a head start. We can sail to where the Buccaneers are and get the suitcase back first!' The fact that she didn't know how to sail was a fact that Flick chose, for the moment, to ignore. How hard could it be?

'We'd need maps,' Avery was saying. 'We could take the ones in Nyfe's cabin – or copy them, that would be better. Maybe do something to sabotage the *Aconite*, too, slow them down a bit.'

Flick nodded. 'Better than waiting here for nothing to happen, right?'

'Right.' Avery said, putting her hands on her hips. 'We can't do anything sitting here. Flick's plan is go, I vote.'

Jonathan had been silent, with his eyes closed, as

they spoke. Now, he opened them wearily. 'Fine,' he said. 'Since we don't have a better plan. But this needs to be as watertight as a mermaid's handbag. One slip-up and Nyfe will have us in the brig for the rest of the voyage.'

'Right.' Flick nodded. 'Now – who's good at sneaking about?'

*

By the pirates' clocks, it was two days of sailing before they reached the Cove of Voices. During the journey, Flick and Avery spent every moment they weren't sitting down for meals doing chores. It turned out there really was a job for everyone on a ship, even if you'd never been on one before. Flick was put to work cleaning the brass in Nyfe's cabin, and Avery found herself peeling vegetables in the kitchen below decks. It was hot and sticky work for them both, but it did give them a chance to start to put their plans into action.

As Flick polished brass, she watched Nyfe. The captain always put her maps and charts away carefully and Flick knew they would be missed if she stole one. So, every time Nyfe left her cabin, Flick took out her waterlogged notebook and biro and copied them instead, a bit each time. From the maps, the Cove of Voices looked to be a long way from the Scattered Isles, and Flick tried hard to ignore the nervous feeling in her gut about her plan.

She was also anxious about the amount of time they were spending here in The Break. Flick liked maths, and she knew that if two days had passed here then something approaching three hours had passed back home. She had told her mum that she would be home before six. And back home it was now gone one in the afternoon.

Avery didn't seem to have any such worries. She used her time in the kitchens to eavesdrop. She could do a remarkable impression of someone who wasn't interested in anything, and barely said a word to anyone as she apparently concentrated on nothing besides chopping and mixing. Clearly, her act paid off, because the sailors thought nothing of talking openly around her, and Avery soon had information about the winds, the sailing conditions, and most importantly, gossip about what might happen at the parley with the mer-people.

She relayed all of this to Flick the night they were supposed to arrive at the Cove as they huddled at the prow of the ship by lantern-light. It was raining, and the two girls held a tar-slicked raincheater over both of their heads, hissing to one another for fear of being overheard.

'I was wrong before,' Avery said over the constant patter of the rain. 'The mood on the ship is that Nyfe doesn't want a real war. She just wants the Buccaneers, and the mer-people on *their* side, to surrender out of fear that they'll be left behind if they don't.'

'I guess that makes sense,' Flick replied, remembering how casual Nyfe had sounded about attacking the other ships. 'She wouldn't risk her own sailors or ships at this point. But why even bother threatening?'

'Power.' Avery shrugged. 'You know what people are like once they get a sniff of it.'

Flick shivered. 'So, Nyfe wants control of all the ships in The Break? And then what? She'll still be stuck here. Even if she gets the suitcase back from the Buccaneers, she won't leave her ships behind.'

'Maybe she expects us to find another solution for her,' Avery said. 'Well – maybe she expects Jonathan to find one. You know what annoys me? She talked about her generation being the ones left trying to fix an unfixable world, but she still expects someone else to do it for her. She sees this as a chance to get some power whilst we, apparently, do the dirty work.'

Flick chewed her bottom lip. 'I don't suppose

Jonathan has given you any ideas about saving The Break at all?'

'No. You?'

The girls looked at one another and pulled identical awkward faces.

Jonathan had spent the last couple of days in his hammock, and nowhere else. The official reason was seasickness, but they both knew it was more than that. He didn't speak unless directly spoken to, had to be reminded to eat and drink, and if left alone would simply stare into space, occasionally crying soundlessly, tears leaking down his face slowly, as if even they had run out of energy.

'I don't know how to help him,' Flick said. 'What do you do when someone's had a shock like that?'

'I don't know either,' Avery said. 'Nothing like that has ever happened to me. In fact, I had so little childhood trauma that I've been forced to develop a personality instead.'

Flick didn't want to laugh, she really didn't, but a bubble of a giggle popped up her throat and ended up as a sort of cackle. She blushed.

'It wasn't that funny,' Avery said, but she looked pleased.

'Obviously.' Flick tried to narrow her eyes at her,

but they both ended up grinning stupidly, then looking away, their breath fogging and mixing together in the small dry space they were sharing.

Flick sighed to herself. She hadn't set out to make friends with Avery, but she didn't seem to be able to help it. She would say something and then catch herself wondering whether Avery had been impressed with it. Or hoping Avery would think she was funny, or clever. It didn't change the fact that Avery still seriously got on Flick's nerves with her messy-but-perfect hair and infectious laugh and that smile that seemed to tug at the corners of your own mouth. Even though she was trying not to be too interesting, everyone on the ship liked her. Flick could see why.

She shoved the thoughts aside. She was supposed to be thinking about Jonathan, Strangeworlds, and finding the missing suitcase. Not Avery.

'I keep thinking about the schism,' she said, to cover the silence she was suddenly aware had been yawning open between them. 'In the suitcase, I mean.'

'What about it?' Avery asked, blinking herself back into the conversation.

'Well, a schism is supposed to be contained inside a suitcase,' Flick said, 'but some of the Strangeworlds suitcases are really small. If you had Nyfe's shoulders then logically you'd never get into them. But Jonathan's never said anything anyone not fitting.'

Avery nodded. 'What's your point?'

'There must be some sort of . . . overspill,' Flick suggested. 'That means anyone can get through a suitcase, even if it's a small one.'

'Makes sense. I mean, as much sense as anything else to do with Strangeworlds.'

'Well . . . what if the overspill could be, I don't know, stretched?' Flick gestured with her hands, like she was stretching a huge elastic band.

Avery stuck her bottom lip out in a way that was far cuter than Flick felt it had any right to be. 'But schisms can't be changed,' she said.

'They can. They can get bigger,' Flick said. 'Did Jonathan tell you about Five Lights?' She quickly told Avery the story. How the Thieves of the city had stolen and bottled so much magical energy that the schism above their world had grown and devoured bits of the world until it was almost too large to be stopped.

'. . . and now, they're releasing all the bottled magic into the sky,' Flick finished. 'To try and repair the damage.'

Avery's eyes were wide. 'You seriously ripped out of one world into another?'

'Well, yeah, I broke out of the Waiting Room.' Flick shrugged, like it was no big deal. 'I had to.'

Avery glanced around, as if looking for someone who might be laughing. 'Are – are you really from Johnnie's world?'

'What?' Flick laughed. 'Of course I am. I've lived there my entire life. You can't live in a world you don't belong in.'

'I suppose not. But, what are your parents like?'

'Just ordinary,' Flick said. 'They're just adults. Human beings. Boring.'

'Guess you just got lucky,' Avery said. 'I wonder if you've got some Mercator blood. You're like Elara Mercator, all over again.'

'I can't move and trap schisms,' Flick pointed out.

'No, but you can open and close them, which is better.'

'I've only done it once!' Flick stretched her arms to try and distract herself from the way Avery's words made her feel like her insides were made of marshmallow. 'And it doesn't help us now. We need to sail a fleet of ships through a suitcase and I am fresh out of ideas.'

'Ripping a new schism open is out of the question, then?'

'It's not like ripping paper,' Flick said. 'Besides, when I did it last time, the whole little world collapsed. It vanished, and pretty quickly. That's the opposite of what we want to happen here.'

There was a streak of lightning across the dark sky. Flick counted to twelve before there was the low rumble of thunder. 'Come on,' she said to Avery. 'Let's see if we're getting close.'

They climbed down the steps onto the lower deck. The ship was slowing now, the Cove of Voices in sight on the horizon like a crescent moon fallen into the sea. They would be there in less than an hour.

Avery blew a low whistle. 'We're doing this, then? Stealing a boat from the Pirate Queen?'

'We've got to,' Flick sighed. 'We can't let Nyfe manipulate this crisis for her own gain.'

Avery pushed herself off the side. 'And we're agreed on number four?'

'Number four,' Flick nodded.

They had agreed to steal Lifeboat Number Four from the side of the *Aconite*. They were also going to disconnect the rudder chain of the ship to delay Nyfe chasing after them. Flick had sketched out a cutaway of the ship that she had seen on Nyfe's desk. Avery, whose dad was apparently a mechanic, had been working on engines for as long as she'd been able to hold a spanner, and reckoned could disable the ship long enough to give them a decent head start.

'LAND HO!' came a yell from the crows' nest above.

It was time.

The parley with the mer-people, and then, their escape.

CHAPTER SEVENTEEN

As Flick predicted, there were more sailors rushing to and fro after the anchor dropped than anyone could keep track of. All the small wooden boats were readied to be lowered into the water to take them right up to the Cove, and Avery placed a bag containing a pack of food and several corked bottles of water into the bottom of Lifeboat Four. With any luck, it would still be there later.

Flick roused Jonathan from his hammock, and directed him to wash, get dressed and eat something. It was like looking after Freddy in some ways, except that Freddy didn't give her dirty looks when she told him he needed to scrub his armpits.

'I do not require babying,' Jonathan snapped as

Flick waved a slice of black bread in front of him. 'I'm just a bit under the weather, is all.'

'And that's fine,' Flick said, trying not to argue. 'Avery and I have got it all sorted. You know the plan. All you need to do is follow us.'

'You mean do as I'm told? Wonderful. I can't wait to be dictated to by a pair of tweenagers.' He pushed his broth away. 'Has it occurred to either of you that I'm going to have to speak up at this parley? We won't be lurking in the shadows at the back, you know.'

'What? Why?'

Jonathan made a *duh* sound. 'Captain Nyfe summoned me here. I'm the one, apparently, who somehow has to get all of these people to another world safely. I think I *might* be required to speak up.' He put his head in his hands. 'I'd sell either one of you for a cup of decent tea, right now.'

Flick felt rather put out. 'We've been trying to think of how to evacuate everyone.'

'Any bright ideas?'

'Not yet.'

'I'm shocked. Well, let's see if we can't at least get my suitcase back first. Your plan had better work, Felicity.'

They joined Avery at Lifeboat Four, and eventually

they were lowered into the sea. Jereme was at the oars again, this time with another sailor Flick didn't recognise. Edony was sitting between them, her drum between her knees. Flick had learnt that the delicate tattoos on her body were actually prayers.

The Cove of Voices was located in a bite-shaped bay on the largest isle of the world. The water was a deep blue that reminded Flick of holiday adverts on TV. The waves didn't crash here; they bobbed and ebbed gently, flowing quietly under large wooden walkways built on stilts that rose above the waterline. Huge ships were tethered out to sea, and from them came a fleet of smaller boats that were being tied off on these wooden jetties.

The walkways joined together like roads, leading from the sea to a flat crescent-moon of pale sandy beach. The sand was pitted here and there with huge grey-white rocks, each one the size of a car.

The Cove of Voices was so enormous that it felt more like a stadium than a beach, with raised platforms built around the edges that looked down onto an area of flat slate next to the water, clearly meant to be a stage of sorts. Flick noticed there was less pushing and jostling than there had been in the cave meeting a few days ago. In fact, all the sailors looked rather fearful and sombre as they climbed ladders onto the high platforms, or else settled cross-legged on the dry sand, eyes on the as-yet empty stage.

As soon as their jolly boat had been tied up, Jereme directed Flick and her friends to a couple of crates acting as seats near the stage. 'Sit tight on these,' he said. 'They'll help you be seen when you're called on to talk.'

He promptly returned to Nyfe's side. She was already standing, hands on her belt, boots apart, staring at the water that lapped at the beach with a thoughtful look on her face. A warm breeze ruffled her clothes, but it made Flick shiver.

'Have you been to one of these before?' she asked Jonathan.

'No.' He shook his head. 'I doubt anyone has been to something like this before, though. A meeting between humans and mer-folk? It's a historic occasion.'

Avery squashed up closer to Flick as someone budged beside her on the crate. Between Jonathan on one side and Avery on the other, Flick felt like a walnut waiting to be cracked open. It didn't help that both of them had very pointy elbows.

The beach was packed now. Pirates were sitting on the platforms, boots dangling down. Small pirate children were sitting on their parents' shoulders or running about underfoot. Taller pirates pushed forward against the shorter, who stood their ground firmly, arms folded and fingertips brushing the handles of their cutlasses. Out at sea, Flick could see the silhouettes of at least a dozen ships, maybe more. If each one was home to as many sailors as the *Aconite*, then there must be thousands of sailors packed onto this beach. How would anyone hear a thing?

There was a great splash, interrupting her thoughts.

In the bay, heads rose. Then shoulders, arms and bodies surfaced, stopping at mid-chest. The mer-folk seemed to be resting on something unseen – some sort of underwater ledge that ran along the curve of the beach.

These mer-folk were not like the ones that Flick had met in the ocean; they had scaley fronds down their arms and chest and through the clear water she also saw the glimmer of scaly fish tails, like mermaids from story books.

Edony, standing a few paces away from Nyfe, banged her drum a few times, and Flick jumped at how loud the sound was. The curve of the bay seemed to act like a giant amplifier that even the mass of pirate bodies couldn't dull.

Nyfe watched the mer-folk crouch at the edge of the

slate stage, then she sat down and crossed her legs so they were not exactly face to face, but closer in height than if she had stayed standing.

The surrounding pirates fell silent. Even the children stopped chattering, clinging wordlessly to their parents.

'Welcome, people of the waves, to this place,' Nyfe said. She didn't have to raise her voice much to be heard. 'We claim no ownership over this cove, nor ruling over this parley. Titles here mean nothing.' She inclined her head. 'In this place, in this meeting, I am no longer the Pirate Queen. I am Nyfe. And I am your equal.'

One of the mer-folk inched closer. Her face was similar to that of the mottled creature that had pulled Flick away from the path of the *Aconite*. Deep black eyes stared from overlarge sockets, and when she raised a hand, Flick could see that her four fingers had deep webbing in-between them.

She spoke, in a high-pitched voice. 'All of you here know me as the Queen of Weeds.' She looked about, her expression defiant. 'In the spirit of this parley, you may know me as Satura.'

'Then, let us talk, Satura,' Nyfe said. 'Let us discuss what is happening to our world, and what we must do to survive it.'

CHAPTER EIGHTEEN

'Our world is collapsing. And we must leave. All of us. Together.'

There was a sudden chorus of upset and fright, as pirates and mer-folk alike shouted anxiously at Nyfe's words.

Not quite all *of you*, Flick thought bitterly. Jereme shouted for 'Order!', but the bellowing only got louder. It reminded Flick of the time the TV had accidentally got stuck on BBC Parliament.

Nyfe looked at Edony, who banged her drum hard with a stick until quiet fell.

'Shut up, the lot of you,' Nyfe said, not raising her voice above a dangerous low note. 'We can argue when we are safe. Every moment lost hastens our demise.'

Satura pushed herself up the rocks. Her flat, muscular

chest was marked with black and green patterns that ran down her skin like drips of paint. 'Our tales say the tears in the sky are other worlds, and I believe you land-walkers say the same thing. If there are other worlds out there, can we consider them as a refuge?'

Nyfe nodded. 'Another world is our only hope, I agree. But to step into another world is not a simple task.'

Satura considered. 'This is magic that the people of the waves do not meddle with. Have you seen it done, Captain Nyfe, this stepping from one world to another?'

Nyfe gave a grim smile. 'There are those who travel between worlds,' she said. 'Those magic-wielders whom we call the *Strangeworlders*.'

There was some uncomfortable shifting amongst the pirates and mer-people. Clearly, they didn't like the sound of magic.

'One of them was supposed to be our ally,' Nyfe went on. 'But, unfortunately for us, he appears to have passed to the next world before we could ask his assistance.'

Flick glanced at Jonathan, whose jaw had gone rigid.

'Who was this man?' Satura asked.

'His name was Daniel Mercator,' Nyfe said. She looked into the audience and pointed a finger directly at Jonathan. 'And he was this young man's father.'

All eyes swivelled immediately to Jonathan, and Flick watched him blush fire-engine red, as though someone was filling him with dye from the feet up. He raised a hand. 'Hello, everyone.'

Satura sat up straighter. 'What business does this boy and his family have in worlds other than their own?'

Jonathan stood. He had put the piratical blue jacket back on over his shirt, and despite the lack of sleep and the emotional wreckage, he looked fairly certain of himself. 'My name is Jonathan Mercator,' he said. He took a deep breath. 'I am Head Custodian of The Strangeworlds Travel Agency. For over one hundred and forty years we have guarded the ways to other worlds. I was summoned here by the Pirate Queen,' he hesitated, 'to take part in this parley.' He swallowed hard. Flick knew he was thinking about who the summons had really been for, and she hurt for him.

Satura cocked her head to one side. 'You guard gateways to other worlds? That is a great responsibility. What do you gain from it?'

'Peace of mind,' Jonathan answered, tiredly.

The Mer-Queen looked sceptical. 'I see. And you think you can help us?'

'Nyfe Shaban thought I could,' he said. 'However, what she wants isn't something that I can provide.' He sat back down, as if his legs weren't capable of holding him up any longer.

'What did you ask for?' Satura asked, looking to Nyfe, who snorted.

'Only what is necessary.' Nyfe waved a hand dismissively.

'We gave you the best solution we had and you rejected it!' Flick cried out, standing up, fuelled by a sudden rage.

Nyfe was glaring daggers at her. 'We are the pirates of The Break and the people of the waves,' Nyfe said, and there was an unmistakeable threat in her voice. 'We *will* find a way out. For all of us – past and present. No matter what it takes.'

Satura gave Flick a look she couldn't read, before turning back to Nyfe. 'I do not foresee solving this issue this evening. And no doubt many of you have fears. I suggest those who sleep, do. And in the morning, we will open the floor to everyone, to hear every idea, and to share our plans.'

'Before you adjourn' – Jonathan suddenly stood

up – 'I must say, Queen of the Mer-folk, that I would rather like the return of my property.'

There was a murmur of confusion.

'Your property?' she said.

'My suitcase,' Jonathan said. 'One of your people took it from us.'

Satura's mouth opened in surprise, and Nyfe's expression turned murderous, her eye flashing in rage as she gripped her hands into fists. 'Mercator . . .'

Jonathan ignored her. He addressed the crowd. 'You see, we *did* have a way out of this world – for some of you, at least. But it was stolen.'

'It's true,' Nyfe cut in quickly, standing up as well. 'Stolen and handed over to those dregs – the Buccaneers.'

Flick expected more shouting, but this time there was only a soft silence, and the sense of menace creeping through the air.

'Captain Burnish has long tested us and our power,' Nyfe went on. 'And now he is trying to keep the way out of this world for himself. This is our chance to rescue those sailors he has lashed to the deck of his rule, to take them under our own flag and help them escape this world with us. Who's with me?'

The question took the pirates by surprise, but after

a second there was a roar of assent. It seemed they were keen on the idea of a battle to rescue fellow sailors from under the rule of apparent tyranny.

Nyfe gave Jonathan a deathly stare as the cheers rang out. She'd been forced to reveal her plans for the Buccaneers, even if she had avoided mentioning what sort of 'rescue' she really had in mind.

Satura turned to one of her people, and spoke quickly, in a language that sounded like a bow drawn over violin strings. Two of the mer-folk dived back beneath the water. She looked at Jonathan. 'Your suitcase was not taken on my orders. We know nothing of it. But our people are sadly divided, much like the humans.'

Jonathan opened his mouth to argue, before Flick prodded him firmly with a finger. He grimaced. 'Very well,' he said through gritted teeth.

Nyfe stretched, the muscles in her arms like steel bands. 'The parley is suspended until tomorrow. Everyone, retire to your ships. Turn down the lights. Smaller boat crews first. My crew, wait here until I give the order.'

Everyone began to move.

'We need to go,' Flick said. 'Quick, before she realises we're gone. Come on!' Avery nodded. Flick grabbed Jonathan by the sleeve and yanked him along.

They scrambled down off the crates, trying to blend in with the moving sailors. No one gave them much of a glance, but that might change when they tried to take the boat. Especially since everyone now knew who they were.

'We could do with a distraction,' Flick said, as they carved their way through the busy walkway. 'Something to take the pirate's eyes off the lifeboats. Especially the sailors from the *Aconite*.'

'Start a fight?' Avery suggested.

'Could do. Between who, though?

'Let's just get to the boat,' Jonathan sighed. 'We'll burn that bridge when we get to it.'

They darted through the crowds, making it out onto the portion of the wooden jetty where their boat was moored. Lifeboat Four waited for them, a dark slice of wood on the water.

Jonathan got to it first and climbed in, picking up the oars as Flick and Avery started to untie the boat from its mooring.

Flick could feel that they were indeed being watched by the surrounding pirates. Curiously, though, not with malice. Perhaps the sailors were wondering why they were leaving when the crew of the *Aconite* had been asked to wait. Flick focussed on the knots, which were surprisingly complicated. If she just kept looking like she knew what she was doing, like she was following orders, then, hopefully, none of the sailors would get too suspicious.

Flick finished untying the knots without incident and she and Avery quickly climbed into the boat. Jonathan loosened the rope holding the sail down, and it billowed out quickly, inflating in the warm air. The boom swung across, almost knocking Avery backwards. Jonathan planted his boot against it to hold it in place. There was probably a better way of holding it still, but none of them had ever sailed before.

'What could possibly go wrong?' Flick asked out loud.

Avery burst out laughing, and Jonathan gave her an incredulous look

But the water was kind, and the wind was kinder. They were quickly blown out into the open water and managed to turn the boat to aim for the Scattered Isles. Flick's sketched-out maps were passed from hand to hand as the three of them set sail away from one bunch of pirates in search of another.

CHAPTER NINETEEN

After about four hours on the ocean, the wind dropped. It dropped entirely, the sail collapsing, hanging from the ropes like wet washing.

Flick pulled at some of the ropes attaching the sails to the mast, but none of them seemed to be the right ones to roll the sail back up. It hung there, casting a shadow and blocking the view so the three occupants of the boat had to lean around it to see where they were going. And where they were going was nowhere.

The boat was bobbing on the slack water like a lazy cork.

All three of them had a go at rowing, but it was like stirring quick-dry cement. No matter how much they heaved, the oars jammed themselves into the water and refused to come up properly, threatening to spring out of their hands. Either they didn't have the right technique, or the water was actively resisting them. Flick didn't like to guess which. She leaned against the mast in the shadows, feeling the utter stillness of the air. It was as though someone was slowly sucking the oxygen out of the world, and, after an hour, Flick caught herself yawning.

'Tired?' Jonathan asked. There were dark purple blushes under his own eyes, and he had hurt his hands trying to get the oars to work.

Flick let her head roll to one side. 'They're going to catch us.'

He shrugged. 'Maybe they're becalmed, too. And they don't have oars, so they can't even *try* to row.'

'So it's a race to see who can pick up some wind first.' Flick looked at the limp sails.

Avery rested her chin on the edge of the boat. 'I always knew I'd die like this.'

'At sea, you mean?' Jonathan asked.

'No – of sheer boredom.'

Flick gave a small laugh. Jonathan went back to the sheet of paper he'd been examining. He had been making adjustments to Flick's copied map as they sailed, though Flick didn't see how he knew what changes to make given there were no landmarks – nothing but water in every direction, right up to the horizon. Occasionally, one of the dark waves would crest and break with white foam, but otherwise there was nothing.

'The wind will come back,' Flick said, not expecting either of them to reply. 'It has to.'

And then, the sun came out.

It dawned suddenly, as though someone had switched on an enormous bulb, bright yellow-white light streaming into the world of The Break through the rips in the fabric of the sky.

Flick jumped as she felt the warmth hit her face. The shade cast by the hanging sails was already only half the size it had been. The daylight bounced off every curve of the water, right into Flick's eyes so she had to scrunch up her face.

'This can't be only one sun, surely,' Jonathan said, putting a hand to his eyebrows to shade his vision. 'It's far too bright. This is the daylight from more than one world.'

'Whatever it is,' Avery said, hunching into what was left of the shade, 'it's hot. And it's getting hotter.'

She was right. The sun, or suns, beamed through the rips in the fabric of the sky, white-hot.

Flick couldn't believe how quickly the air started to cook. She, Jonathan and Avery took large gulps of the fresh water they had, their bodies crying out for hydration as the air started to bake. Flick trailed her fingers in the ocean surrounding them, splashing the seawater up her arms as the heat really started to make itself known. When the water dried on her skin, it left streaks of white salt behind. Flick wondered if the salt would dry her skin out even more, and suddenly felt rather frightened. She could feel the sun crisping her hair and draped her jacket over her head like a scarf to try and stop the top of her head catching fire.

The heat and light were relentless. Flick felt certain that it would have to stop eventually, run out of energy somehow. But it didn't. Avery's spiky hair flattened itself against her skull, and Jonathan's glasses kept slipping down his nose with sweat.

'We need to make a shelter,' Flick rasped. 'Help me.'

Together, they lifted the oars and leaned them against the mast. Jonathan wrapped some rope around them to hold them in place whilst Avery and Flick cut the bottom of the sail and dragged it and their jackets over the long sticks to make something like a tepee-style tent. Then they tried to shelter beneath it.

'We've got about a litre left,' Avery said, weighing

the water bottles in her hands. 'I think. And that's each.'

'Try and use the shade before drinking the water,' Flick gasped from next to her. She could feel the searing heat coming through the sail, threatening to roast her. The three of them were leaning together, taking shallow breaths.

Avery let her head loll onto Flick's shoulder, but Flick couldn't even find it in herself to properly acknowledge it besides wishing it wasn't so heavy and sweaty.

Jonathan licked his dry lips. 'I suspect we may have made an error in leaving the *Aconite*.'

Flick didn't have the energy to answer. She could feel sweat running down her back. It didn't make her feel any cooler, just damp and uncomfortable. She wondered vaguely how long it would be before she was turned into a raisin.

Avery slipped down, lying in the belly of the boat, her dark eyes staring up at nothing. Jonathan poured some of the precious water into his hand and rubbed it over his face.

Flick realised she couldn't even feel scared. She was too warm.

She wondered, just as her eyes closed, if they ought

to have got in the sea, or if the water would have somehow magnified the heat and made it worse.

And then, she didn't think anything at all.

*

She had the sensation that they were on the move, again. There was a shadow – a vast shadow, like a mountain looming over the tiny lifeboat.

Flick thought she ought to say something, maybe wake up one of the others, but then it was like they were flying . . . the wind was back, but it was blowing in the wrong direction. They were moving into the wind.

It was like they were being carried in the hand of a giant.

*

She woke up, but she couldn't open her eyes.

I'm blind. I've gone blind.

She sat bolt upright, hand flying to her face. Her fingers met something cold and soggy where her eyes should have been, and for a horrifying moment Flick was certain that her eyes had melted into goop and that was all that was left of them – but then she smelled it.

Cucumber.

Or something like it.

She touched the soggy substance again and brought her fingers to her nose. Definitely cucumber-y.

Probably not one wrapped in plastic from Tesco, either.

She let her hand drop in relief.

'Oh, you're awake at last.' A voice came from the left. Flick reflexively turned her head. 'We didn't want to wake you up before you were ready, and you needed a bit of treatment anyway. Ready to risk losing the bandage?'

'What's wrong with my eyes?' Flick asked.

'Nothing, I hope. But you were in the sun for goodness knows how long, and that's not good for anyone. You've got some bad sunburn on your arms too.' Hands, rough at the fingertips, started to undo the bandage. 'Now, when I take this off, don't start rubbing at your eyes. I'll get you a cloth. Thank Jones you had that sail over your heads or you'd have a face like a boiled beet.' The pressure of the bandage gave way, and cool air kissed over Flick's face.

She sighed in gratitude. 'Thank you.'

'Well, I think that's done the job. The swelling's gone down. Nothing like a tea and gourd compress for soothing the eyes.' A cold, damp cloth was put into Flick's hand. 'Be gentle with yourself.'

Flick did as she was told, carefully wiping the cloth over her face, forehead, nose, cheeks and chin, before doing her eyes last. Her eyelids were covered in some sort of gloopy mess, and it took several wipes to gather it all out. When Flick finally opened her eyes, her vision was blurry, but a few blinks soon cleared it, and she found she was below deck on a ship.

A woman in a dark blue dress, belted at the waist, was smiling at her. 'There, now. Right as rain.'

'Thank you.' Flick handed the cloth back. 'Where am I?'

'You're in my nurse bay, onboard the *Serpent*,' the woman said. 'We picked you up. Captain Burnish ordered you brought back to health.'

Captain Burnish? This is a Buccaneers' ship, Flick thought, half-relieved and half-nervous. 'That's kind.'

'No, that's fair,' the nurse said. 'We owe you nothing, now.' She turned away, and Flick couldn't help feeling as though she'd leapt from the fishing net into the saucepan.

'Where's everyone else?' she asked, trying to ignore the way her heart was thundering.

'Your friends?' The nurse indicated a corner of the cabin with her chin. 'Over there.'

Flick turned, and saw Avery and Jonathan asleep on separate benches. Avery had a fantastic thin blistered line of sunburn down one cheek, but Jonathan seemed unharmed, aside from the bandage over his eyes. As if knowing he was being watched, he gasped and sat upright suddenly, pulling at the bandage.

'What in the world – oh my – have I been—?' He scrabbled at the scrap of cloth.

The nurse went over to help him, and Flick climbed down from the shelf that had been her makeshift bunk. Her joints were aching, and she was so sore that she felt as if she'd been rolled down rapids in a barrel, but she was alive. They all were. Whatever Captain Burnish had in mind for them now, they owed him their lives.

She remembered the weird flying sensation she had felt. Surely they hadn't really been taken through the air? That had to have been the heatstroke.

Avery was shaken gently, then, and sat up with the same panic as her cousin before being calmed down.

Flick stared around the cabin. There were dried herbs hanging from the ceiling, clay pots and bottles stacked in boxes. There was a big bottle of black ink and a selection of needles lying in a box beside it. There were also skeins of wool and cloth hanging from hooks drilled into the walls.

'Where are my glasses?' Jonathan demanded as soon as his face was clean. 'I need them to see.' Without the frames on his nose, his eyes looked small and weirdly naked.

The nurse shrugged. 'I think the sailors on deck were having a scrap over them.'

'They can have a scrap over *my dead body*,' Jonathan said, standing up in a vibration of rage. 'Those are *mine*.'

'I don't think they'd mind fighting over your dead body, to be fair,' she said. 'Ask for them back yourself.'

Jonathan squinted at her. 'Are you one of the Buccaneers?'

She laughed. 'Is that what Nyfe's gang of hooligans is still calling us? Yeah, we're the Buccaneers, if you like. But we'd prefer to be called Captain Burnish's crew. I'm Marcie.'

'Burnish is the one who rescued us?' Avery asked.

'Well, in a fashion. You were delivered to us.'

'Delivered?' Flick's mind went back to the flying sensation. 'Delivered by who?'

'Ask the captain yourself. He'll want to see you now you're awake.' Marcie climbed the ladder up and out of sight.

Jonathan glared after her. Then squinted back at Flick. 'I can't see a thing.'

'Are you seriously that blind?'

'I can see where you are, but I wouldn't want to chance the ladder. Who steals someone's glasses, I ask you?'

'Someone who has no chance of getting a pair any other way?' Avery suggested. She gingerly touched her sunburn. 'Ouch. This smarts.'

Jonathan groped his way over to a water jug, before dipping a finger into it and licking it to confirm it was safe. He didn't bother searching for a cup. 'Looks like the Buccaneers found us,' he gasped, after guzzling half the jug.

'Yeah, but they're not happy.' Flick took the jug off him and had a swig. It tasted stale. 'The nurse said something about them not owing us anything now. I don't like the sound of that.'

'I don't like it, either,' Avery said. 'They want a clean slate so they can, what – make us walk the plank without guilt? I know we wanted to find them, but is anyone else getting a bad vibe?'

Flick and Jonathan were saved the trouble of answering by the sound of heavy boots stomping down the ladder. A man with wild grey curly hair and a beard to match crashed down into the cabin. He had a green dragon – the long Chinese kind with a snake-like body and flaring nostrils – embroidered onto the front of his dark shirt. His trousers were heavily waxed, like the ones sailors on board the *Aconite* had worn, and his boots were knotted firmly around his ankles.

He was the captain. He didn't have to say he was; he radiated a captainness that needed no introduction. He gave them all a quick once-over. 'No injuries?' he barked.

'No, sir,' Flick said, adding the *sir* without really thinking about it.

The captain took a pair of glasses from his pocket. 'These yours?' He offered them to Jonathan.

'Oh, yes. Thank you.'

'You're welcome to them. They didn't work for Old Samm. Said they made his eyes even worse.' He sniffed. 'You came from Captain Nyfe's ship.' It wasn't a question. 'Well, now. What would you be doing in my waters in an *Aconite* jolly boat, hm?'

'We were coming here to find you,' Avery said. 'We're not trying to start a fight or anything.'

The man raised his eyebrows in a *you-don't-say* expression. 'No, I didn't think the three of you would be up to that task. A bunch of dried-up jellies if ever I saw them. You know what I'm thinking?' He leaned a hand on one of the benches, and gave a cheery smile that went nowhere near his eyes. 'You might not be here to fight, but you don't fool me.'

Flick blinked. 'What do you mean?'

Captain Burnish turned his eyes on her. 'We know Nyfe Shaban's game. Thought she'd appeal to our better nature, did she? Well, I'm sorry to say . . . I don't have one. I reckon that you three,' he flicked his free hand and suddenly there was a knife in it, 'are spies.'

Flick went stiff all over in fear. The captain hadn't lunged or moved at all, but the knife in his hand looked extremely sharp. She raised her hands, slowly. 'We're not spies,' she said. 'The opposite, actually. We stole the boat without Nyfe knowing. We were trying to get away from the *Aconite*.'

'You expect me to believe that you were able to steal a jolly boat from the Pirate Queen? Why would you risk doing that?'

'We know about the end of the world,' Flick said. 'And we want to help.'

Captain Burnish scoffed. 'I never heard such rubbish in my life. I don't know what your game is, but I don't trust liars *or* thieves. Get yourselves up on deck. There's things need settling.'

And with that, he hauled himself back up the ladder.

CHAPTER TWENTY

They had no choice but to follow.

As soon as Flick climbed up, shouts and jeers hit her ears, making her duck her head to try and shield herself. She'd been lucky at school, never bullied beyond having her tie sprogged and that one week where everyone pretended her name was something that rhymed with *Flick*. But this shouting was hateful and unpleasant. The pirates were laughing and egging one another on, stamping on the deck and clapping their hands.

Avery glued herself to Flick's side as soon as she climbed up, and Flick was weirdly grateful for it.

But Jonathan, climbing up last, went through a face-journey that started at shocked, hurtled through anger and ended up at the extreme nonchalance that

Flick knew meant he was one twitch away from exploding. A sailor flicked one of the embellishments on the shoulder of his jacket, and Jonathan slapped his hand sharply away without even looking at him.

The captain leaned again the mast, waiting for them. 'This way, little spies. Let's see if we can't get all this straightened out.'

'Fat chance,' Avery muttered as they walked over.

The jeering died down as Captain Burnish raised his chin a little.

'You were delivered into our waters by our mer-folk allies,' he began. 'They say you sailed straight from the Cove of Voices, which proves you're part of Nyfe's crew. There's only one way to decide if you're lying or not. A trial.'

There was an uproar of cheering from the crew.

'A trial?' Flick asked.

Burnish's grin widened through his beard. 'Oh, yes. But, since we don't have time to assemble a court back at Dagger's Island, we'll do this the old fashioned way – and let the gods decide whether or not you need punishment.'

'What's that supposed to mean?' Jonathan elbowed his way forward.

'It means,' the captain said, 'that we have one short,

sharp fight. The gods give strength to the one they know is in the right'

'That's ridiculous,' Avery said, saying what Flick was thinking. 'The winner will be the one who's best at fighting.'

Burnish shrugged, but there was a sparkle in his eyes that showed he didn't necessarily disagree with Avery's words. 'That's how we settle things on the *Serpent*, lass.'

'Fine. Fine! What's it to be, pistols at dawn?' Jonathan drawled, folding his arms. His eyebrows twitched as one of the surrounding men drew a nasty-looking cutlass.

'We favour swords on this vessel, lad. And why wait until dawn?' the Buccaneer grinned, showing teeth so brown they might have been made of wood. 'Afraid to fight, little spy?'

'Don't point that at me,' Jonathan sniffed, looking down his nose at the cutlass. 'You'll have someone's eye out.'

The captain laughed and looked at the three of them. 'How about it, then? Either you fight to prove you're *not* here on Nyfe's orders, or else you go for a long walk off a short plank. What's it to be?'

Flick's insides went cold. How could any of them fight the captain?

But Jonathan shrugged as if nothing in the world could interest him less. 'If you like.'

Flick tensed. 'Jonathan . . .'

'One on one?' Jonathan ignored her. 'No ganging up from either side?'

The captain glanced at Flick and Avery, clearly wondering what exactly they were capable of ganging up on. 'Aye.'

'And the winner calls their own terms?'

The captain tipped his head to one side. 'If I win, you get off my ship in the manner of my choosing. Exactly what are *you* proposing, should you beat me?'

'A truce, and a few favours.'

'Ha! You take me for a fool, young man? Me? Captain Ezra Burnish, leader of the Buccaneers, a man who'd throw away a few unspecified favours? Never. Not in a month of daylight!'

There was a chorus of laughter from the rest of the Buccaneers.

Flick glowered at them, her fingers tingling as she balled her hands into fists. To Flick, magic always felt as if it were only a touch away, but now, as her fear began to twist into anger, she felt as though it was unfurling, like a snake that had spotted its prey. If this went on, she wasn't sure what she might do.

'Besides,' Captain Burnish grinned, 'it's a big ask from a flowery wee lad, the most cutting thing about him being his clever words.'

The crew howled louder.

Flick gritted her teeth and looked at Jonathan. She expected him to be flushed with anger, but he stood patiently, perfectly still on the deck, hands clasped behind his back like a teacher who is waiting for the giggles to stop so he doesn't have to shout when he starts dishing out the punishments.

Gradually, the laughter died down.

Flick watched Captain Burnish's expression change, melting from amusement to some sort of irritated confusion. In that moment, Flick could have believed that his crew had been laughing at *him*.

Jonathan smiled humourlessly. 'So you won't fight me? *Flowery* little me is too much for you?' The unspoken *coward* hung in the air, like a dark cloud ready to burst.

Burnish stood straighter. He drew his own cutlass, and lifted it slightly, the point aimed towards Jonathan with a casual sort of menace. 'You must have a death wish.'

Flick inhaled sharply. *A death wish*. That was what she had been thinking, without realising it. Jonathan was acting as though he was happy to throw his life away. She suddenly wanted to step between him and the cutlass, but her boots seemed to be drilled onto the deck.

'I simply wish to beat you, and call my terms,' Jonathan said, checking his fingernails. 'That is, if you've recovered your nerve enough. Cap-tain.'

Burnish went red, blush staining his skin like blood dripped into water. 'Get this boy a blade,' he snarled.

Jonathan started unbuttoning his jacket. 'Would one of you hold this for me, please?'

'You,' Flick gawped, grabbing the jacket, 'are actually, properly insane. How can you be going ahead with this monumentally stupid plan?'

'What's stupid about it?' Jonathan stretched his arms over his head.

Avery and Flick stared at each other in disbelief for a moment. Avery threw her hands in the air, speechless.

'Oh, let me think,' Flick said, her voice slipping up an octave in sarcasm. 'Maybe the fact that you're going up against *pirates* with *swords*? Just surrender now, we'll take our chances. We'll get on better without you bleeding everywhere and alerting the sharks, anyway.'

'You're being hysterical. I've as much chance as

anyone. More, actually.' He rolled his neck, working the cricks out.

'More? What do you—'

A muscular woman in a red shirt pushed Flick to the side, and shoved a sheathed sword into Jonathan's arms. 'Your blade, boy,' she said. 'And be grateful the popular vote was to give you something with an edge.'

'Oh?' Jonathan popped the blade up slightly to see it. It was indeed very shiny. 'I would have thought you'd be more than happy to present me with a disadvantage.'

'I would have been,' she snapped. 'But the captain believes in honour. If he gets a new sword, so do you. And believe me' – she looked him up and down and snorted – 'you're going to need all the help you can get, lad.'

'Thank you,' he said, as if he'd been complimented.

'Don't cut yourself before it starts,' she called as she walked off.

Jonathan drew the cutlass all the way out. It looked lethal – the steel was so sharp that Flick couldn't see the edge. It made the very air feel cold. Avery pressed her knuckles to her mouth.

'You're really going to do this?' Flick asked. 'Jonathan – he doesn't care that you're a kid' – she ignored Jonathan's look of disdain – 'or a Mercator, or part of The Strangeworlds Society. He's going to run you through! Don't you care?'

He looked right at her. 'You think I don't care,' he said.

'Well, you're not acting like you do!' she hissed.

They glared at one another, and then Jonathan pulled her by the arm, close to him, so he could whisper. 'I know what it looks like, through your eyes,' he said. 'But this isn't a death wish. I promise you that.'

'But he might kill you,' Flick insisted.

'Not if I get him first.' Jonathan let her go. 'Trust me?'

Flick opened her mouth to argue again. But what could she say? She just nodded. *Yeah, I trust you, you madman*, she added silently. *Don't you dare prove me wrong.* She stepped back to stand beside Avery, who gave her a very tight-lipped smile.

The Buccaneers had formed a circle on the deck, and Captain Burnish had taken off his hat and rolled his sleeves up. He had a tattoo on each forearm and one on the back of each hand, the ink so fine-lined and bright it looked new.

Jonathan stepped forward, into the circle.

And immediately darted left as Burnish's sword slashed at him.

The crew laughed.

Jonathan actually grinned back. 'What – are we not bowing first, like gentlemen? I thought you'd like me to expose the back of my neck.'

Burnish swung again and again and Jonathan had to step quickly out of the path of the sword. The *Serpent*'s crew were jeering and laughing. Jonathan avoided the swipes, yet never tried to raise his own blade to retaliate.

'Stop playing with the lad, Captain!'

'Show him what he's made of!'

Avery bit her thumbnail. 'What is he *doing*? Why isn't he fighting back?'

Flick shook her head, watching Jonathan dance neatly back again, his weight on the balls of his feet, sword held loosely at his side. 'I think he's reading him,' she said softly. 'Working him out.'

Jonathan suddenly lifted his sword. His arm came up like a released spring, the blade cutting up hard at the top of Captain Burnish's arm. The sword sliced through the thick canvas sleeve and kept going, across the man's chest.

The captain threw himself backwards too late, snarling. A thin line of blood blossomed through his sleeve.

Hope leapt up Flick's chest.

The Buccaneers were quieter, now – their captain had been wounded. The boy from another world wasn't entirely clueless. The cheers had turned to mumbles of concern.

But the captain quickly recovered, getting closer until the two men were within spitting distance, their cutlasses striking hard against one another.

Jonathan was suddenly knocked off-balance, and the two of them separated quickly, swords held up defensively as they circled each other. Jonathan made as if he was going to swing again, but at the last second feinted to the right, coming up again quickly to jab the captain sharply in the ribs.

Flick gasped, hands flying to her mouth.

But Burnish seemed not to feel the wound. He punched Jonathan on the shoulder hard enough to make him gasp, and slashed at his legs, missing by a hair as Jonathan threw himself to the deck and rolled, coming up again quickly to parry another blow, block, and block, and stab again, this time puncturing the leather vest the captain wore, and making him howl.

It wasn't deep – there wasn't even any blood on Jonathan's blade as he got to his feet and stepped backward – but it made Burnish clamp a hand to his chest, a look of rage on his face.

'Oh god, he's going to kill him,' Flick breathed, every cell in her body turning to ice.

Jonathan clearly suspected the same. He kept his cutlass up, his other arm out for balance as he watched the injured captain like a hawk. 'Give it up, Captain,' he called. 'Accept that we are not spies or your enemies, and we'll call it a draw. No need for anyone to lose face. Or *a* face.'

'You got lucky, lad,' Burnish snapped back. 'But you can't rely on luck. Where'd you learn to fight like that?'

'I was the British Junior Fencing Champion in 2013,' Jonathan smirked.

Flick put her head in her hands. Jonathan thought he was up to the task of fighting a pirate, when really he'd merely had a very expensive hobby.

But the crew weren't laughing. They were looking at one another and frowning. 'Champion?' one of them murmured to the other.

Captain Burnish moved his hand from his ribs. A pale smear of blood was on his palm.

'That's twice you've made me bleed.' He feinted to one side, but Jonathan was wise to it, keeping his feet flat on the deck, his sword raised and ready, the wiry muscles in his arms braced. 'You say you're a champion;

well, I say you've got the spirit of the lionfish on your side. And she has a sting, if you get too close.' He lunged, swiping to and fro. Jonathan had no choice but to parry, ducking out of the reach of a punching fist, only to be kicked smartly to the deck. He landed hard on his back and swore loudly as Burnish's sword smashed into the woodwork beside his face. The blade stuck.

Jonathan scrambled away a second before Burnish wrenched it free. Jonathan kicked him hard on the kneecap, making the man stumble and loosen his grip on the cutlass.

Jonathan dived forward.

Flick thought he might stab the man and covered her face in horror.

But he didn't.

Jonathan grabbed the captain's sword arm at the wrist, and pushed it up, holding it too far away for Burnish to stab him. Burnish twisted expertly, but Jonathan was ready for it, and got inside his grip – his back against Burnish's chest, still hanging on to the captain's arm. Burnish tried to shove him away but Jonathan hung on like a deadweight. He clawed frantically at Burnish's hand, trying to prise the man's grip open to make him drop his sword.

'You think you can get my blade off me, boy?' Burnish screamed into his face. 'I'll die with it in my hand!'

'You might,' Jonathan said through gritted teeth. 'But not today.' He twisted sharply, and managed to get his own sword pointed up, held just by his fingertips. He aimed it towards where their hands still scrabbled together. And stabbed up.

Flick's mouth dropped in a silent scream.

Jonathan's blade pierced his own hand, and Burnish's as well.

Both men yelled and fell apart, the two swords clattering down to the deck.

Jonathan dove to the floor and snatched up both swords before Burnish could realise what had happened. He raised them both.

Blood was running down his wrist, his glasses were dangling off one ear, and he was heaving, but he held the swords steady. 'I think you ought to yield, sir.'

Burnish spat. His hand was bleeding, and so was his arm and chest. None of the wounds were bad, but they were wounds all the same. He was without a sword. And his crew were tense, around him.

'I really don't wish to become a murderer,' Jonathan added, his voice softening just a little. 'This is just for show, isn't it? No need for anyone to be the loser, if we were simply demonstrating what we could do? An exchange of skills?'

Realisation blossomed in Flick's mind. Jonathan was offering the captain a way out. Call this off, and you won't have to say I beat you. Save face, and no one had to be the loser.

Flick lowered her hands. Jonathan really was the biggest idiot she'd ever known, and she wouldn't swap him for anything.

But Captain Burnish sighed. 'No, lad. You won this. I don't mind admitting that. Everyone here saw.' He smiled. 'I don't mind losing to a champion.'

'Only a junior champion.' Jonathan lowered the blades slightly.

'Then there's more to come.' Burnish walked over, holding out his non-bloodied hand. 'I yield to you, boy. Let everyone take note, this lad and his companions are our allies. They are safe on this vessel, and any that sail under our flag.'

There was a moment's pause from the surrounding pirates before a great crashing cheer sounded, and once again the deck was pounded by boots. Flick almost laughed. The pirates weren't really bloodthirsty – they just liked a show, it seemed.

Jonathan dropped the swords and shook the man's

hand. His own was bleeding steadily, colouring his shirt sleeve.

'What's your name, lad?' Burnish asked.

'Jonathan Mercator.'

'Well, Mercator, you should have that hand seen to. It's hurt.'

'Not badly.' Jonathan examined his hand. The webbing between his thumb and index finger was punctured. 'I hope.'

Burnish tutted. 'You're either brave, or stupid.'

'Perhaps a little of both.' Jonathan looked over at Flick and Avery. 'This is Felicity, by the way. And my cousin, Avery.'

'Ladies,' Burnish gave a bow. 'Apologies you had to see that.'

'It was fun,' Avery said.

Jonathan swatted her away and spoke to Burnish again. 'We meant what we said – we fled the *Aconite* to come here. Firstly, because there is something to warn you about, that concerns you and Captain Nyfe. And secondly, to reclaim some property.' He waved his injured hand and blood went splattering through the air, landing on the Captain's jacket.

Flick rolled her eyes. 'Have you got a doctor on this ship?'

'Aye. Tessa!' Burnish yelled. Then looked back at Jonathan. 'Stolen property, you say?'

'Yes. We heard a rumour that it might have been delivered to you.'

Burnish stroked his beard into a point before letting it fluff out again. 'I'm not in the habit of receiving stolen property, despite what Nyfe Shaban thinks. But it sounds like there's a tale to tell, there. After your hand is seen to, I think.'

A woman appeared at Flick's elbow. She was about four and a half feet tall and wearing a waxed apron. 'Yes, Ez?'

'This lad's done himself a mischief. See to him, send them to the mess, and then to my cabin.'

'Aye.' Tessa took hold of Jonathan's arm. 'You'll be lucky if you haven't damaged the nerve.' She turned it over. 'What a damned stupid thing to do.'

'It made him let go, didn't it?' Jonathan's bravado, running out of adrenaline to power it, was giving way to shaky rudeness. He'd gone rather pale. Flick watched him take careful steps as they all went down into the bowels of the ship.

Tessa snorted. 'As if Burnish was going to run through a wee lad like you. He's as soft as sand at low tide, that man. He's had six children to knock the rough edges off him. He talks tough, but he's like a cockle.'

'White and lumpy?' Avery asked.

Tessa laughed. 'Aye, maybe. But soft on the inside, too. You've got to warm him up a bit to find it out. You follow me to the mess. I'll sort you out at my table, and you can get some stew in you. D'you like octopus?'

*

Jonathan's hand wasn't as bad as it looked. Once it had been cleaned up, and he'd proven he still had the feeling in all of his fingers, Tessa bandaged his thumb against the rest of his hand. It made it difficult for him to hold his spoon, but it was better than nothing.

When they got to Burnish's cabin he was waiting behind a desk, wearing a new shirt, the sleeves rolled up to his elbows. Flick could see now that his larger tattoos were both of mer-people – a male and female, both with fish tails and looking at one another across the man's body, their watery surroundings spilling down onto his hands. She realised that the bottles of ink and the needles downstairs in the medical area had been a tattooing kit.

'What did they feed you on the *Aconite*?' Burnish

asked, as Tessa closed the door to his cabin. 'Blind soup? You look half-starved, the lot of you.'

'Blind soup?' Flick asked.

'Boiling water,' Tessa said, opening a cupboard. 'Sometimes with a bit of bacon on a string dropped into it. When it's boiled, you take the bacon out and dry it, save it for another day.'

'So it's just water?'

'Water and dreams.' Tessa brought out a wicker basket and lifted the lid. She set it on Burnish's desk, taking out two apples and a knife. She quickly chopped the shrunken fruit into slices.

Flick watched curiously as Burnish allowed Tessa to use his desk as a table. She'd thought Tessa must be the ship's doctor, but she seemed very familiar with the captain. The little woman replaced the basket, and then sat on a bench at the side of the room.

'Right.' Burnish picked up a sliver of fruit. 'I believe we agreed to a truce, young man, and some information. What is it that you want to know?'

Jonathan inched his chair closer. 'We lost a suitcase. And we heard a rumour the mer-people who took it from us might have brought it to you.'

Burnish gave Jonathan an even look. 'A suitcase? You're one of those folks from another world, aren't you?'

They all nodded. Flick felt some of the anxiety she'd been carrying give way slightly. At least that was one thing they didn't have to explain.

'Nyfe summoned us here because your world is shrinking,' Jonathan explained. 'She thought we could help evacuate everyone to another world. But without our suitcase, we can't help anyone, even ourselves.'

'I'm sorry but I can't help you either,' Burnish said. 'The mer-folk haven't brought anything to us except you.'

'Us?' Flick asked.

'Aye. The Mer-Queen found you adrift at sea and carried you to our waters. Her subjects alerted us to you when you were close, and we hauled you aboard.' He scratched at his beard.

Flick remembered the sensation of flying. The rushing through the air. Had they really been carried by a mermaid? It made about as much sense as anything else.

Avery leaned forward. 'Nyfe wants to threaten you into giving up the suitcase she thinks you're hiding, and you don't even have it. She wants to start a war.'

Burnish chewed this over for a moment. 'No,' he said eventually. 'I don't think she does want a war. I think she wants a surrender. She wants my ships and crew to come under her flag. And she must be assuming that you can somehow find a way to get her crew *and* her ships out of this world, otherwise she wouldn't bother. If she can escape this world with a bunch of new ships in her armada, she could rule whatever world we end up in. This is her chance to scare my ships and my crew enough into leaving me and joining her. She'll tell them she's the only one with a way out of this world. Well . . .' he snorted. 'She won't get a surrender from me. I'll call her bluff. She won't follow through with a fight. She wouldn't risk damage to the *Aconite*, not now.'

He seemed so sure that Flick couldn't help believing him. She took a piece of apple. It was dry and fluffy, but sweet and very welcome.

'Do you think Nyfe would ever leave her ships?' she asked.

Burnish sat back in his chair, hands folded across his chest. 'No, she won't want to leave her dead.' He chuckled at Flick's dubious expression. 'Oh yes, the dead are aboard those ships,' he said. 'These, too, but we don't pay them any mind, so they stay silent. The Pirate Queen and her folk, well, they don't know when to leave well enough alone. They believe in their dead so much that they're almost alive again. The trouble with living your whole life trying please the dead is that the dead don't live in our world, and they never did. I don't mean another world like you do, I mean times have changed. Tradition is just pressure to do what the dead once did. It's not necessarily good, and certainly not worth prioritising over people living and breathing and struggling right now.'

A shudder ran over Flick's skin. She couldn't get used to these conversations about ghosts and she didn't like that Jonathan was having to listen to this sort of thing. His face had taken on the vacant, glazed look he'd worn on the *Aconite*, as if he was tuning out the conversation.

'No,' Burnish repeated. 'Nyfe is going to die on the *Aconite*, one way or another. Who knows when, or how. But she will.'

Tessa sighed. 'That doesn't mean we feel the same here, mind.'

'Oh, bless you, no.' Burnish smiled. 'Show me the way to a new world, you lot, and I'll start packing my bags right now. I'm not too foolish to know a way out when one is offered to me.'

'But there's the mer-folk too,' Flick said. 'They need to go from water to water.'

'Aye. That's a good point,' Burnish nodded. 'Can

you not go home and find a watery place for them and us all go together, like?'

'We can't go anywhere right now,' Jonathan said. 'We need the suitcase back.' He rubbed at his forehead with his unbandaged hand.

Burnish stroked his beard again as he thought. 'I think our best bet would be to go to the Scattered Isles,' he said. 'Talk to the mer-folk there, find out what's going on. They'll tell me what they'd never tell Nyfe. She wants to be in charge of them, I just want to exist alongside, you understand? They're good people to have on your side. Despite what some people say.' Burnish glanced down at the artwork on his skin. 'I could tell you some stories. You grow up hearing that one lot of people are the enemy. But then you meet them, and you realise . . .' He shook his head.

Flick said, 'People are just people.'

Burnish nodded. 'You've got the truth of the matter right there, young lady. But this sort of talk usually requires a mug or two of ale, so let's get back to the task at hand.' He unrolled a circular map, and jabbed a finger at a few blobs of grey in the blue of the sea. 'Now, then. That there's the Scattered Isles. It'll take two days to sail there, unless the mer find us first.'

'Is that likely to happen?' Flick asked, trying to do

fast maths in her head and work out the amount of time they'd been away. Two days was twenty hours times two and divided by eighteen . . .

'Anything could happen, world being the way it is.' Burnish stood up. He looked the three of them over, and his gaze rested on Jonathan. 'You're grieving, young man.'

Jonathan's blank face turned defensive. 'How – yes, but—'

'I've seen that look too many times.' Burnish drew a circle around the edges of his own face. 'Worn it plenty, too. And I know you're trying not to think on it, because you think your friends need you to be strong, but that's a lot of seagull-doings. Throwing yourself into fights? Trying to float like sea foam over the depths of your own feelings? That don't work for ever.'

Jonathan blushed.

'You got to think on it sometime, lad, or else it'll eat you from the inside out.'

Jonathan frowned. 'And how am I supposed to do that?' he asked.

Burnish smiled sadly. 'The sea takes what it wants,' he said. 'And sometimes it wants what you'd rather die than give up. And it leaves you alive for a reason. Six children I've watched Tessa bring into the world,' he jerked his thumb at the little woman, who, Flick realised, was obviously his partner. 'Six. And only two of them still breathe. My son, Ari, he's the best tailor you could hope for when cloth is scarce. He's below decks.'

Flick stared. 'What about the oth—'

'Tell the lads to set up some bunks,' Burnish said loudly to Tessa, interrupting Flick before she could finish her question. 'We're heading south. Towards the edge.' He looked back at the three travellers. 'I hope there's enough time left in this world for all this. Gods help us.'

CHAPTER TWENTY-ONE

The Scattered Isles were not as large as Flick expected them to be. They had been a cluster of green and brown blobs on Captain Burnish's map, and when they appeared on the horizon, they looked much the same.

'I thought they'd be bigger,' Flick said.

'No, no.' Tessa, standing beside Flick, Avery and Jonathan on the deck, shook her head. 'They're only wee. You can walk around the largest in a couple of hours. But people generally don't. They're not for us, you see?'

'They belong to the mer-folk?' Avery asked.

'And the gods made sure of it. The waters here are too shallow for the ship. We'll drop anchor soon, and carry on by jolly boat.' Tessa pulled her knitted cardigan closer. Above them, the tears in the sky were dimming. The darkness of another world's night would be upon them soon, though by the ship's clock it was only just early afternoon. 'I don't like sailing this close to the edge,' she said. 'It reminds me how little time our world might have left.' She sniffed. 'Excuse me. I'll be needed below.'

Avery chewed her lip. 'Yeah, I think I'll go below as well,' she said, and followed Tessa down the steps and out of sight.

Flick watched her go, tingling with worry and nerves. 'Do you think she's upset?'

'Probably,' Jonathan said. 'I know I am.'

Flick looked at him. 'I'm—'

'Don't say you're sorry,' he said, 'it's getting incredibly boring.' He sighed, and stretched against the gunwale of the ship. 'You know what the most tedious thing is? Sometimes, when I'm busy doing something, I forget. And then I'll think *oh, wasn't I supposed to be sad*? and feel ten times worse for it.'

Flick wished she could think of something to say that wasn't those two little words, again. She settled for patting Jonathan on the arm.

'LAND AHEAD!' someone yelled from above. 'WEIGH ANCHOR!'

Burnish came up from below decks as the anchors, one either side of the ship, crashed into the water. 'HANG TIGHT!'

Flick gripped the railing as Jonathan did the same, and the *Serpent* rose up on a wave, groaning and pulling against the anchor chains, before eventually smashing down onto the skin of the ocean, water pouring over the prow.

'Everyone all right?' Burnish looked about and got calls of assent. 'Right. Load up a jolly boat, quick as you can.' Sailors scurried to do as he ordered. 'Pack it up for an overnight, and don't forget the fresh water. Enough for,' he paused, and looked over at the people on deck, 'four.'

'Four?' Flick asked.

'You three, and me,' Burnish answered.

CHAPTER
TWENTY-TWO

The jolly boat was lowered into the water, with the three of them and Captain Burnish inside it. There was a hamper of food in the middle of the boat, and a flexible waxed sheet that would do for a shelter if they got caught in a storm.

Flick gripped the side of the boat, and watched as the vessel was loosed off, and Burnish took hold of the oars.

'I'd ask for a hand,' he snorted, pulling staunchly, 'but none of you look like you've done a hard day's work in your lives.' The boat skimmed smoothly through the water. 'Must be an easy life, on land.'

'Our planet is mostly water, actually,' Flick said thoughtfully.

'And yet you choose to stay on the land?'

'Not everyone does. There's lots of ships. But not everyone works or lives on them.'

Burnish rolled his shoulders, the oars cutting through the bobbing water again. 'Seems a queer way to behave, if you ask me. If most of your world is water, why would you choose not to see it?'

Jonathan gave a weak sort of harrumph.

'Oh, aye, except maybe young green-gills over here.' Burnish's smile widened into a grin. He fished in his pack and brought out a telescope. 'It won't be too long, lad,' he said. He handed the telescope to Jonathan. 'Just keep your eye on the isles for me, and make sure they're staying still.'

Avery caught Flick's eye. She smiled, but it looked like a different smile to her usual grin. This one was softer. As if it was asking a question.

Flick's stomach tightened. She smiled back but it was the sort where your mouth stretches, but your eyes don't bother to focus.

Avery's smile wavered, and fell. She looked away.

Something like regret blossomed in Flick's chest, and she wanted to apologise and smile properly. Because they were pretty much friends, now, weren't they? But . . . Avery was from another world. Not this one, and not Flick's. If they did become friends, if they did get close to each other . . . she might never see her again.

Flick tried to put a lid on the aching feeling in her chest. She had no right to be thinking about future losses when Jonathan had already lost everything. She looked at him, and asked, 'How much further?'

'It's close,' Jonathan managed to croak. He lowered the telescope. 'Oh, not that close. Maybe less than one hundred metres?'

Burnish looked over his shoulder. 'Right. Keep an eye for me. You see that inlet with the arch overhead? We're headed through there. Direct me into it, keep me away from the rocks.'

'Er, all right.' Jonathan looked over. 'Um. Slightly to the left?'

'The what?'

'Left, your left!'

'That's port, you daft duck,' Burnish dug into the water with an oar. 'I'll make a sailing man of you yet, Mercator.'

They sailed under the stone arch, which appeared to have been made purely by the wind and the waves. The jolly boat fit easily, and they arrived in a cove where the water lapped at a cropping of rock, just flat and low enough to clamber up onto.

'The mer-folk will be in the cove round the other side,' Burnish explained, 'but we can't sail up to them – it's not polite, you see? We'll tie off here, and walk the rest of the way. We'll leave the hamper on the shore, it'll only slow us down.' He unrolled some rope. 'You girl, hop out and wrap this around that rock.' He handed the rope to Avery, who did as she was told, wrapping the rope around a sticking-up rock that had been worn smooth in places by years of other ropes being tied around it.

'That'll do, just to hold it for a moment. Out you get,' Burnish pulled Jonathan to his feet and all but bowled him onto the shore. Flick followed, catching herself before Burnish disembarked as sure-footed as anything. He took the rope from Avery and tied it off in a simple knot.

'How far is it to the mermaids?' Flick asked.

'Mer-folk,' Burnish corrected. 'They're not all women. How would that work? And not far. About half an hour.'

They started walking. Flick felt slightly anxious to be leaving the boat behind, but there was nothing to be done about it. It wasn't as though anyone was going to come along and steal it, she thought, and even if they did, Tessa could launch them another.

'Are there any rules for talking to mer-folk?' Avery asked.

'There's nothing in this world's guidebook,' Jonathan said. 'I checked, last night. But there's nothing mentioned. It went on at length about the pirates, though.'

'Oh, aye?' Burnish looked over his shoulder. 'What does your wee book say about us, then?'

'That you're to be respected, but that you can be beaten,' Jonathan replied, without missing a beat. 'Also that you place a lot of value on debt, and honour.'

'That's true enough. I haven't forgotten I owe you a favour, lad.'

'Thank you.'

'As for the mer-folk,' Burnish gently nudged a crab out of the way with his boot, 'you'll want to keep your wits about you. They talk with gilded words, particularly when they want something. Especially those the same size as us. The wee ones, well, they don't cause too much trouble, unless you harm one of them by accident, and that's easily done.'

'What about the bigger ones?' Flick asked, remembering the mer-person who'd said their people could be of great sizes. 'Aren't some the same size as whales?'

'Only seen two of the giant ones in my lifetime. And that's two more than most folk ever see, though there's meant to be a great many in the Depths. Don't worry your head about them.' He sniffed. 'The Mer-Queen herself is one.'

Flick stopped walking and Avery crashed into her. 'But – but we met the Mer-Queen. At the parley!'

'Did you heck.' Burnish laughed. 'Nah, you met the *voice* of the queen. Like a messenger, only more official. The queen will have a spokesperson, like a voice for herself, to talk to the likes of us.'

'Captain Nyfe doesn't have a spokesperson,' Flick said. Away from the *Aconite*, the "Pirate Queen" title sounded a bit silly.

'Oh, *her*.' Burnish snorted dismissively. 'Far too high and mighty for her own good, that one. Queen, my soggy backside. She's no more royalty than any other leaders of the past. I've known the Opal Bride, Cut-Throat Angel . . . I even remember old Drowned Rat, from back when I was a boy. One hell of a leader, he was. Used to drink beet-wine and tell his enemies it was rat's blood, for strength. Course, drinking rat-blood is like trying to take a sup of cold tar, so everyone who believed him thought he was mad and dangerous, which was the point. Nyfe Shaban is the same. Trying to scrape up a little more respect than she might otherwise get.'

'I thought she won her title, though?' Flick asked, curious to hear another view of the woman who seemed so revered and feared amongst her own crew.

'And we saw her break a man's arm with one punch when he challenged her,' Avery added. Flick shuddered at the memory.

'Oh, aye. She can fight,' Burnish said. 'And command, she's good at that, too. But she has too much ambition. She wants to be a real queen, in command of it all, but she forgets her sailors are real people, with thoughts of their own. You build up enough armour around yourself, and you find it difficult to move. That's when you get toppled by someone who's more nimble, you see?'

Avery frowned. 'You think she needs to change?'

'Be more open to change, at any rate. You heard how she talks about us. Like we're thieves and good-for-nothing. All because we won't bend the knee to her! Have I treated you badly?'

'Well, you did try to stab me,' Jonathan said fairly.

Burnish waved a hand dismissively. 'That was a

matter of honour. Nothing to do with manners, or what sort of a man I am. And besides, I wouldn't have killed you.'

'No?'

'No, I wouldn't have done that. You're just a kid. I might have cut one of your ears off, though. Would've made those spectacles difficult to keep on, wouldn't it?' He laughed uproariously.

'Hilarious,' Jonathan said, drily. 'But if you want to escape this world safely, why didn't you attend the parley with the pirates and the Mer-Queen's spokesperson? It was a peaceful zone.'

'Peaceful to her friends,' Burnish sighed. 'There's some grudges Nyfe won't be shifted on. Now, hush. We're close.'

They had been walking up a shallow incline, which now plateaued before grading sharply downwards again. Flick supposed they had reached the middle of the island, though in the gloom it was difficult to tell. Her brain was trying to tell her it was getting late, but her body wasn't tired yet, and knew she hadn't been awake long enough for it to be really night-time. How did anyone regulate their sleep pattern in this world?

Burnish led the way down the slope and Flick and the others followed him. They copied where he put his hands and boots, subconsciously trusting the man not to slip.

'There. You see them?' Burnish murmured, pointing down.

Flick stared, but saw only a mirrored circle of water within the crescent of land, and several raised stones jutting from it. Clearly not a place to land a boat. 'No,' she said.

'We'll get closer, seeing as you're unlikely to get taller in a hurry.'

A little further, and Flick could see more of the cove. The water gently lapped at the rocks and there, half-submerged on the jutting stones, were mer-folk.

They looked the same as the others Flick had seen – bald, and scaly, and nothing at all like picture-book mermaids.

'Hello, there!' Captain Burnish yelled beside her ear, distracting her. He waved at the mer-folk in the water. 'Hello!'

Heads turned. A couple of the mer-folk vanished beneath the waves, but others waved back and beckoned.

'Right, down we go,' Burnish said to them. 'Remember what I told you. Keep your wits about you.'

They descended quickly, coming out onto a shoreline

of smooth black rock that looked almost melted – volcanic, perhaps, Flick thought.

Burnish approached the water, smiling broadly, and reached out a hand to a mer-person, who swam up and took it. 'Well met, Katyo. You look in fine health. Have you done something different with your gills?'

'You can't charm me, Ezra,' Katyo said, letting go of the captain's hand. He flashed a smile of pointed teeth. 'I know you're a married man.' He put both his hands on the ground and heaved himself up and onto the rock.

It was then that Flick saw Katyo was not like the fish-tailed mer-woman from the pirates' parley. As he dragged himself up to sit on the rocks, he revealed a thick mass of tentacles that started at his waist and flared outwards like a skirt. They deepened and darkened in colour from a brownish grey at the point where they met his torso to a reddish-black at the tips.

Flick realised she was staring. Avery and Jonathan were, too. She snapped her mouth shut and smiled. 'Nice to meet you.'

'And you, human girl,' Katyo nodded. He had a handsome face, and turned it towards each of his visitors, one by one. Flick wondered if he thought they were strange looking.

'You can survive out of water!' Jonathan choked out, breaking the mood.

'Indeed.' Katyo turned dark eyes towards him. 'Though we primarily use gills, some of us have a secondary respiratory system that allows us to respire through our skin, for a little while. Perhaps ten of your minutes. But it is difficult, and uncomfortable.'

'Like trying to breathe at altitude, I suppose,' Jonathan mused.

Captain Burnish and Katyo exchanged puzzled glances, then shrugged.

'Kat, we're here about a suitcase,' Burnish said. 'A box, with a handle, and a lid. Have you seen it?'

Katyo nodded. 'I know of it. It is in the Queen's possession.'

Flick's heart leapt – the suitcase wasn't back in her hand yet, but it suddenly seemed a lot closer.

Burnish said, 'It belongs to these children. They need it back, Kat, it's important.'

Katyo looked doubtful. 'I understand the object was taken for the purpose of negotiation with the Pirate Queen. As we are openly allied with you, Ezra, we planned to offer her a gift – something she desired. So, we were forced to steal it. To give it up now would weaken our position.'

'She can't be trusted with it,' Flick said desperately. She stepped closer to Katyo, trembling with nerves but determined to speak. She could still feel the wrench of the suitcase being pulled from her hand. 'Nyfe is planning on threatening Captain Burnish's crew with war to frighten them into surrendering to her, and the suitcase will give her more power than she already has. She could say that only sailors who swore to be part of her crew could use it.'

The mer-man's expression had become deadly serious. 'She has not offered a peaceful joining of crews?'

Burnish snorted. 'As if she'd offer me that.'

'If the Pirate Queen gets the suitcase, she'll force all of us to do as she says,' Flick said. 'And that means helping only the people she wants to help. If you give her the suitcase, that doesn't mean she'll help you.'

Katyo sat up, his skin changing from grey-brown to scarlet. 'Is this true? She means to use this crisis to increase her own forces? The whole world is crumbling and she has only her own interests at heart?'

'For a change,' Burnish muttered.

'Please,' Flick said. 'We need it. We all need it, really. We know what's happening to your world, and . . . if we have the suitcase back, we promise to try to help everyone.'

Katyo's expression softened slightly. The red bled back down his body. 'You truly want to help?'

Flick nodded. 'I'm not sure how much help we can be or how many people we can save. But without that suitcase we're no help to anyone at all. And . . .' She glanced back at Avery and Jonathan. 'And it's our job to help. We're members of The Strangeworlds Society. We've promised to look after every world we can. But to do that, we need you to trust us.'

Out of the corner of her eye, Flick saw Burnish give an approving nod.

'I suppose we have nothing to lose by trusting what you say,' Katyo said slowly. 'You can hardly run back to the Pirate Queen whilst Ezra has you under his hand. I shall relay what you have told me to our Queen, and request the suitcase's return for you.'

Jonathan sagged in relief. 'Thank you.'

Katyo nodded to say *you're welcome*. His dark eyes stayed focussed on Jonathan for a long moment. Flick wondered if he could read grief in his face, just as Burnish had. Then he quickly dropped backwards, and disappeared beneath the skin of the water.

Jonathan abruptly sat down, as though stunned by the news that the suitcase might be within their grasp. Flick was about to go over to him when there was a great splash of water, and Katyo heaved himself back onto the rocks.

'The message is on its way,' he said. 'I cannot go to the depths, where the Queen dwells, but I would trust my messengers with my life.' He looked at Jonathan sitting on the ground, then back to Flick. 'Is he well?'

'Not really,' she said. 'But I hope he will be.'

Katyo nodded. 'The suitcase – it is a portal of magic, is it not?'

Flick was pleased to be able to talk about something she was sure of. 'The suitcase takes us back to our world,' she said. 'Back home we have access to lots of other worlds, too, in other suitcases. Once we can go back, we can search for a different world for you. But . . .' She trailed off.

'But?' Katyo prompted.

'I'm sorry,' Flick said. 'But the only way through to a new world would be through another suitcase. I don't know if you've seen the size of it?' She gestured with her hands to show the dimensions. 'It's not large. I know for a fact that not everyone and everything could fit through it.'

Katyo ran a finger over his mouth before speaking. 'So not all of us could leave. But it is a way out for some, at least?'

'Yes. I'm sorry.'

'You apologise a lot, girl.' Katyo's tentacles darkened even further, and Flick wondered if they reflected his thoughts. 'I would not wish to abandon those of us who are too big to escape. Is there truly no way to expand the escape route?'

Flick felt her face prickle. 'No,' she said. 'None that we know of.' *Or have tried*, she thought guiltily.

'Then it is a case of sacrifice,' Katyo said. His dark skin paled. 'And a dishonour many would rather not live with.' His black eyes rested on Flick's face.

There was a splash. 'Katyo,' a mer-person's high voice called. 'The Queen sleeps. Her attendants will alert her of your guests when she wakes.'

'Can't you wake her up?' Avery asked.

'No!' Katyo looked horrified at the very idea. 'Our Queen might be a giant of these waters, but she is over a century old and very fragile. She rests. And you will wait. I trust you brought supplies for yourselves?'

'I'll go back for the hamper,' Burnish grumbled. 'You three wait here. And watch your lips, all of you. You're guests here.'

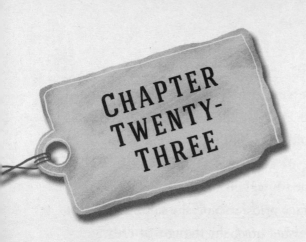

CHAPTER TWENTY-THREE

Flick leaned against the wall of the cove, and watched, smiling absently, as Jonathan politely turned down an invitation to a private swim with one of the mer-women.

'Madam, your affections could not be more poorly aimed,' he said. 'And besides, I don't swim.'

Avery was sharing some of the picnic with several mer-babies and children, all of whom had taken a shine to her.

Flick shifted against the cold rocks. She knew she was being antisocial, but she couldn't help it. Her mind felt as if it was going through a blender.

The conversation with Katyo had only made her even more painfully aware of their problem. The problem of how to get everyone out.

The solution was to make an existing schism bigger, that much was obvious.

Suitcases were holding places for schisms. The schisms couldn't get out, and they welded themselves into the suitcases the way water fills a sink. The schism *was* the suitcase, in a way. Back when Flick had first joined The Strangeworlds Society, Jonathan had told her that schisms could not be destroyed or created by people.

But then, in the City of Five Lights, Flick had done just that.

Desperate to save her own world, and to put an end to the tyranny of the notorious gang of Thieves, Flick had first created a schism – tearing her way out of a tiny holding cell of a world. And then she had destroyed a schism – grabbed hold of a suitcase, and demanded that it *close* permanently, trapping the Thieves inside in another world.

Flick fidgeted. She still didn't feel good about what she had done, but it had been a necessary evil. She'd saved the world of Five Lights – as well as her own and countless others – from being exploited by the Thieves' thirst and greed for magic.

It seemed appallingly unfair that here at The Break, even though the pirates didn't hoard magic like the thieves in Five Lights had, their world was somehow having it stolen nonetheless. This place had weeks left, and then . . . it would vanish. As if it had never existed at all.

A thought stirred at the back of her mind. A seed of an idea, germinating through worry and desperation. What if she could somehow make a schism bigger? Surely, if she could close a schism, she could expand one? But, in her heart she knew it wouldn't be the same process at all. A bigger schism would need to eat more magical energy from somewhere. It would devour this world even faster than it was already being consumed, and she, Flick, would be responsible for that destruction.

The thought made her feel sick. She couldn't possibly suggest it to Jonathan. If she tried it, and it all went wrong . . . she could never forgive herself, if she even survived.

She looked over and saw Jonathan sitting by himself now, looking out at the sea, but apparently seeing nothing. He wasn't doing a lot of blinking. As Flick watched, he bent forward and pressed his face into his raised knees.

She got up and went to sit beside him.

He flinched slightly, acknowledging her being there,

but didn't speak. That was fine, Flick thought. She wouldn't have known what to say, anyway. She just watched him breathe, his dark coils of hair spilling over his arms like a hood, hiding him.

The rock they sat on was letting the cold through Flick's trousers.

'When I was fifteen,' Jonathan said suddenly, raising his head, 'we went through a suitcase for my birthday. It wasn't too long after my mum died, and I was still learning about Strangeworlds. We went to a world far more technologically advanced than ours. Flying cars, teleports, the lot. The sort of thing I used to draw pictures of when I was small. I'd dreamed of that sort of thing, and watching the silvery streets and the rockets was incredible. But what I remember the most is being on this shuttle. My dad must have thought I was asleep and he let out this big sad sigh, like he'd been holding it in all day, and he just put his head down . . .' Jonathan lowered his own face back onto his knees. 'I never said anything to him but I knew how he felt. Like . . . everything we did was a distraction from what was really hurting. Mum being gone, I mean. That's how all this feels. It doesn't feel real, any of it. How can there be a world in danger if my dad is dead? Doesn't the multiverse know *that* should be the most important thing happening right now? Everything else should just stop, out of respect.'

Flick felt as if her heart weighed as much as an anchor. 'It's the most important thing to you,' she said.

'But it shouldn't be.'

'But it is. That's not a bad thing.'

'The Strangeworlds Society takes care of other worlds. Head Custodians aren't supposed to be like this.' Jonathan lifted his head back up. 'I want to cry all the time, but it won't always come out. And that just makes me feel like an over-inflated water balloon, about to burst at any moment.'

They were quiet for a moment, and Flick looked up at the sky. The streaks of black were interrupted by streaks of blue, as though the sky had been raked through by the claw of something gigantic.

'What are you thinking?' Jonathan asked.

Flick shook herself. 'Um. The tears, in the sky.' She pointed, slightly embarrassed to be changing the subject from Jonathan's grief. 'Are they schisms?'

But Jonathan seemed grateful for the distraction. 'No, they're actual tears. Rips, in the sky. Like this world is a tent, and it's been slashed.'

'That doesn't make any sense. What about the atmosphere?'

'Perhaps it healed, but transparently. Those clear spaces above might be scars.'

'That sounds too good to be true.'

'Doesn't it? But unless you have a rocket hidden in your backpack, I doubt we'll ever know.'

Flick tucked her hair behind her ears. 'You think worlds can heal?'

'Five Lights is healing. But for this place, it's too late. Too sick to get any better.'

'But in Five Lights, it was the Thieves taking the magic,' Flick said thoughtfully. 'What or who is taking it here? And why now? The pirates aren't doing it.'

Jonathan pushed his glasses up his nose. 'If I knew that, Felicity, I would certainly tell you,' he said.

Flick looked at him. 'Your dad came here, didn't he? Do you think he knew something?'

'It was on his list. Perhaps he . . .' Jonathan stopped. Then shook his head.

Perhaps he found out too much, Flick thought.

'He would want us to help, though,' Jonathan said after a moment. 'If we could.' He pushed his glasses up his nose again. 'There might be something you could do, something that doesn't involve a suitcase. Don't tell me you haven't been thinking about it.'

'It won't work,' she said.

'You ripped a world open before.'

'Yeah, and look what happened! The whole little world collapsed. Even if I could rip a new schism here, I would have to keep The Break from collapsing whilst holding a new schism – a BIG one – open at the same time. I don't know how to do that. And I can't exactly practise.'

'Mm. I suppose you're right.'

They watched Avery laugh as a mer-baby bit into a soft fruit, making a face of utter disgust.

'If the Queen returns our suitcase, I think we'd do well to go straight back to Strangeworlds,' Jonathan said. 'Dry off, get more supplies, and then we can find a water world for these people. We owe them the option to run to another world, if they want to at least. They can always refuse.'

'Nyfe won't go for it.'

'Right now, I'm struggling to understand her pig-headedness,' Jonathan shrugged. 'Her ship is special to her, but if she chooses to value it over her own life and the lives of her crew, that's not something we can change. We'll tell the truth to everyone we can, and people can make their own decisions.'

'Are there other water worlds?'

'Oh, yes. A great many. I don't see finding an unpopulated one being too much of a problem.'

Flick considered. 'I think you're right about giving them the option. We can only offer what we have. I don't know how to stomach leaving people behind, though.'

'Well, unless you work out how to hold an enormous schism open, you'll have to,' Jonathan said, getting to his feet. 'Look – they're waving us over.'

They got up and walked quickly over to where Burnish and Avery were already waiting with Katyo.

'The Queen has awakened,' Katyo said. 'You will need to sail out, away from this island and into the vast ocean to meet with her.'

'Why?' Flick asked.

'She cannot surface here,' Kayto said, his tentacles flexing. 'She is of the deep. Sail out and she will find you. We have brought your boat around.'

The mer-people had indeed pulled the jolly boat around. It was beyond the cove, away from the rocks and shallow water.

'More swimming?' Jonathan groaned.

'Can you not swim?'

'I can, if I absolutely must.'

Katyo looked at Burnish. 'Will you come?'

'Not I.' He shook his head. 'It's not my time to speak to Leviatha.'

Promising to see Burnish again shortly, the three of them went to the water. Flick kicked off her shoes, as did Jonathan and Avery – they had learned that much, at least. Katyo took all three pairs and held them above water-level as he splashed into the sea with a sigh of delight, his chest rising and falling as his gills took over.

'It isn't far,' he said.

Flick gritted her teeth as she stepped into the water. It was no warmer than before, and immediately her feet felt like blocks of ice. She waded further, hands held up as if she could prevent them from getting wet at all—

when the surface beneath her toes fell away sharply, and she dropped under the water like a stone.

'There's a ledge there,' she gasped, surfacing, more embarrassed than anything else.

Avery and Jonathan made noises of distaste, but jumped into the deeper water with more grace than Flick's anchor impression.

When Flick reached the jolly boat, she reached up for the side to pull herself in, but it was surprisingly high.

'Here.' A mer-woman who looked a lot like Katyo appeared and wrapped six of her limbs around Flick's waist and thighs, then pushed her up out of the water as if she weighed nothing. Flick tumbled into the boat.

'Thanks.'

'Not a problem, girl. There are dry blankets under the benches. You should take your wet layers off.'

'I would, but I'm not sitting half-naked in a boat with these two.' Flick's teeth started chattering as Jonathan and Avery landed, one after the other, in the bottom of the boat.

'Please yourself,' the mer-woman said. 'But you will die of cold before you die of shame.'

With averted eyes and embarrassed blushes, the three of them stripped off their coats and trousers, leaving only their shirts and pants on and bundling themselves into the thick blankets.

There was no need to worry about who would be rowing, as the mer-folk were pulling the jolly boat along as if it weighed less than nothing.

'I'm not certain this is worth losing toes for,' said one of the blankets in a Jonathan sort of voice. He sat in the bottom of the boat, his legs up, knees against his chest. 'Why couldn't we have gone somewhere warm?'

'Like a desert?' Flick shivered.

'Ha,' Avery tried to laugh but it came out like a cough. 'We'd be in one now, if that letter hadn't come.'

Flick was puzzled. 'Wh-what do you mean?'

'The House on the Horizon, remember? It's in a desert.'

'The D-Desert of Dreams,' Jonathan shuddered.

'I should have come to you sooner,' Avery said miserably. She'd clearly been stewing this guilty admission up for a while. 'The custodian who lives there – Danser Thess – might have been able to help you find Uncle Daniel, since he was looking for him himself. I was too late to tell you about it.'

Jonathan pushed his blanket down a little. 'Even if you came as soon as you heard it might still have been too late. It's been months since Dad . . . disappeared. "Too late" might have been weeks ago. And we can still go to the House, to find this Mr Thess and ask him why he was searching for my dad. We can do that if we get back.'

'When we get back,' Flick smiled.

'When,' Jonathan agreed.

The boat glided through the water with ease, and the cold wind bit into their cheeks. Overhead, the darkness lent to the ocean by other worlds was beginning to lighten, though it was really coming close to the end of their day. Flick shut her eyes for a second. She imagined this must be what jet-lag felt like.

'Why do you think Burnish is helping us?' Avery asked.

Flick opened her eyes. 'I think he knows that if he doesn't, he's condemning himself, and all his crew, to death. We're his only way out. Everyone's only way out.'

'No pressure, is there?' Avery sighed.

But Flick wasn't listening. She was looking over the prow at the blank expanse of flat water. 'I think we're close.'

Jonathan reached for his trousers. 'Wet through or not, I'm not meeting a queen in my pants, thank you very much.'

They all struggled back into their clothes which, although damp, didn't seem as cold as they expected.

Katyo pulled himself up on the side of the boat as they started to slow. 'She is below,' he said, his voice low in reverence. 'The proposal you've made has been explained to her, and she wishes to discuss it with you. And, if you are lucky, you may learn something, too.' He dropped back down with barely a splash.

The mer-folk pulling the boat let go, and the jolly boat drifted slightly, before settling into a gentle spiral on the water, turning on the invisible current.

A shiver ran down Flick's spine, settling somewhere around her middle.

The air felt as though it was being held back in the lungs of the ocean.

The mer-folk had disappeared.

It occurred to Flick that, if their plan had been to bring them out here to die, she and her friends had allowed it to happen without a murmur of complaint.

A fresh wave of gooseflesh broke out over her skin. She swallowed, her ears roaring with the quiet of the ocean. The silence had weight, but it also felt empty, as though the emptiness was something Flick was carrying and couldn't put down. She'd brought them here, after all. She'd lost the suitcase. If she'd just held on tighter, they wouldn't be here right now, drifting on a mirror of flat water with no sign of life or land. She shut her eyes, trying to get a grip on the anxiety creeping through her veins.

Then, she felt cold fingers brush against her own.

Flick opened her eyes.

Avery's eyes met hers, and she smiled. Warmth blossomed through Flick's bones, glowed like embers in her face. She looked away to hide the sudden blush, just as Avery did the same.

Oh.

And Flick knew Avery was thinking the same thing. And it felt wonderful and terrifying at the same time.

Wordlessly, they linked pinky fingers and held on tight.

And then . . .

Then, the water rose.

It looked like a duvet, shifting as a sleeping body turns beneath. The grey-blue water stretched in a dome before it broke on a rising deep grey and black surface. Water streamed down like a waterfall over a head, a flat nose with a single horizontal nostril, the thick curves of a neck and shoulders.

Flick realised in astonishment that she was looking up.

'Oh my god.'

The body continued to rise from the water, higher than a house, then three houses, wider than two buses, each roll and curve of dark skin folding into another. The face that looked down on them was impassive, with glowing yellow eyes framed by thick translucent fronds of skin, so dense that they almost passed for plaits of hair, running down from the scalp.

Flick gasped as she felt the boat rise into the air, gripped in a hand that had swept out of the water with a sort of heavy grace. The webbing between each of the four digits was as wide as Flick was, and she held on tight to the side of the boat as the Queen of the

Mer-People, a giant of the water, brought their tiny boat up close, so they could look her in the eye.

The Queen's eyes glowed, like the bulb on an angler fish. Her face was almost expressionless, her jawline was soft, and her chin and neck were obscured by thick folds of fat.

Flick realised she was kneeling on the bottom of the boat. And so were Jonathan and Avery. That felt right. You knelt before a queen. And this mer-woman was undeniably royalty.

The Queen smiled, then. A slow drag of her lips that curved upwards, before she spoke. 'You are welcome in my ocean, little ones.' Her voice was a deep rumble that hurt Flick's ears, though it was obvious the Queen had tried to keep her volume down as much as possible.

'Thank you.' Jonathan spoke first. 'We're honoured to meet you in person.'

The Queen's smile widened and she nodded once. 'You have lost your magical box.'

'It was taken,' Jonathan said, carefully. 'When our boat was capsized.'

To Flick, this sounded almost like an accusation and she glanced up nervously.

But the Queen didn't appear ruffled by it. And why

would she be? She could squash Jonathan like a soft-shelled baby crab. 'Your box shall be returned to you,' she said. 'But first: I understand you have offered help to my people.'

'Yes,' Flick said quickly, and the lamp-like eyes of the Queen turned to her. 'We can help some of your people escape this collapsing world. But – but we can't save everyone. We can only take those who can fit through the suitcase. The box.'

The Queen regarded her, unblinking, for what felt like a long time. Then she sighed, and it was like a sharp blast of wind across a harbour. 'I am over a century old, little ones. My parents live still, in the dark depths of the beneath. The surface dwellers say this world is a circle, but they forget the ocean. This world, the water and the surface, was once a cylinder two-thirds filled with water. The collapse that has been happening, this disintegration of our world, affected the edges of the ocean before it reached the surface or the sky.

'Now, our world is shaped like a cone. It is wider at the brim than it is in the depths. And, once, my people were scattered all over the world. Those with fish tails lived closer to the surface. In temperate waters, the tiny ones made their homes, and my family swam in the depths, lighting our way with song and luminescence. We knew there was something wrong when Katyo's people came to us, begging for space above our feeding grounds, that they might share this part of the ocean with us. After them, came the tiny ones, afraid and weeping. The cold-water ones came last, obstinate and distressed at what was happening. And after that, we were too many in too small a space. Fighting was a regular occurrence. The ocean was ribboned with blood. And then, Nyfe Shaban came, offering the chance of a solution, if we would follow her rule.'

'But you didn't accept?'

'Some did, including my own spokesperson. The fear of the end of the world has torn our people into factions. A great many have declared they will follow the Pirate Queen rather than me. But, I have never met a human I would trust to deliver on their promises,' she said. 'I have seen too many of my children and subjects in their nets. And besides, they offered no real solution. Only the amassing of an army.'

'An army?' Flick frowned.

The Queen nodded again. 'Captain Nyfe has not united anyone. She has driven a wedge between them. She has *made* enemies by deciding anyone not with her is against her. We do not care what she does, whether she rages, or pillages, or sails clean off the edge of the world. But when she creates enemies where there were none, she threatens more than battle.'

'She would declare war,' Jonathan said.

'And claim it was for the good of those on her side. No doubt, on some level, she thinks she is doing the right thing. Every villain is the hero of their own story. Nyfe is no different.'

'But you're . . .' Avery gestured at the Queen's height. 'You could fight her. How would Nyfe ever hurt you?'

'Can the great whales of your world not be cut down?'

Flick thought of harpoons. Of sharpness and blood. Of micro-plastics, oil, poisons, everything that could, and did, kill. Her heart sank down into her boots. 'Yeah,' she said sadly. 'They can be.'

'Humans have always made war,' the Queen said. 'That is not new. They are a warlike tribe. I believe that they will, given the chance, fight themselves into extinction. But it does not have to be now. It can be prevented.' She moved slightly in the water, her immense size utterly graceful.

Flick wondered what form of sea creature the

Queen might be if she lived on Earth. Katyo was clearly similar to an octopus, and Satura's tail was like a fish's. But the Mer-Queen was too big to be like either of them. There were barnacles on her shoulders and elbows like freckles, and seaweed growing in the cracks of her skin. She could be a blue whale, Flick thought. Or a vast shark. But one that lived in the darkness, weightless and peaceful, and undisturbed.

Flick thought of the environmental posters in the library. The plastic bags exchanged for paper in the supermarket. The images on television of the struggling sea life, tangled and dying, wrapped in mankind's rubbish.

Save the Whales.

She was about to abandon the Queen to a terrible fate, and there was nothing she could do about it. The helplessness she felt was as sharp and painful as a knife-edge.

'We can't save all of you,' Flick said softly.

'I know,' the Queen said. 'But you can save some. Many. It will have to be enough.'

'We can try to save more,' Jonathan said. 'We will try.'

'It is enough to know that some will live.'

There was a splash below and the Queen raised up

her other hand. On the palm of it was the suitcase. It was wet through, but still tight shut.

Relief shot through Flick like wildfire, and if she hadn't already been kneeling her knees would have given way. They had a way out. They could go home.

Jonathan gave a sob of joy and stepped onto the mer-woman's hand to pick the case up, hugging it like it was his firstborn. 'Thank you. Thank you so much.' He looked down, and realised where he stood, and blushed. 'Oh. Sorry.' He stepped back into the jolly boat.

The Queen smiled at him. 'I am glad it has been returned to you. Now, how soon can you arrange for my people to leave?'

'We need to go home, first.' Jonathan patted the case. 'And find somewhere for you to live. Somewhere empty, watery, and peaceful. We shall be as quick as we can.'

'Time does not move for your world as it moves for ours, little one.'

Flick had lost count of how long they'd been at The Break. If anything slowed them down, The Break could crumble to pieces without them.

'I promise I shall be as fast as I can,' Jonathan was saying.

'That will have to be enough.'

'We'll do our best,' Flick said. 'To come up with a way to help you all, I mean.' She blushed, feeling useless.

The Queen closed her eyes as she nodded. 'Very well. I shall have Katyo's people take you back to the Scattered Isles, and you may make your way to Captain Burnish's ship from there. We will wait, little ones. And if you never return,' and now her voice became hard, 'the last thing we shall remember of you, will be your betrayal.' She lowered their boat gently back into the water and began to sink back down. 'But if you do return, and help who you can, Queen Leviatha will sings songs of you until the ending of all worlds, whensoever that will come.'

And with those words, she disappeared back under the water.

As soon as she had gone, Jonathan quickly put the suitcase on the bench and undid the catches.

'Is it all right?' Flick looked, anxiously.

'Yes, it'll take more than water to damage this.'

Struggling slightly with his bandaged hand, he lifted the lid, and the warm scent of books and dryness and *home* flooded out into the freezing air. He looked at Avery. 'Want to go first?'

She shook her head. 'I'm not coming. Someone needs to tell Burnish where you've gone.'

'You can't stay here!' Flick cried. 'This isn't your world, and you've been away for so long already.'

'Good incentive for you to come back for me, then.' Avery folded her arms. 'Come on, think about it. If we *all* vanish, they'll never trust us again.'

Flick wanted Jonathan to argue, but instead he nodded. 'You're sure about this?'

She gave a curt nod back. 'Jonathan, you know very well I'm sure about this.'

Flick wanted to drag Avery into the suitcase and tell her to stop being stupid, but the fact was, she was right. If they all left, Burnish would think they had abandoned him. But if Avery stayed, she'd be all on her own, time crawling past for her as it flew by back in Strangeworlds.

They'd come back for her, of course they would, but it seemed so grossly unfair to leave her behind by herself.

'But,' Flick started to say, 'but what if I stayed with—'

Avery's eyes glittered. 'Flick,' she said firmly, 'look after him.'

Flick knew what she meant. Jonathan had already lost nearly everyone. Flick couldn't ask him to go back to Strangeworlds on his own and risk losing the two people he had left.

'I will,' she said.

Flick watched Jonathan clamber into the suitcase and disappear and, with a final look back at Avery, she climbed over the edge of the case and caught hold of the handle, pulling it back through with her, into a familiar world.

CHAPTER TWENTY-FOUR

'We haven't got a lot of time,' Jonathan said, as they tumbled back into the travel agency. 'If my maths is correct, and it usually is, we've got just less than fifteen hours here to get back to The Break before it's a mere quarter of the size it is now. And that's assuming it continues to crumble at the same rate it has been . . .'

He went over to the mantlepiece, and picked up one of the clocks, setting it down on the desk.

The hands of the clock were moving swiftly, turning smoothly around the face much faster than they ought to. 'This is the time Avery is running on in The Break.'

The sheer magnitude of the task ahead of them suddenly seemed to have physical weight, and Flick wanted to put her head down on the fireside-rag-rug and fall asleep. She blinked hard to clear the mist from her eyes. 'What's the plan?'

'Let's start with finding them a safe world, one with water,' Jonathan said, flinging his jacket in the direction of the sink in the kitchen. 'We'll go through all the cases now. If you can take down any from the wall that look suitable, I'll head down to the Back Room.'

Flick nodded, then looked at the mantlepiece, at the clocks.

And froze.

'Jonathan.'

'Of course they'll need some land as well,' Jonathan said, dragging the huge trunk out from the disused fireplace. 'But that should be simple enough . . .'

'Jonathan.'

'And we need to take waterproof trousers with us this time. I'm sure I have some around here somewhere. For Avery, too. I'm sure she can suspend her sense of style for a few hours for the sake of keeping dry—'

'Jonathan!'

'What?'

Flick pointed at the clock, the one that showed the time at Strangeworlds. 'It's gone five.'

He looked at the clock, then stared at her, blankly. 'And?'

She lowered her hand. It felt so trivial, compared to the task at hand. But she had to. She had to say it. 'I need to go home.'

'Don't be absurd,' Jonathan scoffed. 'How can you possibly want to *go home* at a time like this?'

'I don't *want* to. But I promised my parents I'd be home by six,' Flick said, her voice very small. 'If I stay now, I can promise you I won't be allowed back ever again. I've only just earned back their trust. My parents will never let me out of my room – let alone the house – if I roll in after six again.'

He stared at her as if she was speaking Martian. 'But – but this is important. We – we only have fifteen hours!'

'I know,' she said. 'But I need to go home. I can't do this to them again.'

Jonathan's mouth opened, and then shut again. His hands flexed on the desk as if he was trying not to tear something in half. He genuinely looked as if he couldn't get his head around what Flick was saying. 'If anyone can save them – all of them,' he said, 'it's you. You know it is. I can search for the right world to send them to, but I can't affect a schism any more than I can breathe underwater.'

'You don't know that I can do anything to help,' Flick said.

'You could stay here and *try*,' he said. 'Not run away.'

'I am not running away!'

He glared at her. 'Yes, you are.'

'I'll come back as soon as I can.' She brightened. 'I can even try and come back tonight, when they're asleep! But I can't promise anything,' she added.

Jonathan pinched between his eyes under his glasses. He was taking very deep breaths. 'Every hour that passes here, eighteen pass in the world of The Break. *Eighteen.* They have less than three weeks left, which means they have fifteen of *our* hours left before they'll be sailing around a puddle – at most. If you're gone until nine tomorrow morning, that's . . . that's sixteen hours from now. It's going to be too late.' He leaned heavily on the desk as though his strings had been cut. 'We've left my cousin there by herself. She'll think we've deserted her. Think of *her* parents!'

'Avery's brave,' Flick said, believing it but wishing she didn't have to say it. 'She'll have had time to tell Captain Burnish our plan by now. She won't think we've deserted her,' Flick said, her voice shaking with emotion. She took a deep breath. 'I have to make a choice here, Jonathan. If I go back to The Break without going home first, I will never be able to come back here, to Strangeworlds. They won't let me, if I frighten them like I did with staying too long in Five Lights. You have to understand that.'

He stared at her. 'You're really choosing them over all this. Over Avery. Over The Strangeworlds Society.'

'You know full well that's not what I'm doing,' Flick said, heading for the door. 'You know I'm not. I don't want to leave you, but—'

'But you might as well,' he said, bitterly. 'Everyone does.'

She paused at the door, her heart hammering in her ears. She knew it was the grief talking, but that didn't mean that his words didn't hurt her. She gripped the door handle. 'I'll be back once my parents are asleep tonight, if I can manage to sneak out,' she said. 'But you should start looking for a world to take the pirates to. In case I don't make it back in time.'

*

It was a terrible walk home. All the way, she worried. She worried about Captain Burnish, and Katyo, and the Mer-Queen, and Edony and everyone on those massive ships, each one of them hoping for a miracle.

Her mum was in when she got home, and she looked pleased and relieved that Flick had stuck to her curfew.

She handed Flick a frying pan and told her to start browning some mince for dinner.

Flick worked mechanically, feeling like a robot whose joints needed oiling. Guilt weighed on her, turning her bones into lead piping, poisoning her every movement. She shouldn't have come home. But she'd had to. She'd *had* to.

She dropped spaghetti into a bubbling saucepan and scowled as she stirred it rather more violently than she probably should have. Boiling water splashed over the side and hissed as it hit the top of the hob, and Flick felt like something inside her was hissing as well.

Jonathan had no right to be cross with her. Just because his entire world was the agency, didn't mean she should feel bad about having real-life commitments.

All the same, her stomach clenched at the thought of the pirates. She pictured Jonathan, alone in the travel agency, surrounded by suitcases and memories and nothing else. And her heart sank. She had promised Avery she would look after Jonathan, and she had left him all on his own. She could have invited him round, or something. Her parents wouldn't have minded, she was sure. He would have refused, though.

What was he doing, right now? Going through the suitcases, probably, in search of a water world. He'd said there were seven hundred of them in the Back Room, so that wasn't going to be a quick task.

Flick checked her mum wasn't looking and took out her phone. Phones were banned in the kitchen in the Hudson household after a memorable soup incident.

You ok?

The reply came back a minute later.

Perfectly amenable, thank you.

I didn't want to go home, you know.

I know. I apologise for not taking your commitments into account. You have been entirely accommodating of mine, after all. I appreciate you saying you will attempt to come back tonight, however I will not be upset if you cannot. Your family being important to you is something I should more than understand.

I'll do my best. See you later. I hope.

I hope so too. For all our sakes.

CHAPTER TWENTY-FIVE

Flick dreamed she was on an island.

It was an island she'd been to before, but it wasn't The Break. It was somewhere she'd been to before that. Somewhere that had frightened her and stayed in her heart for longer than it was welcome.

She knew it was a dream because she wasn't struggling to walk up the sand dunes. She felt her feet glide over the sand (though not really, because you can never really feel your feet in dreams), until she reached the cliff-top.

The lighthouse at the top was bigger that she remembered, though dream-structures tend not to be entirely accurate. This being a dream, there was no time at all between her reaching the cliff-top, and her hand pushing open the door.

It was as she remembered – as good a replica as her dream could create, anyway, having only been in the space once. But some places require only half a visit to be imprinted on our minds. The lighthouse was one such place.

Flick walked over to the desk on the opposite side of the room. The photographs pinned around the desk showed colourful swirls. Flick knew they should have been photos of people, but as that fact wasn't important to the plot of her dream, her brain had lazily decided not to illustrate them properly. She wasn't here for the photographs on the wall, anyway.

She was here for the—

'What are doing here?'

Flick jumped and turned around. Her dream splintered, jarring as it was derailed, sent somewhere it hadn't planned to go.

A man with long greying hair and pointed ears, a brown apron over his clothes, sat in the middle of the wrought-iron staircase.

'Tristyan?' She stepped closer, confused about what the apothecary from another world was doing in her dream.

'Felicity.' He smiled, and, just like when they first met, Flick knew she had seen that smile somewhere before. Then he stood up and walked down the iron steps to the ground. 'Is this *your* dream?'

'I think so.' Flick was trying to keep hold of her dream, but she could feel her grasp on it starting to slip. 'What are you doing in it?'

'Now, there's a question. How's Jonathan?'

'I don't know, I haven't seen him for a while.' *That's not right*, Flick thought, *I saw him today.*

Tristyan nodded. 'Ah. So, why are you here?'

'I was . . .' She looked back at the desk. The photographs were gone, and all that remained was the wooden box she'd knocked to the floor the time she'd been here before. There was a dent on the side, and Flick felt guilty about it.

Was the box what she'd come here for? She couldn't remember. She tried to reach for it, but her dream-arms wouldn't do as they were told.

She looked back at Tristyan. 'How can you be here?'

'Perhaps I was dreaming of this place too.' He came over and lifted the box in his hands. Flick wished she had been able to pick it up. It looked smaller in his spidery grip, and his thumb tapped on the latch as if impatient. The box was here for him, then, not for her. Then why had she come here?

Flick tried to stay in the dream, though already the walls of the lighthouse felt shadowy, and she could almost feel the pillow under her head. There was a buzzing sensation in her body – the vibration of her alarm trying to wake her up. 'Tristyan, was this your home?'

'No.' He raised the lid of the box. 'But I remember it.'

Flick had the sensation that she was falling. She wanted to stay, to see what was inside the box, but . . . Tristyan closed the lid. 'I fear your dream is ending, Felicity, as mine is merely beginning.'

'How come we can talk?' Flick whispered. 'You're not a dream. Am I a dream?'

'I don't think so,' Tristyan said. 'I think we simply have a lot in common.' His face suddenly misted over, and Flick knew she was barely asleep at all any more. 'Perhaps we shall meet again.'

Flick could feel herself dissolving, the world around her melting into consciousness. 'I'll – I'll come and see you!'

Tristyan turned to her, looking pleased at the idea. 'I hope you will. Both of you.'

And then Flick opened her eyes and the man, the lighthouse and the world of her dream all disappeared.

Flick turned off her alarm and stared at the ceiling

for a moment. It was one in the morning, and the world felt heavy and still. Her dream was very loud in her head.

Whatever that had been . . . she didn't have time to worry about it. She had to get back to Strangeworlds.

*

She ran through Little Wyverns and was gasping for breath by the time she got to The Strangeworlds Travel Agency. She crashed through the door.

'Here,' she panted, bent double and holding her chest. She looked up and gawped. It looked as though a herd of wildebeest had stampeded through the travel agency, followed by a small hurricane and a tsunami. There were always suitcases stacked around, but this was an explosion of luggage. Jonathan had clearly been thorough in his search for a new watery world.

There was a smashing noise from the kitchen area.

'Bit tense, are you?' Flick asked, picking up some of the suitcases and putting them into the bay window to make a path through the shop.

'I am not tense!' came a shouted reply. There was another *smash* that sounded like the teapot. Flick stacked some more of the suitcases away, and after a moment, Jonathan came through from the kitchen area, looking mildly harassed.

'You made it, then?' he clipped. 'Good. Another six days have gone by in The Break, and I don't feel easy about it at all. And searching for a new world hasn't been quite as simple as I'd hoped. Nothing's been totally right yet – more of the worlds are inhabited than I'd anticipated. But there are a handful left still to check.' He gestured to a fairly small pile heaped onto his armchair.

'Should be a cinch,' Flick said, rolling her eyes. 'Right then. Which case is next?'

Despite the time pressure and the worry, Flick's skin now prickled with excitement. *This* was what The Strangeworlds Travel Agency was about – hopping into different worlds as easily as stepping from one room into another. This was what she loved.

Jonathan passed her the top suitcase and as she popped the catches a grin escaped from her mouth. This was serious, of course it was, but it was still magical. A warmth spilled out from the suitcase, along with the rushing sound of waves. Flick looked at Jonathan. 'Ready?'

He cricked his neck. 'Of course.'

They stepped inside. And immediately plummeted

straight down into water, dropping like stones. Jonathan yelled as he smacked into the water like a starfish, somehow managing to keep the suitcase handle in his hand.

Flick kicked hard, pushing with her arms, and broke the surface, gasping. Jonathan paddled over, the suitcase floating helpfully. The water was calm. Flick looked around them. There was nothing but the flat shine of water, mirroring an orange-pink sky, as far as she could see.

Jonathan spat water out of his mouth and tried to wipe the splashes from his lenses. 'Well, this is bleak,' he said. 'And damp. I had *just* dried out.'

Flick spun around. 'I can't see any land. But that doesn't mean there isn't any, I guess.' She looked down at the reddish water, wondering how deep down it went and what might be lurking within. Her stomach swooped as her brain conjured up ideas about sharks and monsters.

'What do we do?' she asked. 'Try and swim for land? We can't stay here.'

Jonathan was about to answer when there was a great mass of bubbles from around thirty meters away. The bubbles rose in the way they do when you blow into a milkshake through a straw, clinging to one another and growing rather than just popping at the surface. In the middle of the bubbling mass, something glass-like and shining rose up, like a great ceramic and glass egg.

Flick didn't know whether to scream or not.

The top of the egg suddenly split away, lifting up like a lid. And a person – if that was the right word – stood up and raised a crooked arm.

Jonathan raised an arm back. 'Seems to be a multiversal gesture, waving,' he said under his breath. He waved cheerily, giving the same false smile he'd given Flick's mum in the supermarket only two days ago.

The person standing in the glassy egg looked somewhat like a frog, if frogs could grow to be five feet in height. Their head was sunken into their neck, their arms crooked as though they were unable to straighten them completely, and their eyes – all four of them – bulged. They croaked something at the two humans in the water.

'We're friends,' Flick called, not sure whether they could understand her, but making an effort to at least sound innocent and calm. 'We were looking for land?'

The frog-like person croaked again, putting their squat head to one side as if asking a question. Their egg-pod gave a soft *beep*.

'I don't think we're going to get very far,' Jonathan said to Flick. 'Language barrier.' He pulled the suitcase close. 'Maybe we should just go. This world is clearly occupied. I doubt they'll welcome several boatloads of pirates turning up.'

Getting back into the suitcase was difficult. In the end, they shoved it open beneath the water and hoisted themselves into it.

The result was a lot of water all over the travel agency. Flick skidded across the floorboards in a torrent of it, almost crashing into the desk as Jonathan tumbled out, wet through and furious. The ocean of the other world continued to pour in, covering the whole room in seconds.

'Oh, for the love of . . .' Jonathan yanked the suitcase shut to stem the tidal wave and pulled a blanket off one of the armchairs. 'We need to clean this up. Grab anything you can!'

Working fast, Flick and Jonathan covered the floor of Strangeworlds with old clothes and towels and blankets until the water was absorbed and the shop looked like it had been attacked by an angry washing machine.

'We'll just have to leave it like this for now,' Jonathan sighed. 'Ready for the next world?'

He selected another of his suitcases at random.

This time, thankfully, they stepped out onto what seemed to be a large wooden walkway.

Flick wobbled uncertainly, trying to find her balance on the uneven wood. As Jonathan pulled the suitcase through behind them, she realised it wasn't a walkway she was standing on at all – it was the branch of a massive tree.

Flick went as still as a statue. A terrified statue. A terrified statue that has just realised it is standing at the top of a massive tree that's moving about in the wind.

She'd thought the trees of the Crystal Forest were huge. But compared to what she stood on now, they were tiny bonsai trees. These trees were *impossible*.

The tree was growing straight up out of the ocean. Flick dropped down onto her hands and knees, frightened she would be blown away like a dry leaf. She dug her fingernails into the bark, hanging on in terror. She could only see Jonathan's ankles, but by the way he was standing he seemed rooted to the spot in fear too. She hoped to goodness he still had a hold of the suitcase.

They were at least one hundred storeys up, maybe more. Flick had never been in a skyscraper, but this tree was taller than any building she had been at the top of.

The water below glittered in the glow of a pale blue sun overhead.

The giant trees were everywhere. They twisted upwards, rising up out of the sea like tower blocks. Each tree had huge flat leaves which were aimed directly at the blue sun. The size and number of the plants was boggling Flick's mind. It was as though she and Jonathan had shrunk as they stepped out of the suitcase.

Gritting her teeth, she lifted herself up slightly to see the view again. The water and the trees seemed to go on for ever, nothing else in sight. An enormous forest of impossible scale. It would have been beautiful, if they hadn't been stuck at the top of it.

'No land I can see,' she said, her voice hoarse.

'I wonder how deep this water is,' Jonathan said, looking nervously over the edge of the branch. He held his arms out to the side, like a child walking on a wall. 'Assuming these trees have roots like the ones on our world, they'd need some sort of soil for nutrients. They don't feel as though they're simply floating.' He bounced slightly on the branch. The bough moved minutely, but it was enough to make Flick shut her eyes and send a silent prayer to whoever might be listening. Jonathan hummed. 'There's no dramatic movement of the branch, even at this height.'

'Wobble this branch again and you'll be finding out how deep that water really is,' Flick hissed. 'Do you mind? I'm trying not to fall to my death here.'

'Sorry. Would this world work, do you think? There's water, and wood . . .'

'What bothers me is the tree roots,' Flick said. 'Would the ships get stuck in them?'

Jonathan pulled a face. 'I didn't think of that.'

Flick sat up slightly. She wouldn't fall off if she sat still, she told herself. 'I don't think this is the one. The lack of land is the one problem, the tree roots is another. And the size of the place! If these are the trees, imagine how big the fish might be!'

Jonathan nodded. 'We aren't getting anywhere. We need an island, an ocean, some greenery . . . Earth would be ideal, but there's no way I'm unleashing Nyfe onto our oceans.'

Something stirred in the back of Flick's mind. A huge body of water, so still it looked like a mirror. A beach, covered with scattered debris of a life that had vanished. A lighthouse.

'I . . . I know one,' she said. Even as she said it, she felt strange. As if she'd told a secret. She wanted to take it back, but it was too late. It was that weird dream that had made her think of the place at all.

Jonathan frowned at her, oblivious to her discomfort. 'What do you mean?'

'You remember that time I had a – a sneaky look in a case?' She blushed.

'You mean when you entered one without my permission?' Jonathan corrected, raising an eyebrow.

Flick shrugged. 'Whatever. Well, there was ocean. And a bit of land. I don't know how much water there was, but it was a lot.' Flick swallowed, thinking of the flat water, how utterly undisturbed it was, the waves barely even lapping at the sand. The *emptiness* of the world had been so vast that even remembering it felt like standing at the mouth of a great dark cavern, the darkness inside too thick to see within.

Jonathan rubbed his chin, where a faint shadow of stubble had started to grow through. 'I know you didn't exactly linger but was there any life?'

'None,' Flick said. 'None on the dry land, anyway. Not even a spider. Maybe there were fish in the water.'

'It does sound ideal, I must admit—'

'But there was the lighthouse,' Flick said quickly.

Jonathan's hand dropped from his chin. 'Ah. Yes. You thought it was a bit . . . creepy?'

She swallowed. 'I can't think how to describe it to

you. It was completely dead. It felt *wrong*. The only thing not creepy about it was your dad's notebook.'

'You saw no people?'

'There were photos, but no one alive. It was like it had been abandoned,' Flick said. 'Maybe there's somewhere better.'

Jonathan pulled an uneasy face. 'I don't like the idea of this abandoned lighthouse. Particularly since Dad seems to have been there and left too quickly to remember to take his notebook with him.' He frowned. 'You said there were photographs there too?'

'Mm. But your dad wasn't in any of the pictures, they were of a family from another world.' Flick remembered something else. 'And didn't you say that the case I went through to get there was locked?'

'I thought it was, but it can't have been.' Jonathan shrugged. 'Otherwise you would never have got in.'

'I've broken out of locked places before,' Flick pointed out. 'Maybe it was locked for a good reason, and I shouldn't have broken into it at all.'

There was an uncomfortable silence.

Jonathan looked at his watch. 'Let's go back to Strangeworlds and find that suitcase. You can investigate that world, and I'll check the remaining water world suitcases. I don't like the idea of us splitting up, but time is of the essence here.'

Flick felt a fresh drop of sour nausea fall down into her stomach.

*

'How long have we been away?' Flick asked as Jonathan dug out the suitcase that led to the lighthouse.

He looked up and checked the clock. 'Just over a week,' he said.

Flick choked. 'That long?'

'Indeed.'

The clock's hands continued to progress around the circle, too quickly. Flick had the urge to put a finger on them to stop them.

'We need to move fast,' Jonathan said. 'You try that case and find out if it's suitable.' He pulled another case towards himself. 'See you back here as quick as you can,' he said, before jumping into it.

The lid shut behind him, and Flick was left alone with the suitcase that led to the dead, silent world of her dream.

She stepped over to it.

The suitcase looked as unassuming as it had before.

Flick put her thumbs to the catches, remembering how stiff they had been to open before.

This time, they flicked up as easy as anything. Flick stared into the suitcase, the sandy air blowing up at her, and felt sick. She hadn't planned to return here. The place frightened her. It had then, and it still did, now.

But she couldn't afford to be selfish about this. It might be just the kind of world her new friends needed.

She stepped into the case, and, with a new-found elegance that she would swear blind she wasn't copying from Jonathan Mercator, took hold of the handle and pulled it through after herself.

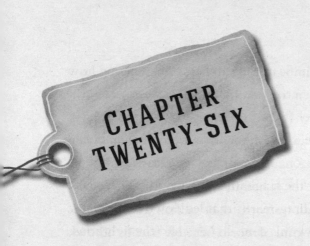

CHAPTER TWENTY-SIX

Flick staggered out of the suitcase, emerging onto the beach she had tried not think about for so many weeks. The stillness of the air, so different from the constant winds and cold blasts of The Break and the warm familiarity of The Strangeworlds Travel Agency, seemed to steal her breath away.

She tried to ignore it, picking up the suitcase. She didn't pull it through with her – if she went too long without going back to Strangeworlds, she wanted Jonathan to be able to come and rescue her. The last thing she wanted was to be sealed away in this place.

The sun was casting pale light down onto the sea and sand. Flick shielded her eyes as she looked around. She was further from the lighthouse than she remembered being last time, but there was a low crop of sandstone to her right and a crunching grass verge above it. She climbed up onto the verge quickly. Somewhere here she knew there was an abandoned picnic. She kept one eye on the sand as she walked, watching out for the gingham blanket and broken glass, and those awful drag-marks that led down to the water.

But, somehow, this time she reached the lighthouse without seeing any of that. As she walked towards the lighthouse, she noticed the vast ocean, the land with sparse patches of grass, and what might be trees in the distance. This could be a good world for the pirates of The Break. She might have found the place for them.

That should have made Flick feel better, but it didn't. She hadn't seen the abandoned picnic this time – where was it? The other side of the lighthouse? It couldn't be – she'd come the same way as before.

Perhaps, a creaking little voice in her head chuckled darkly, *someone else has been here, and cleared it away.*

Flick attempted a Jonathan-style eye-roll, cursing her imagination. Who else could have come here? Who else had a suitcase? Flick pressed the heel of her hand to her forehead. There were too many questions. Who was taking the magic from The Break? What had Daniel Mercator been doing here? And who had last seen him?

Had it really been the people who ran the Strangeworlds Outpost in Five Lights, Greysen and Darilyn Quickspark who saw him last? And now she thought about it, who was the man who had wandered into Tam's forest with a gun, scaring the children?

She reached the lighthouse and leaned against the side. The Strangeworlds Society should be solving *those* mysteries, not trying to work out how to get a galleon through a suitcase. This was the problem with the multiverse, she realised. You tried to fix one problem and then another one comes up and you're so busy trying to fix the new one, that the first one gets forgotten about. And that could be dangerous.

In the quiet of this empty world, all of Flick's held-back worries were rising to the surface. And the words of Glean, that sinister leader of the Five Lights Thieves, suddenly rang in her memory louder than a church bell.

'. . . *why was The Strangeworlds Society formed in the first place? To protect the worlds? Protect them from what? From whom?*'

Something, or someone, had been stealing magic from the world of The Break. Not the pirates, they were innocent (at least in that regard). And the Thieves were locked away in another world, so they couldn't be to blame. But . . . the Thieves of Five Lights had been afraid. They had been running from something. Something they thought Flick and Jonathan ought to know about.

'. . . *We have never been safe, not for one single moment. The multiverse is in more danger than you realise.*'

What if whatever The Strangeworlds Society had been formed as a protective force against, and whatever was taking the magic from The Break . . .

What if it was the same thing?

Flick pushed herself off the wall of the lighthouse. She couldn't see the whole picture yet, but she felt as if she had been handed several puzzle pieces. She just needed time to sort them out.

And right now, she didn't have time. She needed to get back to the agency and tell Jonathan the world seemed suitable, even if it was still very unsettling.

She looked up at the lighthouse.

Last time she had been here, she had gone inside, seen the emptiness of the place, but also the pictures on the walls, the paper-covered desk with its boxes and frames.

She could go in again.

She could also go straight back to the travel agency.

Flick bit her lip guiltily as she turned towards the door of the lighthouse and pushed it open.

It swung inwards with less resistance than the last time.

The interior of the lighthouse didn't feel as creepy as the beach. Whether that was because it was warmer, or the fact it had thick protective walls, Flick wasn't sure. But as she wedged the door open with the suitcase, she felt her shoulders relax a little.

'Hello?' she called.

Obviously, there was no answer.

She stared around the empty space, her eyes resting on the black iron spiral staircase in the centre. The sight of it nagged at her, like she ought to remember something about it, but she didn't know what. She walked over to it and touched the cold metal. She had been too nervous to climb it, the last time she was here.

The memory of her dream stirred, like a cat stretching in its sleep.

She put one foot on the bottom step. She shouldn't be nervous. Hadn't she broken out of a locked world? Hadn't she stood on the hand of a gigantic mer-queen? She could climb this staircase.

Gripping the banister, Flick went up. The staircase coiled tightly, and the steps were slim, but it didn't take long to reach the top. She stepped up onto solid floorboards.

No one had been here for a long, long time. Her shoes left marks behind in the undisturbed beige dust. Above her, the roof curved like a little cap on a too-large head. The space where a lantern or bulb would sit was empty. The glass of the dome itself, which looked like a single curved pane from the outside, was revealed to actually be several dozen slices of glass neatly pieced together and sealed.

The lighthouse tapered upwards as it rose, so the space at the top was no bigger than the box-room back at Strangeworlds. There was a dusty pile of sheets and clothes, a small collection of empty glass bottles, and a woven basket containing some old toys.

One of the toys – a stuffed rabbit – glared at Flick with its one remaining glass eye. Flick had an urge to turn it to the wall. Then, something clicked in her head.

She went quickly back down the staircase and into the main room. She went over to the desk. The evidence of her sending things clattering to the floor on her last visit was still clear. There were papers, that slim wooden box, and framed photographs stacked up haphazardly on the desk. She went through them quickly.

There they were. The two photos she had remembered.

In one photo, a father and mother stood outside a shop, holding a baby each. In the other, the same father and mother sat on a beach with just one child, a young daughter, all laughing together. Behind the child, lying on the beach blanket, was the very same one-eyed rabbit Flick had just seen upstairs.

And then, Flick's heart seemed to stop.

She hadn't expected to stare into a face she knew in the pictures.

His hair was darker and his face sharper, but it was definitely him. Holding a baby in one photograph, and his daughter's small hand in the other, was the man who had patched up Jonathan's wounds after they had escaped the City of Five Lights. The man who Flick had thought she'd recognised.

She *had* seen him before then, but in a photograph.

Smiling out of the pictures at her was the apothecary, Tristyan Thatcher.

CHAPTER TWENTY-SEVEN

'Well? We're running out of time and options,' Jonathan said, as Flick stepped back through the suitcase.

He'd clearly been back for a while – the wet towels and clothes had been piled into the kitchen area and the travel agency floor was now only slightly damp. 'Mine was a waste of time – there was plenty of water but the land was solid rock, no soil or plant life at all. How was yours?'

'Same as before,' she said, closing the suitcase lid with her foot. She was carrying the photographs.

Jonathan was facing away from her and looking at the bookshelf. 'I've been trying to find the guidebook to your lighthouse world and get some more information,' he said. 'I'd like to know some of the history, at any rate.' He paused. 'My dad might have taken the guidebook with him, of course . . .' He stopped, curling a hand into a tense fist.

'Jonathan,' Flick said, coming over to the desk. 'You need to take a look at this.' She put the frames down.

Jonathan turned, and raised his eyebrows in surprise. He touched the picture of the family of four. 'Tristyan!'

Flick pointed to the other photograph. 'Tristyan said he lost someone because of Strangeworlds. I wondered . . . well, there's only one child in the second photograph,' she said quietly.

Jonathan was looking troubled. 'How did these come to be in an empty world? He said he didn't travel by suitcase.'

'Maybe he was lying.'

'Perhaps. Or perhaps these photos belonged to someone else.' Jonathan dragged his hands down his face. 'We don't have time to think about this now. Is the world suitable for the evacuation, do you think?'

'I think so,' Flick admitted. 'It's got what we're looking for.'

'Then we can at least begin to rescue people from The Break. That's what matters now, not whether Tristyan has been there.'

'Rescue *some* of the people, you mean.' Flick picked Tristyan's younger family picture back up and looked at it. Her time in the quiet world of the lighthouse seemed to have amplified all her feelings. She was tired and angry and disappointed all at once, and she didn't know how she was managing to feel it all without dissolving.

Jonathan sighed. 'Some of the people are better than none,' he said, though he sounded as bleak as she felt.

Flick couldn't take the hurricane of feelings any more. 'It isn't fair!' she exploded. 'Why should some of the people be rescued just because they're fortunate enough to fit into our suitcase, and others not?'

'It's the only plan we have!' Jonathan retorted.

Flick clenched the picture frame in her hands. 'We're failing them. And we're supposed to just be OK with that? What about all those mer-folk who will be left behind to die? Those people who – who don't *fit* into our plan? We are *leaving* them! And they'll know! They'll have to watch while everyone else goes to a safer place, and then – and then . . .' Flick's whole body was fizzing from the inside. She gripped the picture frame so hard the glass shattered in her fingers, falling to the floor of the travel agency. Her arms tensed, and her chest was so tight she felt as if she would explode, but then . . .

'Get me,' she forced out between her teeth.

'What?' Jonathan said.

'Suitcase,' she said. 'Get – me – one.'

Jonathan moved fast, grabbing the suitcase that led to the world of the tall trees. He opened it in front of Flick, not even bothering to kick the broken glass away.

Flick exhaled . . .

. . . and the sides of the suitcase began to strain. The leather-stitched edges creaked and bent. They pulsed and stretched. Then . . . they gave way, collapsing open. The schism inside – a dark red magma flow – became edged in white. It swelled out of the suitcase and kept on widening. It was *growing*.

'Oh my god,' Jonathan breathed, backing away.

Flick could feel the edge of the schism in her hands, in her mind, pulling at something inside her, wanting to make her fly, vanish, explode.

'I have to stop,' she gasped. She released her mental grip on it and the schism snapped shut.

The bright red and white light became a thin glowing line, hovering in the middle of the travel agency, before it gave a final glow of desperation, then vanished, leaving nothing behind. Not even the suitcase it had risen from. There was simply a space on the floor, and pieces of broken picture frame.

'Felicity?'

Flick could hear Jonathan, but it was as though he was a voice on the TV. Something that could easily be ignored. It wasn't important.

'Felicity, can you hear me?'

The voice was strangely insistent, though. She stared, slowly realising that she wasn't really seeing anything.

Something shook her arm.

She turned her head to look, each tiny movement feeling as difficult as trying to shove a tractor through mud. There was a hand on her arm. And her arm was on the floor.

And so was she.

'Flick!'

She took a deep breath, her chest rattling like it was throwing off an illness. She wanted to cough. It felt like someone was sitting on her chest. 'Hhrr . . .' she managed to say.

A puff of relieved breath cut through the air. 'Come on, Felicity, that's it.'

Jonathan.

Flick raised a hand. Or, she tried to. It felt like her body was made of lead.

Slowly the ceiling of the travel agency sharpened into relief, and she sat up shakily.

Jonathan was kneeling next to her, a look of wonder and horror on his face.

'You – you *vanished* that suitcase,' he said. 'You made the schism inside it move. And – and get bigger. How did you . . .?'

'I don't know,' she said. 'I – I was just so angry.' Flick put a hand to her chest. The ache had gone, but she suddenly felt bone-tired. She could have put her head down on the floorboards and gone to sleep. She swayed and caught herself on the floor. 'I'm really tired,' she said, stupidly.

Jonathan grabbed a cushion off the closest armchair and put it behind her in case she should fall backwards. 'I don't understand how you did that. Where did the magic come from?'

Flick pressed a hand to her forehead. 'It was like, I knew there was energy – magical energy – in the world inside the suitcase. And I could use it. So, I did.'

'You used magic from another world to expand a schism?' Jonathan looked as though he was losing his grip on reality. 'How did you know what to do?'

Flick couldn't answer. In the moment, it had felt as natural as breathing. She had torn a hole between two worlds before using magic. Now she had used it to expand a schism. Magic was a multi-use tool, like a

Swiss Army knife that could be used to cut or saw or magnify.

She looked around the travel agency. She had always felt as though the place buzzed with potential. Now, the cases seemed to literally vibrate. She didn't need to ask whether Jonathan could feel it, too; she knew he couldn't. She put a hand into her pocket and took out the little brass magnifying glass. She held it up close to her eye.

The travel agency looked the same as it always did. The suitcases they had recently travelled through glowed a brighter gold than the others and there was a fine mist of magic in the air, but nothing to show that anything extraordinary had just taken place. Flick lowered the magnifying glass, wondering.

Jonathan picked up the photograph that had fallen out of the broken frame. He turned it over. 'There are names on the back of this.' He handed it to her.

Flick looked at the neatly written names.

Aspen, Tristyan, Clara and I

She turned the picture back over, feeling a penny drop. '*And I*. Whoever wrote this, it wasn't Tristyan,' she said. 'It did belong to someone else, after all.' Flick's eyebrows went up as she remembered something else. 'Aspen! Wait—' she snatched at her backpack and dug out her copy of the Strangeworlds' *Study of Particulars*. She turned to the first page and jabbed a finger at the names written there.

Property of:

Anthony Mercator, 1900

Juliet Mercator, 1970

Aspen Thatcher, 1982

'Aspen Thatcher,' Flick sighed. 'They must have been married, her and Tristyan.'

'And she was a member of The Strangeworlds Society,' Jonathan said. 'Oh, that's very sad.'

'Sad? Why?'

'Remember what I said about living in a world that isn't your own? If she was from our world but chose to live with Tristyan in another . . .' He pulled a face. 'They wouldn't have had long together. Not the lifetime they would have wanted.'

Sorrow welled up in Flick's chest. 'What about the babies?'

'I suppose that would depend where they were born,' he said. 'You can only live in the world you're meant to be in, after all. And if Aspen owned this handbook nearly forty years ago . . .' He let the implication hang unpleasantly in the air.

Flick clutched at the only straw she had available to her. 'Tristyan said he had *lost* someone, right? Not that they *died*. She might have just come home, to our world.'

It was still heart-breaking. To not be able to see someone you loved, ever again?

How could you go on?

Jonathan winced, clearly feeling the same. 'Let's assume for the sake of our emotions that Aspen Thatcher did come back. She might have had her children here. For all we know, they could still be out there. So could she.' He looked up at the window as if expecting to see three faces looking back at him.

Flick squinted at the photograph. 'But how would it even work? Babies born to parents from different worlds? One parent wouldn't be human.'

'Similarities are far more common than differences,' Jonathan said. He looked back at the photograph. 'It's happened before. Look at Avery's lineage,' he added.

Flick stood up. 'We should put this picture somewhere safe. Whoever wrote those names on the back might still be out there. They might walk through the door, one day. You never know.' She looked up at the clock, and gasped. 'We've wasted time. We need to get back to The Break. And then I need to . . .' She looked at her hands. 'I need to make a schism big enough for them to get through. All of them.'

'Can you do it?'

'I don't know. Jonathan, the amount of energy that took was . . . it was enormous,' she said. 'I don't know how I could have made it any bigger without bits of our world starting to get pulled in.'

He snapped his fingers. 'That's it, then.'

'What?'

'Collapse their world,' he said, as if he was suggesting something as simple as stacking bricks. 'The Break. The circle. Collapse it. Use every drop of magic in the place to widen a schism enough for everyone to get through. You could do it.'

Flick stared. 'I – I don't know if—'

'There's no time for *I don't* know,' he insisted. 'You just widened a schism right here in the shop. You have to try. You have to. If you don't save them, no one will.'

Flick shut her eyes for a moment. 'Even if I could do it, I don't know how long I'll be able to hold it open.'

'We'll tell everyone to be ready.'

'But those ships . . . it will take ages.' Flick shook

her head. Then looked up. 'Unless they're already travelling at speed.'

Jonathan tilted his head to one side. 'Go on.'

'Moving things have energy of their own,' Flick said. 'I could use that energy to keep the schism open. They'd need to have the wind behind them,' she said, looking into the middle distance as her mind raced, forming a plan. 'They'd need to be going full-tilt, one after the other, building up as much energy as they could, and . . .' She blinked. 'I think they need to go over the edge.'

'Excuse me?'

'If I could stretch the schism to be open beyond the edge of the world, and the ships could sail over the edge, I mean right over, into the empty space, they'll have even more magical energy. And it'll help me keep the schism open for longer. The ships would have to go first – so I could use their momentum, and so they could carry as many people as possible.' Flick pressed a finger to her lips. 'I still don't know how long I could hold it, but that would all help.'

Jonathan took a deep breath. 'You want Nyfe and Captain Burnish, and all their people, to sail right over the edge of their world, in the hopes of falling into a new one?'

Flick nodded.

'Right,' Jonathan said. He unbuttoned his cuffs and pushed his sleeves up to the elbow. 'We'd better get back to them before it's too late then.'

CHAPTER TWENTY-EIGHT

'We're going to do *what* now?' Captain Burnish looked over his clasped hands at Jonathan and Flick.

'I know it sounds a bit mad,' Flick said.

' A bit,' Burnish repeated. He looked at Tessa, who gave him an expression that said *these children have lost their minds*.

Avery was giving them the same look, from extremely tired eyes. Staying for so long in The Break had clearly taken its toll on her. When Flick and Jonathan had arrived back on the ship, she had looked like she didn't know whether to laugh, cry, or punch them both in relief. She'd settled for screaming *Where have you been?* at them, and then taking them immediately to

Captain Burnish. Flick had been so pleased to see her alive and in one piece that she wanted to cry.

'It can be done, can't it?' Jonathan asked. 'You can sail over the edge?'

'You *can*,' Burnish said, eyebrows going up. 'You probably shouldn't, however.'

'It's been done before?' Flick asked.

Burnish leaned back in his chair. 'Yes. It has been done.'

Tessa nodded. 'They thought, back in the old days, that the world was a ball. That you could sail all the way around it and come back up on the other side. Some folks went sailing.' She shook her head. 'They never came back.'

Everyone went quiet.

'My world is a ball,' Avery said.

'Ours is a ball, too,' Flick added.

'Fascinating.' Burnish rolled his eyes. He looked weary. The *Serpent* and the other Buccaneers' ships had spent the last week sailing in wide circles around what was left of the world, with the *Aconite* and Captain Nyfe in an endless chase. The Mer-Queen and her people had slowed some of the pursuing ships, but with Burnish ordering his allies not to harm anyone, all they could really do was try to outrun the other pirates until Flick and Jonathan returned. They were all at the end of their tether, in more ways than one.

Captain Burnish stood up and rolled his shoulders back. 'No more running away. If this is to be our way out, let's run towards that, instead. Tessa, tell the lads to get their ships together. Get word out to the Freemariners, and . . .'

Tessa looked up at him. 'And?'

Burnish sighed. His eyes met Tessa's. 'We need to tell Nyfe.'

Tessa's lips went thin. 'Tess,' Burnish said gently, 'she's our girl.'

Avery dropped the tin mug she was holding.

Flick looked at Jonathan, whose eyebrows had disappeared into his hair. It was a surprise, but at the same time . . . not a surprise at all.

'She left us,' said Tessa.

'Doesn't change the fact she's ours,' Burnish said. 'I've lost four children, Tess. Don't ask me to stand here and make it five.'

Tessa closed her eyes for a moment. Then opened them and nodded. 'I'll get the word out. All the birds. I'll ask Katyo to assemble his people. Where's the meeting point?'

Burnish smiled. 'The Scattered Isles. We can get

everyone there and make for the edge of the ocean. Together.'

Tessa nodded, and walked from the room with all the regal elegance of a queen, closing the door behind her.

Captain Burnish waited until the door was closed, before looking at Flick. 'You didn't know?'

'I thought, maybe she could be yours,' Flick said. 'But Tessa seems to dislike her so much.'

Burnish sighed and looked at the ceiling. 'Look, kid, you don't get to choose your family. And sometimes, you don't like the ones you're handed.'

'But she's her daughter?'

'And mine,' Burnish shrugged. 'And I love them both. But one of them hates me because I wanted her to wait before trying to take control of the armada. Another can't forgive me for losing four of our children already.'

Flick blinked. 'And now Nyfe's your enemy?'

'She'd say that. But I'd still do anything to keep her safe.'

'Why didn't you want her to be the leader?' Avery asked.

Burnish cracked his index knuckle with his thumb. 'There's wanting to lead, and there's wanting people to just do as you say. It's all right to want both. But if you want the latter, you need to be able to do the former. If she'd waited a few more years, I would have handed these ships over to her, gladly. She would have learned, by then, that leadership isn't about threatening people and saying your sword is bigger than theirs. It's not about making the people you're supposed to be leading too afraid to ask for help. No one should be afraid of their leaders. And when enough people think their leaders are unjust, they rise up.' He picked his cutlass off the desk, and shoved it into his belt. 'Even without the circle collapsing, Nyfe's days as Pirate Queen would have always been numbered.'

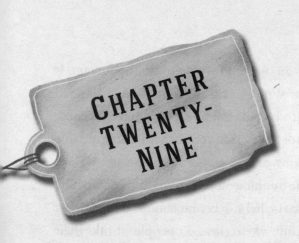

CHAPTER TWENTY-NINE

'She wants to speak to you,' Katyo said, as he surfaced beside the jolly boat. Flick and Avery had been sitting in it for hours, receiving messages from the various ships scattered around the world. Everyone, it seemed, was willing to bank everything on what must have seemed like a very foolish plan.

Everyone, that is, except Nyfe.

'When you say "speak to",' Flick said, 'do you mean "throttle"?'

Katyo smiled. 'I suspect she honestly wants to talk. Or at least, her crew wants her to. The *Aconite* is a ship full of frightened people. If Nyfe doesn't show willing, she'll face a mutiny.'

Avery frowned. 'What if some of her crew want to join us, but some don't?'

Katyo shrugged, his skin fading to a pale grey that deepened to almost navy blue at the tips of his tentacles. 'The *Onslaught* has plenty of room aboard it.'

Flick nodded, thinking. The *Onslaught* belonged to a group of pirates called the Freemariners, who seemed to be somewhat like Switzerland – they didn't take sides with anyone. They also happened to have the largest ship on the water, four times the size of the *Serpent*.

Flick had talked to the captain of the *Onslaught* herself, onboard the *Serpent*. The captain's name was Nicylo Bee, though everyone called her the Stinger. She had thick dreads of hair that went down to her waist and she listened patiently to Flick's explanation, before asking a question.

'And if your plan fails,' she had said slowly, 'what will happen to my ship and my crew?'

Flick had wished she could lie. 'I think they wouldn't come back.' The truth had been eating at her for a while. She couldn't be sure if her plan would work at all as there was no way to test it beforehand, and if it didn't . . .

The Stinger had pursed her lips. She wore a yellow

and black striped neckerchief around her throat. 'So if we try, and we fail, we die.'

She stood and went over to the window in Burnish's cabin. Outside, the ocean of The Break looked peaceful and calm. It was amazing how easily it could trick you into thinking there was nothing wrong.

'The *Onslaught* can carry a bigger crew than any other ship,' the Stinger had said. 'I understand what you say about energy, and a ship full of sailors will have more than an empty one. But, child, do you know what you are asking?'

Flick had nodded. 'I'm sorry.'

The Stinger had given her a small smile. 'I'll sail the *Onslaught* over the edge of the world for you. I don't want it said that, at the end, I was too afraid to try. Any sailor can choose whether or not to join me.'

Flick had felt her throat contract painfully. Every sailor was risking so much. They were willing to try, just for the tiniest sliver of hope. 'Thank you,' she had said.

The meeting stayed with Flick long after the Stinger took a jolly boat back to her own ship. Thinking about it made her feel strange inside. Her fingers prickled, and she tugged her sleeves over her hands. The more she thought about the schism she had to make, the more she seemed to want to do it. It was as though there was a second Flick, buried somewhere within her, that was in charge of the magic. That Flick was desperate for another go. The Flick who was in charge of keeping herself alive was trying not to think about what might happen when they tried it.

She looked back at Katyo, who seemed to know she was struggling with the enormity of what she had to do.

'Nyfe is close. Are you ready?' he asked. 'To speak again to the Pirate Queen?'

'I guess we don't have much of a choice,' Flick said. 'We need to give Nyfe's crew a chance to escape, even if she says no. I don't want to leave anyone behind.'

*

'I'm coming with you,' Jonathan said, when Flick told him where she was going. 'She summoned me in the first place.'

'Yeah, but you're not the one who's got to . . .' Flick mimed ripping something with her hands. To her surprise, her fingers felt suddenly hot, and she suspected if she had looked through the magnifying glass she would have seen sparks. She dropped her hands down quickly.

No one else seemed to have noticed.

'I might not have to *do* the actual tearing,' Jonathan said, 'but I like to think I could sell the idea rather convincingly.'

Avery raised an eyebrow and folded her arms in an admirable impression of her cousin.

'He just wants to come to make sure we know who's in charge,' Flick grinned at her.

'That's not accurate.' Jonathan blushed.

'Yeah? You don't trust us, then?'

'No, I – I mean, of course I do, but—'

'But you're in charge?' Avery suggested. 'Because you're a *grown-up*?' She smirked.

'No! We're a . . .' Jonathan cast around for the right word, '. . . team,' he finished pathetically.

Avery laughed, but Flick decided to let him off the hook. 'Right then, team,' she said. 'We'll all go over. Tell Nyfe this is her last chance.'

'Burnish's sailors are hoping to condense themselves onto four ships,' said Jonathan. 'One of them being the *Onslaught*. We'll need to tell Nyfe she'd have to do the same with everyone sailing under her flag.'

Flick shivered. 'Jonathan, I don't know how long I can hold a schism open. I have no way of testing it. It could be five hours. It could be five seconds. What if it's not enough for even *one* of the ships?'

'Felicity.' Jonathan clamped his hands down on the tops of Flick's arms. 'Don't start beating yourself up before you've even tried.' He squeezed her arms. 'You did something in the City of Five Lights. You did the impossible. It wasn't a fluke, or a mistake. It was something you did, something that probably only you can do. You're the best chance we have of being able to help everyone in this world. And if you try, but it doesn't work . . .'

Flick swallowed. 'I—'

'I won't think less of you at all,' Jonathan interrupted. 'No one will. I promise you that. You could never be a disappointment, or a failure, Felicity.' He gave her arms another squeeze, before letting go and standing back.

Avery looked from one of them to the other. 'Yikes. I thought you guys were about to kiss.'

Flick looked at her in unbridled disgust as Jonathan pretended to be sick. 'That's *really* not—'

'Good,' Avery said. 'Now, unless you've got another heart-to-heart planned, we need to get going. We have a fleet to rescue.' Her tone was stern, but her eyes were glittering with mischief.

Flick pressed her lips together to hide a smile and followed Avery out of the door.

CHAPTER THIRTY

Captain Burnish was determined to go to the *Aconite* with them, but Tessa put her foot down.

'We need you here, Ezra,' she insisted. 'We have several ships to try and organise. The Freemariners will help, but they need leadership.'

'You could handle it,' Burnish pointed out.

'I could,' she said, 'but I'm not the captain.'

Burnish rolled his eyes. 'Fine.'

'We'll be back as soon as we can be,' Flick said.

'Unless she throws you all in the brig and the entire plan goes to heck,' Burnish sniffed.

Avery glanced at Flick and pulled a face. 'Is that likely?'

Burnish shrugged. 'I'd say anything's likely, these days.'

*

Katyo hauled Flick and Avery's jolly boat through the water, towards the water-surrounded stones of the Three Maidens, where the *Aconite* was anchored. The Three Maidens weren't so much islands as slender towers of rock, jutting up out of the ocean like fingers poking through holes in a blanket. Their tops were covered in thick mossy grass that trailed downwards like long strands of hair which was presumably how they had got their name.

Katyo held their boat steady alongside the bulging hull of the *Aconite*. Flick, Jonathan and Avery could hear jeers and shouting from on board but it didn't seem to be directed at them. It was just general raucous shouting. The sound of people who were restless and spoiling for a fight.

It was Jereme who climbed down the rope ladder to help tie their small boat to the side of the ship. His face was drawn, and there were dark smears under his eyes as though he hadn't slept in days.

'Brave of you to show your faces again,' he said gruffly, knotting the rope.

Flick didn't rise to the bait. 'Is she really going to talk to us or is she planning on taking us hostage?'

Jereme snorted. 'She needs to make a show of listening, even if she doesn't act.'

'But her crew deserve a chance to escape this world with us!' Flick cried.

'Aye, we do.' Jereme gave a sad smile. 'And, personally, I thank you for coming. I'm interested to hear what you have to say.' He shrugged. 'But you know what they say . . . you can lead a bird to seed, but you can't make it feed.'

They climbed up the ladder. Halfway up, Flick's arms started to tremble. Was this really wise? She'd run away with one of Nyfe's boats and now she was undermining her authority by offering her crew an escape.

Avery nudged her leg. 'Flick, what's wrong?'

Flick realised she'd stopped climbing. 'Nothing.'

She carried on again up to the top, where she was greeted by a whole bunch of restless pirates, grumbling and snarling. Captain Nyfe Shaban was leaning against the main mast, arms folded across her chest. There were two cutlasses in her belt and a look on her face that told Flick in no uncertain terms that the chamber-pot was about to hit the propeller.

Flick was extremely relieved when Avery clambered to stand beside her, a very Jonathan-like expression of distaste on her face. 'This is cheery,' she said under her breath. Jonathan himself looked extremely nervous, but said nothing.

Nyfe pushed herself off the mast to stand straight. 'Let's hear it then, this great plan of yours,' she barked.

Flick steadied herself, forcing her feet to stay where they were, and not take a step backwards. 'It's the same plan we offered you before,' she said loudly, so the rest of the crew could hear her over the wash of the waves against the ship. 'Except this time there's a chance – just a chance, mind – that I could get your ships through as well.'

Nyfe's eye narrowed as her crew began to mutter amongst themselves. 'What's changed?'

Flick wondered how to explain. 'You see, we worked out—'

'You worked out,' Jonathan corrected.

'I worked out how to do it. How to hold the schism inside the suitcase open to let something big like a ship through.'

Nyfe narrowed her eyes. 'But?' She was too clever by half.

'But I wouldn't be able to do it for very long,' Flick admitted. 'You'd have to decide now whether you're joining Captain Burnish and the Freemariners, including Captain Bee. Captain Burnish is already moving his crew. The mer-people are ready to come as well.'

'How would you get a ship through that tiny suitcase?' Nyfe asked. 'Tell me.'

Flick wished she had better words. 'I can make it bigger. I can't explain it in any more detail than that. It's magic. But to do so . . . I have to destroy this world.'

There was uproar. The crew crashed about on the desk, shouting and roaring, until Edony appeared with her conical coat and drum. Eventually there was silence again.

Nyfe hadn't taken her eyes from Flick's face. 'Then you're not giving us a choice,' she said. 'It's an ultimatum. Either we follow you, or we die.'

'You're going to die anyway,' Flick said bluntly. 'The Break is falling apart – weeks left at the most. Trust me. Please.' She stepped closer and lowered her voice so no one else could hear. 'Your father doesn't want to leave you behind.'

Nyfe flinched but recovered quickly. 'I doubt that very much.'

'He said so,' Flick said, stepping closer still. 'He said you're still his girl. He doesn't want to leave you behind.' She looked up at Nyfe's face which, for the first time, wore an expression of uncertainty.

'He's scared,' Flick went on, taking advantage of Nyfe's hesitation. 'But he knows he needs to try. He wants you to try, too.' Flick raised her voice again. 'Captain Burnish is ready to sail right over the edge of the world to save his crew. Captain Bee, too, and the other Freemariners. Will you join them?'

There was a roar of agreement from some of the crew, and Flick squared her shoulders.

'We're aiming for the edge of the world. The *Onslaught* will sail over first as it's the biggest. If you want to join us, you need to decide which ships to save because you can't take them all. It's time to decide what's more important to you – people, or things. Dump everything you think you can survive without, load up with fresh water and food, and follow us. I'll send a signal, to tell you when to set off.'

Nyfe held a hand up. '*You'll* tell us? On your own?'

'She won't be on her own.' Avery folded her arms, and Flick felt a rush of heat go through her body at this fierce display of camaraderie.

Nyfe shook her head. 'You girls are brave, right enough, but you're not sailors. You shouldn't be out there by yourselves at the edge of the world.' She stuck her chin out, then unhooked the eyepatch from her face. A sphere of a frosted glass eye stared out unseeingly from beneath. Nyfe held the patch out to Flick. 'If it's magic you're searching for, I think you might need this.

Handed down from captain to captain, and now back to a Strangeworlder.'

Flick took it. 'What is it?' It was heavier than she would have expected.

Nyfe smiled as she took a spare eyepatch from her pocket. 'Lift the embroidered part.'

Flick lifted the embroidered material. It reminded her of those glasses that have a flip-down part to turn them into sunglasses. And below the embroidered cover was a small oval of glass. 'Is this . . .' Flick raised it to the sun. 'Is this a magnifier?'

Nyfe nodded. 'Never knew why we hung on to it, to be honest. I suppose we were just waiting for you.'

Flick closed one eye and looked through the glass. Happiness washed through her as the magical sparkles flickered into her vision as if greeting her, swimming through the air in a golden haze she knew and loved so well.

'This is perfect. Thank you, Captain Nyfe.' She lowered the glass. 'So, are you joining us?'

Nyfe finished tying the new patch behind her head and nodded. 'Aye. If Burnish can do it, so can we. I'm going with you. To the edge.'

CHAPTER THIRTY-ONE

Dawn was breaking in another world, shining down on the ocean as Flick, Avery and Nyfe rowed out in the small boat to the edge of the ocean.

Jonathan had gone ahead to the world of the lighthouse. They'd agreed that it might make it easier for Flick to stretch out the connecting schism if there was someone she trusted on the other side of it.

Flick had expected to be able to see a sudden drop on the edge of the world, but when Nyfe dropped the anchor, she could still see water around them, stretching off into infinity.

'Are we close to the edge?' she asked.

Nyfe put a hand to her ear. 'Listen.'

Flick leaned over the side, listening hard. There was a faint *hiss* coming from ahead of them. 'What is that?'

'The ocean spilling over the edge,' Nyfe said.

Avery and Flick both looked shocked.

'Don't believe me? Watch.' Nyfe picked up an old bolt from the bottom of the boat and lobbed it like a cricket bowler. It sailed through the air, and then dropped down. Flick waited for the splash, but it never came.

'It's gone over the edge?' she asked.

Nyfe nodded. 'We're always closer to the edge than we think.' She adjusted her new eyepatch.

Avery frowned. 'But if the water spills over, why hasn't the ocean all drained away?'

'It falls back down as rain. What – are you simple?' Nyfe turned to Flick. 'You ready?'

Flick nodded. 'I think so.' She tapped her fingers on the suitcase. It seemed to buzz under her touch.

'All we have to do now is wait for the *Onslaught* to get close enough.' Nyfe looked back across the water. 'Once it gets up to speed it takes a very long time to stop. They'll be using both the oars and the sails, and the wind is on their side. They won't be able to stop if you're not ready in time.'

'Thanks for the pep-talk,' Flick sighed. She flexed

her hands. Her fingers and wrists felt tingly and achy, as if they knew what was coming. She pulled Nyfe's old eyepatch from her pocket and wrapped it around her head. Nyfe helped tie it into place, the embroidered part lifted so Flick could see through the glass underneath. She squinted through the glass of it. It was amazing, being able to see magic while having her hands free.

There was a lot of magic concentrated around the edge of the circular world, like a golden ring holding the whole thing in place. Except Flick knew that the world *wasn't* being held in place. What was causing this magical barrier to fail? The question didn't just nag at her, it stomped around, demanding attention she couldn't really spare.

Flick pushed the magnifying patch up onto her forehead. 'When I was in Five Lights, I could see the magic drifting away into the giant schism. This magic isn't drifting anywhere. It's just sitting there. Everything should be fine.'

Nyfe nodded. 'And yet, the circle still collapses.'

Avery pursed her lips. 'Always in big chunks at a time? Not gradually?'

'You remember watching it break away when you first arrived? That is how it happens.'

Flick looked up at the sky. The golden sunlight was growing stronger now, making yellowy spots on the ocean. 'Something must be taking it. Or someone.' As she said it, she knew for certain that what she said was true. Her blood seemed to sing with the truth of it. But who would need such a large amount of magic in one go?

Nyfe followed her gaze upward. 'If it is a *someone*, I'd like to show them what the sharp side of a cutlass feels like.'

'Yeah, that'd show them,' Avery said vaguely. She was looking at Flick, who wasn't really listening.

Flick looked down at her hands. She could only think of one thing that would need such a large amount of magic at once: opening a new schism, like she had done in Five Lights.

But no one else could do what she could do.

Not even Elara Mercator, the very founder of The Strangeworlds Society, had been able to open schisms of her own.

Surely . . . surely, it couldn't be that?

'I can see the *Onslaught*, dead ahead,' Nyfe said, shaking Flick out of her thoughts. The woman was looking through a brass telescope. 'It's already got some speed, girl. You'd best move fast.'

Flick didn't bother asking for the telescope. She could already see the shape of the enormous ship approaching at a tremendous speed. Barrelling straight towards the end of the world.

Nyfe collapsed the telescope. 'Shouldn't you do it now?'

Flick shook her head. 'No, I need as much energy as possible. And that means waiting until the ship actually tips over the edge.'

'What?' Nyfe spun around so suddenly the boat rocked violently.

'A falling object has energy,' Flick said. 'Energy is magic. Magic is what I need to open this schism. If I open it too soon . . .' She swallowed. 'I don't know how long I can keep it open.'

Nyfe's expression was so hard you could have broken a chisel on it. 'Some of my crew are aboard that ship.'

'So let me do what I've got to do!' Flick snapped. 'You're not helping.'

Nyfe looked back at the approaching ship. 'You know,' she said, after a moment's silence, 'you'd make a good captain, one day, with that attitude.'

Avery nodded. 'She's right.'

Despite it all, Flick had to smile.

Flick could see the individual sails of the *Onslaught* now, each one big enough to wrap up a house. As it bore down on them she could make out the figurehead – a twisted carving of two women embracing.

The ship wasn't slowing down. If anything, it seemed to be getting faster. Flick could see the *splash splash splash* of the oars jutting out from the sides. The sailors pulling on them must be afraid, worried this wouldn't work, and yet pulling as hard as they could because the little girl from another world had told them to give it everything they had. Flick could see the full bellies of the sails now, and understood just how much force this ship had behind it.

She'd asked for everything they could give her.

It looked as though she'd got it.

Behind the *Onslaught*, following in its wake, were the other ships determined to try and cross to a new world. The *Aconite*, the *Serpent*, the *Watchman* and a dozen others, sailing with all their might into an uncertain future. And the mer-folk, swimming beneath the waves, occasionally surfacing to see if they were close, like whales breaching. There were even littler splashes beside the ships that Flick thought might be sea creatures, racing the pirates to the way out.

Flick had never felt smaller in her life.

It was time. Hands shaking, Flick picked up the lighthouse-world's suitcase and flicked the catches open before dropping it into the water. The suitcase opened like a book, floating quickly towards the edge of the world. The suitcase buckled and hesitated at the waterfall, wobbling and splashing but not quite going over the edge.

The *Onslaught* was now only the length of a playing-field away. It was barrelling forward faster than Flick had imagined a ship could move.

Flick braced her feet in the bottom of the boat.

The *Onslaught* came closer, closer, closer, too close –

– the suitcase was pushed forwards by the waves and disappeared over the rim of the world.

The *Onslaught* reached the edge a moment later –

– and teetered.

Though it hovered at the edge for only a split second, Flick felt as if she could see everything happening in slow motion as the magic in her blood came to life. The ship's enormous wooden frame groaned as it pitched forward, prow-first. The sails sagged, and the ship became a deadweight. Flick caught sight of the sailors on deck, hanging on to the rigging or tied to whatever they had found.

The ship tipped over halfway.

Flick breathed in, and everything seemed to freeze for an instant.

And then immediately sped into real time again.

The *Onslaught* went over the edge like a cannonball. And fell.

It was now, or never.

Flick pulled the magnifying glass back down over her right eye, shutting her left. Her view exploded into luminescence, and she could see glittering magic shooting up from the *Onslaught* as it fell.

Flick gritted her teeth. She let the tingling feeling in her fingers shoot outwards, meeting the glimmering magic in the air, and gathering it up like candy-floss in a machine. She could sense the suitcase, which was falling through the air scarcely ahead of the ship, the schism inside it waiting for her like so much bunched-up elastic.

All she had to do was stretch it out.

The magic in the air, guided by Flick's mind, seized hold of the suitcase's schism. And pulled.

Find Jonathan, she told it. *Find the lighthouse.*

The magic responded gleefully, as if she had told it a delicious secret. A swarm of glittering magic dived off the edge of the world, dragging the schism free of its suitcase prison, gathering more and more energy as it went. The schism rose into a golden mist that condensed into a line that was more red than gold – like a wound in the sky only Flick could see.

All this happened so fast the *Onslaught* had only just dropped out of sight when the explosion came.

Flick couldn't just *see* the glowing line in the air; she could also *feel* it. And she felt it as it darkened, deepened, turning from red to black as it reached across the space of the multiverse that was the emptiness between worlds.

And then it broke through.

It all happened in a single heartbeat.

Blue-white light suddenly streamed upwards in a blinding FLASH.

Avery gasped, and Flick realised the flash must have been visible to the naked eye.

A tear, a schism, a gash the size of the biggest ship in the fleet, hovered a few feet below the edge of the world. It was as clear as the rips in The Break's sky.

*

The *Onslaught* dropped like a wooden whale through the portal between the worlds. It hit the water below with a *SMASH*, the prow splintering as the force of the drop took its toll. The ornamental figurehead broke off the front, the carved embrace splitting in half as it was forced into a new world.

The water the ship landed in rolled like steel, rising up in a wave that carried it away through the new ocean before crashing hard against the beach and dunes. The oars were broken off, the polished wooden body was wounded, but the ship had made it through. And, from the happy shouts on board, so had the crew.

Jonathan, clinging to the railing at the top of the lighthouse, yelled in delight at the sight of it, waving as the invalided ship began to slowly drift away from the schism, as if it were limping.

*

Above, in the pirates' world, Flick felt as if she could see it all happening at once. She could feel the pulse of the schism, smell the saltwater from another world, and hear the rush of approaching ships and mer-people from this one.

It had worked.

It was working.

'They made it,' Flick whispered. Her arms were aching already. 'They're through.'

'How do you know?' Nyfe asked urgently.

'I just know.' Flick twitched as she felt a piece of the pirates' world suddenly break off and vanish, reduced to pure magic to feed her new schism.

'Flick?' Avery grabbed her arm.

'It's crumbling. The circle. This world. The rest of them need to leave, as fast as they can!'

In her mind, she could see the schism, hungry for magic, devouring the world it had been born in. There was no time to lose.

Nyfe pulled a small glass crystal from her sleeve. She blew on it, hard, and it glowed a brilliant blue before she smashed it between her palms. The light went shooting into the sky before exploding like a firework. A signal for everyone to haul as fast as they could.

Immediately, there was a great surge beneath the water as the mer-people began to pick up speed. And even though Flick was starting to tremble with the effort of keeping the schism open, she gasped at the sight of the great Mer-Queen raising her head and shoulders above the surface.

Moments later, like a school of brightly coloured fish, the mer-people jumped from the water in an arc, over the edge of the world. They fell down gracefully, dropping into the waters of their new home like pebbles scattered into a pond. They were joined by sea creatures of all colours, tentacled monsters that looked like balls of slimy sting, and lithe sharks all leaping as one from the old world to the new. The larger mer-people, each one the size of a house and with glowing eyes, followed behind. Leviatha herself went last, heaving her enormously strong body from the water of The Break in a sort of roll. Her lower half was the thick blue-grey of a whale, scattered with barnacles that looked like beauty-spots and grey jagged scars that spoke of a life full of stories. She tipped over the edge and hit the water below with the same grace as the rest of her people, crashing into the depths so that water splashed upwards into the old world in the shape of a crown.

And with a CRUNCH loud enough to be heard on the other side of the world, another piece of the world broke off and vanished to feed the schism. Flick had to allow it to happen. She had to keep feeding the schism its magic, or else it would consume the people, the ships, the world and her.

The schism was turning to her, and it was as though she could see its evil grin.

I will win, it seemed to say.

Flick made a noise of effort, somewhere between a grunt and sigh. *Not today*, she thought back, as loud as she could.

The *Serpent* came then, Captain Burnish visible hanging from the rigging. He gave Flick a salute before his ship plummeted through the schism.

Flick gasped.

The CRUNCH this time made Nyfe clamp her hands over her ears like a child. Avery looked around wildly, eyes wide with fright.

A fizzing feeling shot up Flick's arms as though she'd just banged her hands hard into a wall. The schism lurched, getting smaller by a couple of meters across. Flick gritted her teeth and tried to force some more magic into it.

'Faster,' she forced out. 'It's – trying – to – close—'

Nyfe cupped her hands around her mouth and yelled: 'COME ON YOU WASTES OF DECK-SPACE. PUT YOUR BACKS INTO IT – DON'T YOU KNOW THIS HAS TO BE FAST?'

Flick couldn't speak. As the *Gilt Princess* tipped over the edge, the balance of magic shifted completely. It was rushing, now, straight through Flick like she was a sieve, and into the gaping maw of the schism.

If she didn't find more magic to feed it with, The Break would be wiped out of the multiverse before the rest of the fleet had made it through.

But there was no more magic.

There wasn't enough spare in the pirates' world.

It wasn't going to work.

The schism was going to close and take what was left of the world with it.

It had all been for nothing. Some of them would be left behind after all.

Flick's arms dropped a fraction and the schism shrank a little more.

She was failing.

A hand touched her elbow.

'Felicity?'

She shook her head.

The touch turned into a grip. 'Felicity. Flick. Look at me.'

Feeling like she was made of lead, Flick turned and looked at Avery. She wanted to tell Avery she was sorry she hadn't been able to do it, but she couldn't speak. It was as though Avery was somehow right there, and a million miles away at the same time.

But Flick could hear her.

'You're doing it,' Avery said. 'You're saving them! You just have to hold on a little bit longer. You're stronger than it is. Aren't you?' She made a determined face and Flick felt her chest clench. 'I know you can do this. You're the only one who can, Flick. You just need to show it who's boss, OK?'

Flick's mind turned back to the schism. The devouring space between worlds.

And she made a decision.

She stopped channelling the magic from the pirates' world. And took it from somewhere else, instead.

Instantly, it was like lightning was coursing down her veins. Magic fizzed through her blood from somewhere else. Not the world around her. Not from the new world below. Not from the falling people moving through the schism.

Not even from any of the worlds visible through the tears in the sky.

This magic was a different kind.

This magic came from inside Flick.

Where the magic in the air and surrounding the schism was the fluttering white-gold Flick knew and loved, the magic that now burned under her skin was the same as the magic at the mouth of the schism – a deep red-black that scalded her blood and shot out of her before she had chance to think that it might not be a good idea to use it.

Avery let go of Flick's arm as though it was on fire.

The schism yawned wider as the magic flowing straight from Flick's heart crashed into it.

Flick barely noticed. Her blood vessels felt as if they had been replaced by electric cables, humming with power beneath her skin. She could feel the magic flowing straight out of her like she was a conduit, a battery, a power-station. She couldn't say how long she stood there. It was enough time for every ship to sail over the edge, though Flick could no longer see them. It was enough time for every mer-person and even every fish to leap from ocean to ocean, though Flick could no longer hear them.

Flick was lost in the power of the magic. Nothing else was real. She didn't even know how to stop.

Eventually, she realised she was falling.

She felt the breakers inside her clanging down, cutting off the power.

And she pitched forward, over the edge of the world, towards a closing schism.

CHAPTER THIRTY-TWO

Jonathan watched from the lighthouse world as the deep red of the schism suddenly contracted. It pulsed for a moment, and then began to close as though someone had tied a string around it.

He grabbed the lighthouse railing. Horror ran through him.

'Oh my god – Flick and Avery, they're not through yet!' He stared at the closing schism in desperation. *All these people saved, and they didn't make it?* He dug his nails into the wood.

The schism closed up completely.

The darkness in the sky was wiped away, replaced by clear blue.

Jonathan sagged against the side of the railing,

his muscles refusing to support him any longer. 'No.' He shook his head. 'No . . .'

'Look! Sir, look!' A sailor who had come ashore from the *Onslaught* shook his shoulder. 'There!'

Jonathan turned so quickly his neck almost snapped. Then he gasped.

Tumbling through the air like dolls were three human shapes. They were buffeted to and fro by the wind, but falling quickly like rocks down towards the water.

'Oh my god, they'll be killed,' Jonathan choked.

But then, there was a huge surge of water. A great shape rose from the depths and leapt, with all the grace of a blue whale, to catch the falling people.

Leviatha caught Felicity, Avery and Nyfe in her hands, then fell back into the water with a thunderous *SPLASH* that rolled out across the ocean.

*

'Wake up, girl. Rise and shine.'

Flick winced with her eyes shut.

Someone tapped her face. 'Come on, get those eyes open.'

'Get out of the way,' another voice snapped. Then:

'Felicity Hudson, open your eyes and sit up this *instant*, do you hear me?'

'Go 'way,' Flick managed to croak.

'Well, if you can be rude there's not a lot wrong with you.'

She heard the smile in Jonathan's voice.

Flick rubbed her eyes before opening them. She was lying on the deck of a ship, several dozen faces peering down at her in amusement and relief.

'She lives!' Captain Burnish yelled into the air. There was a roar of appreciation from behind him, and several sailors broke out into applause.

Flick sat up and was immediately flattened again by several blankets being thrown at her. She hadn't realised it, but she was wet, and though this world was warm, she was getting cold. She tucked one of the blankets around her shoulders. 'Where's Avery?'

Jonathan jerked a thumb over his shoulder. 'In the sickbay. Don't worry,' he said, as Flick made to get up. 'She's fine. Promise.'

Flick rubbed her forehead. 'What about Nyfe?'

'Up and about as soon as her boots touched the deck.' Jonathan rolled his eyes. 'She's talking to Katyo now. They're sending out parties to map this world.'

'Never a wasted moment, is there?' Flick smiled as

she was handed a cup of fresh water. She wasn't thirsty, but felt that she probably ought to drink it. She sipped. 'So, what happened?'

Jonathan sat down beside her. 'What's the last thing you remember?'

'I remember trying to keep the schism open,' Flick said, avoiding mentioning the red-hot darkness that had seemed to come from deep inside herself. She couldn't talk about that yet. Especially not with half of the *Serpent*'s crew listening in. 'And then, I remember falling . . .'

'Mm.' Jonathan pushed his glasses up his nose. 'Yes. I saw you fall.'

'Bet you enjoyed that.'

'It was about as much fun as snogging a sea urchin.'

'And Leviatha caught us.' Flick smiled as the memory came rushing back to her.

'Oh, you remember that? Yes, she caught you. Brought you straight to us before going back under. Amazing, really . . .' He trailed off. 'You know, no one quite knows what to do with you. Captain Burnish wants to give you a title, but you're not a pirate or part of any crew, so there's a bit of discussion there. But everyone's so grateful. I've already declined two offers of marriage on your behalf, I hope you don't mind.'

'No, that's fine.' Flick drained the cup. 'Thanks.'

'Not at all. I figured you'd rather not have a husband with wooden teeth.'

Flick didn't reply, just watched the sailors bustle around the ship, making it seaworthy again. On the island with the lighthouse, she could see a scouting party already walking off in search of food and water.

'I told them the lighthouse is out of bounds,' Jonathan said. 'They were more than happy to agree to leave it be. I doubt they'll want to stay on this island, anyway. None of the people here were made to stay still for very long. They're seafarers.'

'Are there other islands in this world?'

'Katyo seemed to think so. He said something about the flow of water indicating more land.'

Flick got to her feet, and she and Jonathan went to sit on the steps that led from the deck to the helm. There were several ships floating close by. The *Serpent* was bobbing about as they walked, and Flick could hear banging and crashing from the outside of the hull.

'They're recycling some of the floorboards to repair the hull,' Jonathan explained. 'I tell you, if they find a forest on this world they're going to think all their Christmasses have come at once.'

Flick frowned. 'They won't chop it all down, will they?'

Jonathan shrugged. 'I doubt it. Unlike the people of our world, the pirates know the value of living trees. They'll take what they need to be seaworthy and be on their way. They've been given a second chance. I can't see them wasting it.'

*

Avery was holding a thick wad of bandage to her face when Flick and Jonathan got down to the sick bay.

'You said she was fine!' Flick shoved Jonathan down the last two steps and ran over to Avery. 'What happened?'

'Freak accident,' Avery said. 'Leviatha got me onto the deck fine, but I tripped over some rope. Caught my face on the edge of a barrel.' She lifted the bandage away to reveal a cut along her jaw, from her chin up to her ear. 'What do you think?'

'Oh, Avery.' Flick's heart sank. 'Your face.'

'Gruesome, isn't it?' Avery tried to smile, but all that happened was her lip sort of wobbled.

'We need to get you back,' Jonathan said. 'You need a proper hospital.'

'I know. Would you tell Burnish and everyone that we need to leave?'

'Of course.' Jonathan went back up the steps onto the deck and disappeared.

Flick looked back at Avery. 'I'm really sorry.'

'Don't be. I'm still the best looking out of the three of us.'

A little bubble of a laugh escaped from Flick's mouth. 'God, you're annoying.'

'I know.' Avery met her eye, and Flick shook her head. The two of them smiled, and Flick wondered if she might actually like Avery *less* if she stopped being so annoying. Avery wouldn't be herself if she stopped, that was for sure. Flick remembered the way they'd held pinkie fingers as they drifted on the ocean, and she suddenly wanted to hide her hands in her sleeves.

As if reading her thoughts, Avery put the bandage back to her face. 'I suppose I should thank you for the whole world-saving thing.'

'I didn't save the world, though,' Flick pointed out. 'I destroyed it.'

'You saved the people. A world isn't just a place on a map. It's the people. It's the way it runs. The friends that hold it together. That's what a world is, really. It's the love.'

Flick didn't know what to say to that. The sensation of The Break crumbling as she drained it of magical energy was still fresh. Even now, she could feel her fingers tingling, her blood singing. She had destroyed an entire world.

And the knowledge that she could do it again frightened her. It frightened her so much she wanted never to talk about what had happened. No one else had ever felt like this. No one else had done what she could do.

Or had they . . .?

Her memory stirred, replaying a thought from just before the schism opened. *The circle's magic was being taken. By something. Or someone.*

Flick swallowed. If there was someone else out there, with the same powers as her, that would make her feel less alone. But maybe they weren't using their powers for good.

The thought made her sit down suddenly on the low bench beside Avery.

'Hey, you OK?' Avery budged up to make room.

Flick pulled the eyepatch out of her pocket. 'Just thinking.' She twisted the strap in her hands, and then pulled it over her head, fitting the embroidery-covered glass over one eye.

Avery was looking at her closely, an uncharacteristically hesitant expression on her face. 'Back there in The Break, it seemed like . . . it seemed like you were out of magic. But then you kept going. What happened?'

'I'm not sure,' Flick lied. How could she say the extra magic had come from within her? How could she ever explain how she'd used some of the magic that powered her own life, but was still here to tell the tale? It was unnatural, frightening, gross. She knew, somehow, that she hadn't affected her own lifespan, either. The magic had almost been . . . created by her. But was that even possible? To create magic? 'I don't know how I did it,' she repeated. 'But I'd like to find out.' She lifted the covering up off the eyepatch and looked through the glass, smiling as a waft of white-gold glitter curtained in front of her. 'Oh,' she breathed, 'there's so much magic here!'

'Yeah?' Avery looked around, blind to what Flick could see.

'So much. It's like we're swimming in it. It's gorgeous.' Flick trailed a hand through the air. 'It must have come through the schism with us.'

'What does that mean? Is it a good thing?'

'I'm not sure, but I *think* it means that the pirates

won't have to worry about losing years off their lives.'
Flick wrote her name in the air with a finger, parting
the particles of magic. 'I think they're going to be just
fine.' She lifted the eyepatch up to her forehead.

Avery nodded. 'You're so made for this. For
Strangeworlds.'

Flick snorted.

'No, I mean it. You care. You care so much. I mean,
lots of people care about money, or whatever. But you
care about the important things.'

Flick looked at her.

Avery's face, half-hidden by the bandage, wore a
soft expression.

Flick smiled. 'Thanks, I guess.' She fidgeted with the
eyepatch, putting it back on and peeking through it at
Avery. A thin glittering line of magic shone where the
cut on her face was healing, and it gave Flick an idea.
'Take that bandage away,' she said happily. 'I think I
can do something about that cut.'

CHAPTER THIRTY-THREE

and, by the authority I have as captain, I would like to present you with this ceremonial whistle.' Captain Burnish handed Flick a small brass whistle shaped like a fish. 'Can be heard over many miles, if you've got the lungs for it.'

'Thank you,' Flick beamed. 'I'll treasure it.'

'And as Commander of the Fleet,' Nyfe added, 'my crew and I would like you to have this.' She snapped her fingers. A man hurried forward, carrying—

'A suitcase?' Jonathan called out from the watching crowd.

Flick grinned as she took it. 'Are you sure you want to give this up?' she asked Nyfe. 'Isn't it handed from captain to captain?'

'It's no use to us,' Nyfe said. 'It never has been, since

it leads to a desert. But you might find it comes in useful. We don't have any need for magical travel. You saved us all, Flick. I'd have you as part of my crew in a heartbeat, you just say the word.'

'Thank you, Captain,' Flick said. 'But I should be going home before it gets too late. I've got to try and sneak back into bed before my dad's alarm goes off.'

'Mm, we're cutting it fine,' Jonathan muttered, looking at his watch. 'It's half three in the morning.'

Flick put the suitcase down and turned to Burnish and Nyfe. 'Can I ask something of you both?'

'I suppose you can ask,' Burnish said.

'Would you shake hands?' Flick asked. Nyfe looked shocked. 'And promise to try and listen to each other, from now on?' she added. 'I'm not saying you have to be friends, but you don't have to be enemies either. Just stop this pointless rivalry. You almost lost a world over it. Don't make the same mistakes again.'

The two captains shuffled about on the deck like they were six-year-olds who had been told by their teacher to apologise.

Flick folded her arms. 'Come on, who wants to be the grown-up?'

Burnish sighed, turning to Nyfe. 'The girl's right. This is a chance for a clean slate. What happened,

happened. Can we start again?' He offered a hand, the mer-person inked onto his forearm colourful in the sunlight.

Nyfe looked at the offered hand, and, for a moment, Flick thought she might refuse it. But instead, she clasped his hand. 'Let the past be the past, eh?' She grinned. 'Dad.'

Burnish blushed under his beard. 'Right you are. No sense in bringing grievances through with us.'

Nyfe nodded. 'I was short-sighted. I can see that much, now.'

'Ambition isn't a bad thing,' Burnish said. 'But it shouldn't come at the cost of people.'

They stared at each other for a moment, then Nyfe gave her father's hand a single shake, before letting go.

Burnish clapped his hands together. 'Now. How about showing your old man around this tub, eh?'

Nyfe grinned. 'This way.' And with that, the crowd of watching sailors began to disperse, and Flick went back over to Jonathan and Avery.

'I think we've been forgotten,' she said.

'Good,' Avery said. 'They don't need us any more.'

'That's the way it should be,' Jonathan said. 'And now, home.' He kicked open the suitcase that led back to Strangeworlds. 'After you, Felicity.'

CHAPTER THIRTY-FOUR

I t was a peculiar thing to step back into the travel agency and find that only two hours had passed since she and Jonathan stood arguing about what to do, but Flick was relieved that this time, at least, she hadn't stayed so long she'd end up in trouble.

Jonathan picked up the suitcase once Avery had clambered out of it, and carefully closed it before placing it on the desk.

Flick raised her eyebrows. 'Not pulling it through?'

'And cut them off from us completely?' Jonathan looked at her. 'I don't think that's a good idea. If they need us again, I'd rather they were able to reach us easily.'

'But what if someone else gets hold of it?'

'Then we'll be ready for them.' He pushed the

suitcase back into its slot in the wall and patted it like it was a good dog.

Avery, who had carried the suitcase Nyfe had given them through with her, put it down on the floor against the desk. The cut on her face had faded to a thin white line. Flick hadn't been sure it would work, but by focussing on the magic of *time* just around Avery's cut, the healing process had been sped up by what looked like at least a fortnight.

She gave Flick a small smile, and Flick returned it. 'Guess I should get going. I don't even know what time it is in my world.'

Jonathan picked up one of the clocks on the mantlepiece. 'I could tell you the time, but the date is another matter.'

Avery grinned, but it dried up very quickly. 'It's been long enough. I feel like I could sleep for a week.'

'I know what you mean,' Flick said, fighting the urge to sink into the closest armchair. 'That was a lot.'

'Especially for you,' Avery pointed out, 'controlling all that magic.'

Flick's cheeks prickled. The secret was bursting to get out of her. 'I . . . don't think the magic was just from The Break.'

Jonathan frowned. 'What do you mean?'

'The magic that was keeping the schism open,' Flick said. 'At the end it was like . . . it was coming from *me*.'

'That's impossible,' Jonathan said.

'I know,' Flick said. 'It's like the magic came from another part of me that I didn't even know existed.'

The three of them exchanged worried and confused looks.

Avery bit her bottom lip. 'When we were on the boat, it was as though you were in another place. Your eyes were elsewhere. Like you could see something I couldn't.'

'I could,' Flick said softly.

'What did you see?' Jonathan asked.

Flick paused for a moment. 'I think,' she said, 'I think I could see what's in-between worlds.'

'There isn't anything between worlds,' Jonathan said dismissively.

'That's what I mean,' Flick insisted. 'The nothingness. I could see it.' She shivered. 'It was so close.'

There was a moment of unease, sinking into the room like a thin film, settling over everything in it.

Jonathan cleared his throat. 'Avery, I'll get your suitcase.' He pushed the footstool close to the wall and reached up for the case.

Avery took a step towards Flick. 'I guess I'll see you around . . .' she said. There was a question in her voice.

Flick stood up. Her face suddenly felt rather hot. She wanted to press 'pause' on time, to work out what to say. She'd had all that time in The Break with Avery, but hadn't actually said what she wanted to say. And now Avery was going away.

Flick swallowed. 'Yeah. I mean – we have to see each other again, really, don't we? You're part of The Strangeworlds Society.'

Please say you are.

Avery went a bit pink. 'I'm not really,' she said, and Flick's heart dropped. 'I'm just Jonathan's cousin, but,' she glanced behind her as Jonathan climbed down holding her suitcase, 'I could always try to come more often. If you wanted.'

Flick looked at the ceiling. 'I do want you to come back,' she mumbled.

Avery raised her eyebrows. 'What was that?'

'You heard.' Flick sighed at Avery's teasing. 'I'm not saying it again.'

Avery's pink cheeks went slightly redder. 'Right.'

From the desk, Jonathan rolled his eyes so only Flick could see. But he didn't look cross.

Flick stared at Avery, feeling as through her tongue

was stuck to the roof of her mouth. She wanted to say something – that without Avery's help she would never have been able to help the people of The Break, that she wouldn't have known how to help Jonathan, that she would have been isolated and alone, and most of all that she was sorry she'd treated her with such suspicion and jealousy when they first met. And also that she didn't want to think about the possibility of not seeing her, even for a little while, because it made her heart ache in a way that was both unfamiliar and frightening. But she couldn't say any of it.

It was awful.

Jonathan put Avery's suitcase on the floor. 'Thank you,' he said to his cousin. 'I doubt we would have managed without you.'

Flick felt a spike of annoyance. How come *he* found it so easy to say?

Avery reached out and hugged her cousin for a moment. 'I will come back,' she said, letting him go. 'I just don't know when.'

'That's fine,' Jonathan smiled. 'I like your surprises.'

'And I am really sorry about Uncle Daniel. I'm sorry.'

Jonathan didn't speak.

Avery turned to Flick. 'See you soon, then?'

Flick inched forward. 'Um. Yeah. Soon.'

Avery's arms flinched, and for a moment Flick thought – hoped – she might go in for a hug, even though Flick didn't know how she'd respond to that, but then Avery was holding a hand out. 'Soon as I can,' she said.

Flick took her hand.

It wasn't a handshake, not really. It was a handhold. But it didn't last for very long. *Like us being together*, Flick thought bitterly as Avery let go and turned to the suitcase.

'Wish me luck,' Avery grinned.

Flick gave her a wave, one not unlike the wiggly-fingered one Jonathan had given Anthony, the handsome rugby-type lad in the supermarket only a few days ago, and she could feel Jonathan giving her a look of glee as she did it.

Avery raised her hand in a quick salute and stepped into the case without another backwards glance. The suitcase snapped shut as she dropped down inside it, the catches bouncing once before clicking closed.

Flick sighed.

Jonathan picked the suitcase up. He gave it a cursory dust with his hand. 'She will come back, you know. I'm absolutely certain of that. You don't need to worry.'

'I'm not *worried*.' Flick shrugged. 'It's just hard, having a friend who lives in another world.'

'I'm sure you can work it out. It isn't as though you're married yet.'

'I didn't think The Strangeworlds Society approved of people from other worlds getting – wait, what do you mean *yet*?'

'Oh, please,' Jonathan drawled, but didn't elaborate. He went over to the suitcase wall.

Flick put what Jonathan had said to one side. There was plenty of time to think about that later. Right now, Jonathan needed her to ask a different question. She looked up at her friend. 'Are you all right, anyway?'

'I'm fine.' But as he pushed the suitcase back into its slot, Flick could see his hands were trembling. Like a sprinter having completed a race, his body was feeling the aftermath of the past few days. The adventure, the news, the grief, the loss were clearly all weighing down on him more than ever in the quiet of the travel agency.

She went over to him and touched him on the arm. 'Jonathan. *Are* you OK?'

He turned. His eyes were shining behind his glasses. 'What do you think?' he asked eventually.

Flick held her arms out.

Three Weeks Later

Flick had suggested they have a memorial service. Jonathan had been dismissive of the idea initially, until he decided he might do something in the travel agency 'for close friends'. But when you worked in The Strangeworlds Travel Agency, you couldn't just invite people by email.

They decided to ask everyone in person, which meant waiting for the weekend, when Flick was available. September had rolled around, and she'd started school. Byron Hall wasn't as bad as she'd thought it was going to be. The place was so small that she had been the centre of attention for a couple of days, but now that everyone had realised she was just like any other kid, she was being ignored – but in a good way.

Jonathan had also gone back to school – to college, at least. Flick didn't like to say it to his face, but she thought it was doing him good to get out of the travel agency. He also got cagey and weird when she asked him about Anthony, so she guessed things were going well there.

The summer temperatures had just started to drop on the day when they made a list of people they wanted to ask back to Strangeworlds to celebrate the too-short life of Daniel Mercator. And the first suitcase they pulled down and jumped into was Tristyan Thatcher's.

They also took with them the photographs Flick had liberated from the lighthouse.

*

'I wanted to ask you,' Jonathan said, 'if you'd come back with us for a day. To my dad's memorial service.'

Tristyan had been very pleased to see them (though to Flick's relief didn't seem aware of the dream they had apparently shared), and had welcomed them into his shop and set about bringing them bitter tea and bite-sized cakes. But at Jonathan's words he froze with a plate in his hand, his face a mask of shock. 'You're certain, then? That he has . . . passed away?'

Jonathan nodded.

'I am so sorry.' The apothecary put down the plate of treats and came over to where Jonathan and Flick were sitting awkwardly on his too-firm sofa. 'How did it happen?'

'I don't know. All we know is that Captain Nyfe of The Break sent him a blood-magic note. To be delivered either to him, or his closest relative. And it came to me.'

Flick's throat hurt as she watched Jonathan speak. It was so final.

But Tristyan looked thoughtful. 'A blood-magic note to pass between worlds?'

'Yes. Captain Nyfe explained how it worked.'

Tristyan shook his head. 'But that's not – wait.' He grabbed a piece of brown paper and a pen from the sideboard. 'Er, Felicity, what is your mother's name?' he asked.

'Moira Hudson,' she said. 'Why?' she watched him write the name on the paper. 'You're not sending her a letter, are you? She doesn't know about Strangeworlds!'

Tristyan didn't answer, just finished addressing the

note before folding it into a crude paper aeroplane. He picked up a glass bead from a bowlful on the sideboard and crushed it hard against the paper, so it shattered in the heel of his hand. But it didn't cut him. The glass melted into the paper like water into a towel, shimmering for a second and then vanishing.

Flick had the urge to run up and snatch it out of his hand. If that letter got to her mother, she'd be in more hot water than someone attending a jacuzzi convention. 'Tristyan, I really don't think this is a good—'

'Just wait.' He picked up the aeroplane. 'And watch.' He launched it into the air.

Flick bit her lip.

The note twirled, dived, and then ... it zipped straight to Flick, landing neatly in her hands. She looked up in surprise.

'What does that prove?' Jonathan asked, as Flick looked at the note, puzzled.

Tristyan smiled. 'Blood-magic notes are not terribly sophisticated, Jonathan. The pirates of The Break are not sorcerers, after all. It takes more than a simple spell to find someone lost in the multiverse. What these sort of notes find is the addressee's *closest* relative, Jonathan – closest in terms of distance.'

The whole world seemed to grind to a halt. Flick dropped the note in her hand.

Jonathan stared at Tristyan, eyes wide. 'Please tell me this isn't a joke.'

'It isn't. The note came through a suitcase, yes? And found you. The closest relative.'

Flick put a hand to her mouth. Hope sprang in her chest. 'So, Daniel Mercator could still be alive?'

'Yes,' Tristyan said. 'He could be.'

Jonathan's eyes were the size of soup plates. He stared for a moment, then crossed the room at a run and hugged Tristyan so hard the man gasped for air. The hug only lasted a few seconds, but it was enough.

'He could still be alive? He could be. He could be!'

It wasn't certainty. It wasn't even a ghost of a promise, but it was enough. It would have to be, Flick thought. They might never find Daniel, or he might reappear at any moment. It was impossible to say. But there was hope now, where there was none before. Jonathan could hope to see him again.

One day.

Jonathan collapsed into Tristyan's chair and covered his face, shaking with emotion. Flick wanted to go over to him and hug him but thought perhaps he needed a moment to himself. His world had been turned upside down yet again.

To give Jonathan a moment, Flick took the photographs out of her backpack and went over to Tristyan, who was looking pleased with himself.

'Tristyan?'

'Mm?' He looked at her, and Flick again had that feeling – that she had looked into his eyes before, in another face.

She held out the pictures. 'Is this you?'

Tristyan took the pictures. His mouth dropped open slightly, and his eyebrows creased. 'Where did you get these?'

'I found them,' she said. 'In a lighthouse in another world.'

'A lighthouse?' He frowned at her. 'What's that?'

'You don't know what a lighthouse is?' She frowned.

'Perhaps I would call it something else,' he said, looking back at the pictures, and putting the one where he was holding a baby on the top of the pair. 'That's my wife,' he said, touching the woman in the image. His finger lingered on her. 'That was my wife.'

'She—'

'Died,' he said. 'A long time ago.' He turned the picture over and read the names with a sigh.

Aspen, Tristyan, Clara and I

'We wondered who the "*I*" was, who wrote the names,' Flick said.

'I wrote these names,' Tristyan said. 'This is my handwriting.'

Flick was taken aback. 'But it says Tristyan, Clara and *I* . . .' She frowned, confused.

'Oh! The *I* doesn't mean *me*,' Tristyan said. 'That's—' He stopped, and bit his lip. 'I can see it's confusing. At the time I wrote it, the *I* was all I could manage. Sometimes, even thinking about someone is enough to make you want to stop existing. And writing their name can be just as painful.'

Flick nodded. 'Is that because . . . in the other picture, there's only the three of you?'

Tristyan put the pictures down on his table. Then he took down a frame of his own from the mantlepiece, and brought it over. A teenage girl with dark ringlets, pointed ears and a laughing smile shone out of the glass. Beside her, a younger Tristyan smiled too, his hair not quite as grey as it was now, his hand on her shoulder, the two of them looking windswept and happy, the moment locked in the frame for ever.

'That's her,' Flick said. 'That's the girl.'

'My little girl,' he said. 'The only one of my children I saw grow up.'

'I'm so sorry,' Flick said. 'I did wonder, when there was only one child, after there were two in the early picture. And Jonathan said you lost someone.'

Jonathan himself came over, then. He looked happier than he had in weeks, but still stunned.

'I never expected the love of my life to come from another world, and when she did, it was heart-breaking.' Tristyan said. 'We tried to make it work. And, for a time, we were happy. We had the twins. But you can't live in a world you don't belong to.'

'Did Aspen go home?' Flick asked.

'No,' Tristyan sighed. 'No, she never went home. She wanted to stay here, with us, her family. And she did, for years. But then . . .'

'I'm sorry.'

He gave her the saddest smile she had ever seen. 'Some people live hundreds of years, Felicity, without knowing how blissful it can be to find the kind of love we had. Yes, it was short. I would rather she had gone home, and lived a long life, but it wasn't my decision to make. I am very, very grateful that I had the chance to love Aspen. And our children.'

'So the *I* on the back of the photo *was* your other child?'

Tristyan nodded. 'My son. The boy of the twins. His mother named him, a name from a holy book in her world. His name was Isaac.'

Flick felt her entire life grind to a halt.

There was a clanging sound in her ears, and a rush of blood. Her face felt as if someone had slapped her, all stinging and full of pressure.

'Clara and Isaac,' Jonathan was saying. 'Nice names.'

'I thought so. Aspen named them both. Felicity? Are you all right?'

Flick put a hand on the counter. She forced herself to look up, past the bottles and jars, and into Tristyan's face. Into his eyes.

She *had* seen those eyes before. In another face, in another world. Those eyes, that expression of loving concern. She knew it. She'd known it all her life.

'What's wrong?' Jonathan asked.

She swallowed. 'Isaac.'

'Yes,' Tristyan said, looking worried. 'Is something wrong?'

She saw it again, that expression she knew. The voice was wrong, the expression was the same. 'My – my dad's name is Isaac,' she said.

There was a silence so deep you could fall through it for a century.

Tristyan spoke first. 'Is that a common name in your world?'

'Sort of,' she said. 'Except, he doesn't have a mum or a dad. He was found. Outside a police station when he was a few weeks old.'

Jonathan's mouth dropped open.

Tristyan gripped the countertop. 'Isaac – Isaac Thatcher?'

'Isaac Hudson,' Flick said. 'When they found him, he had a letter with his name on it—'

'Hudson was my wife's *middle* name,' Tristyan said. 'Her mother's surname. She was Aspen Hudson Thatcher, and I took her surname when I chose to leave mine behind . . .'

The two of them stared at each other.

Flick could see it clearly now. The deep brown eyes that were her own father's, in another head. The curve of his chin, the rise of his knuckles on his broad hands.

'You look like her,' Tristyan said, breaking the silence.

'My Aspen. You . . .' His eyes suddenly shone. He came around the chair, eyes on Flick as though she might disappear if he so much as blinked.

'I have her *Study of Particulars*,' Flick almost whispered. 'Aspen's Strangeworlds Society book. I read her name in the front. She's my—'

'Grandmother,' Jonathan said.

Flick looked back at Tristyan, who was leaning against the chair, his hand braced on the back of it as he gazed at her. 'And – you're—'

'I didn't know you even existed,' Tristyan said softly, reaching out a hand.

She stepped towards him, then stopped. 'What happened to my dad?' she asked. 'Why didn't you keep him? Why didn't you *want* him? You kept your daughter, but gave him away, why?'

'We had no choice,' Tristyan said. 'The twins were of different worlds.'

'You belong to the world you're born in,' Jonathan said.

'No. Not always,' Tristyan said. 'Sometimes, you belong elsewhere. The twins were born here, and they were thriving at first, but then . . . Isaac got sick. Nothing could make him better. I tried, and so did others. Aspen decided to take him to her world in search of more doctors.' He shut his eyes for a moment. 'Isaac started to recover as soon as she took him through the suitcase. He was meant to be in her world. When he was well again, Aspen came back for Clara. But as soon as Clara was taken from this world, she sickened in the same way. They were born together. But the multiverse intended for them to live apart.'

'But Aspen could have gone with him!' Flick's voice cracked. 'His mother could have stayed with him in her world, and you with Clara in yours!'

'I wanted Aspen to stay with Isaac, truly I did.' Tristyan shook his head. 'But that isn't how the story goes, in this case. Aspen chose to remain here. We asked Nicolas Mercator to find a good home for Isaac, and he promised to.' His expression darkened. 'Being left outside a police station is not what we thought would happen.'

'He was never adopted.' Flick's tears started to brim. 'He lived in children's homes until he was eighteen, and then he was on his own until he met my mum and they had me . . .' She brushed the wetness from her eyes, angrily. 'You never once wanted to check on him?'

'Of course I wanted to,' Tristyan said. 'I've thought about him every day since the day we left him. But what good would it do him to meet me? To learn he's from another world? That his mother is already dead, his sister moved away and his father a lonely old man with nothing to offer? What good would that do anyone at all?'

'He'd know he has a family,' Flick said. She walked away, and then back again. She felt utterly torn, stretched in two different directions.

Tristyan looked at her with those familiar eyes. 'I would very much like to be your family now. If you'll have me.'

One half of Flick wanted to run out of the door, or back into the suitcase and slam the lid. The other wanted to go over to this man, this grandfather she had never known, who looked so very sad and lonely, and hug him.

In the end, she stood still. 'I don't know what to think about this.'

Tristyan gave a laugh that was barely more than a breath. 'Likewise. This is . . . I mean, I always *hoped* Isaac would have a family of his own, but to meet you . . .'

Flick stared at her hands. Hands that had wrought magic, and ended worlds. Was this the explanation for her magical ability? Tristyan was from another world, and so a part of her was too.

'What are you?' she asked. 'What am *I*?'

Tristyan's eyes sharpened. 'You're mostly human. Your grandmother Aspen was, for certain. And I assume your mother is. But at least one quarter of you is something else.'

'And what is that?'

Tristyan stood straighter, putting his shoulders back. 'We are called the *Seren*,' he said. 'And it is my people who created schisms.'

ACKNOWLEDGEMENTS

The Strangeworlds Travel Agency had a rather different birth than we were anticipating. It arrived during the Pandemic Lockdown of 2020, when shops were closed and schools were shut and no one was travelling very much at all, magically or otherwise. Without having such a fantastic team of publishers and supporters behind me, I don't know where I, or my books, would be! So this is a huge thank you not only for all the work that has gone into *The Edge of the Ocean*, but also for all that which helped Flick and Jonathan to take their first magical steps into our world. To everyone who read *The Strangeworlds Travel Agency* and took Flick and Jonathan into your hearts, I send so much love and gratitude.

I owe a thousand thanks and more to the team at

Hachette Children's Group, including my wonderful editor Lena McCauley, who has helped *The Edge of the Ocean* make as big a splash as possible. I am proud to be part of your crew! Also my publicist Dom Kingston and marketing whizz Beth McWilliams, both of whom have worked themselves silly in this challenging new world of virtual events and video calls. To the rights team, who have ensured that Flick and Jonathan still get to travel to new countries, I thank you so much! Flick's dream of travelling has come true for her after all.

The Strangeworlds Travel Agency wouldn't have gone anywhere without the tireless efforts of the amazing booksellers who put it into the hands of readers – booksellers rock! To all the independent bookshops that put *The Strangeworlds Travel Agency* into the window, into readers' hands and into their hearts, I can never thank you enough. A special thank you must go to the QBD booksellers in Australia, and also Dion, Louise, Tsam, Gavin, Layla and Helen for all their support; it really means the world to me. Likewise to the bloggers who gave up their time and space to talk about my book: thank you so much to Steph Elliott, Jo Clarke, Imi, Samantha Thomas, Scott Evans and ReadingRocks for all your loveliness.

Shout-out to Peter and Steve as well, for once again being excellent sensitivity readers. I owe you so much.

Thank you to Samuel Perrett and Natalie Smillie for once again turning pages of words into a beautifully designed book with a cover to die for. Thank you as well to the artists who took Strangeworlds and made their own art with it, particularly Joel and Andrew – your fan art and creations are amazing.

To everyone in my Strangeworlds support bubble, thank you for putting up with my nonsense and hourly crises. Particularly Darran, Alice S-H, Nick, Charlie, Alice O, Hux, El, Mia, Olly and Sana, all of whom have received more than their fair share of terrible memes this year. And Nicole, my partner in grime, you know which bit of this book was written especially for you.

Thanks to Michael Sheen for growing an excellent beard and providing the inspiration for Captain Burnish. Thanks also to Klaus Badelt and Hans Zimmer for producing the *Pirates of the Caribbean: The Curse of the Black Pearl* soundtrack, which I have played approximately seven million times whilst writing this book.

To my agent Claire Wilson, who really is as wonderful as the legends claim, I owe a pirates' hoard of gratitude and thanks. I will sail under your flag to the edge of the world and back again.

And to my family, for the space and time and listening ears, I love and thank you all. And Anton and Joseph, I love you both more than I can say. Let's set sail for the next adventure.

LOOK OUT FOR ANOTHER MAGICAL ADVENTURE!

COMING SOON
BOOK 3
IN THE
STRANGEWORLDS
· TRAVEL AGENCY ·
SERIES